SUICIDE
SQUAD

SUICIDE SQUAD ™

THE OFFICIAL MOVIE NOVELIZATION

Based on the Warner Bros. Pictures Film

Written by David Ayer

Based on the characters from DC Comics

Novelization by Marv Wolfman

TITAN BOOKS

33614057721960

SUICIDE SQUAD
Print edition ISBN: 9781785651670
E-book edition ISBN: 9781785651687

Published by Titan Books
A division of Titan Publishing Group Ltd
144 Southwark Street, London SE1 0UP

First edition: August 2016
10 9 8 7 6 5 4

This is a work of fiction. Names, characters, places, and incidents either are
the product of the author's imagination or are used fictitiously, and any
resemblance to actual persons, living or dead, business establishments,
events, or locales is entirely coincidental. The publisher does not have any
control over and does not assume any responsibility for author or third-
party websites or their content.

A CIP catalogue record for this title is available from the British Library.

Printed and bound in the United States.

TO NOEL AND JESSICA

ALWAYS

PART ONE
THE SEARCH

ONE

June believed with absolute certainty that unless she successfully completed her mission by midnight the next day, her dreams were going to kill her.

Staring past the thick jungle, to the distant mountains shrouded in perpetual mist, shimmering in the blinding glow of dusk, she shivered at the thought that to reach its base they'd have to drive through the thick, often impassable vegetation, for another eight hours at least. Possibly much longer, and over a meandering, unmarked, and treacherous path.

Then once they made it through and found the base, they'd still have to locate the cave entrance. Unless, as she feared, it had been long buried and lost beneath the tangled undergrowth. Which, of course, meant she would die.

What could possibly go wrong?

June had already accepted the sad fact that the nightly dreams that forced her to this desert, and to this one particular mountain, wouldn't end until she found whatever was waiting for her inside.

Yeah. Whatever is waiting.

The woman who haunted her nights gave no clue as to why June was being compelled to leave her home and travel halfway around the world, all to search for some potentially nonexistent will-o'-the-wisp. Yet if she wanted to live—and she did—June had no choice but to do as she was told.

Told by a voice in a dream.

June thought she just might be going off the deep end.

By the time she pulled her Rover to a stop, the mountain was hidden in total darkness. Night had an annoying way of falling all too fast here in the furthest corner of nowhere, and without convenient GPS towers to help guide them, they would definitely lose their way. Best to start again at dawn.

"Let's call it a day," she said. "Cover the equipment and pitch the tents."

Manuel and Luis, the two mountain guides she had worked with for the past several years, jumped from the open cargo bed. It was filled with all the necessities June needed for any manner of archeological digs, and they stretched a protective canvas over them. Rainstorms were all too common in this area, as June had sadly learned on more than one previous expedition.

"Tomorrow's gonna to be a helluva busy day," she added in Spanish. "We have to find the cave before nightfall."

"We will reach the mountain by afternoon," Luis said as he began to set up his tent, "but your maps do not show where the cave is hidden. It could take many days more."

"I don't have several more days. Hell, Luis, I may not even have one full day. Tomorrow is do-or-literally-die day."

"But, senorita…" Manuel began. Before he could finish, June paused in setting up her own tent and turned toward the bulky man.

"Manuel, please. You know I prefer just 'June.' Or 'Doctor Moone,' if you keep insisting on being so damned formal."

"I know. We both know. It is habit to comfort the less informed, who only know of this region from your movies. We apologize, but I was about to say, Luis and I will take you to the mountain as we promised. And to the cave. But as we told you, we cannot go beyond the opening rooms with you."

"I was hoping once we got there your curiosity would change your mind. I really need you. Both of you," she added for emphasis.

Luis hammered the final tent peg into the jungle floor, cleared his throat, and turned to his old friend.

"She does not understand," he said. "I do not believe she can." He looked back to June, and drew a long breath.

"Doctor Moone," he continued, "you know Manuel and I are not just guides. Our people have lived in and cultivated these mountains for thousands of years, for they have always offered great spirituality. Since time began they were believed, and still are believed, to be portals to the Gods and especially to Inti, the Sun God, our Supreme God.

"It is here, during times of war and famine, that our sacrificial Capacochas were offered to appease the Gods. There is simply no other more sacred place to honor our dead. To this day our people continue to make offerings here, lest evil spirits rise yet again."

June suppressed a momentary smile as she shook her head, but she said nothing.

"Senorita... Doctor Moone, I know your countrymen believe differently than we, and we respect your beliefs—but whether you understand ours or not, please accept their importance. These mountains you seek may not be Everest, the 'Mother of the World,' but they are sacred to us."

"It is not that we do not want to go inside with you," Manuel said as he pulled the tent rope over to the peg and tied it in place. "We cannot."

He turned back to the tent and pulled at the cord. It was taut. He gave an accepting grunt. "But we will take you there tomorrow, wait for your return, and pray the spirits keep you safe."

Over the past few years Manuel and Luis had come to deeply respect the young archeologist and would do anything she asked of them.

Not this, however.

"Okay," June relented. "You're right, and you know I do accept your beliefs, but is it all right for me to say I hope you're wrong?"

"We hope so, too, Doctor. For your wellbeing, more than ours."

June unfurled her sleeping bag and crawled inside. It was a moonless night. She stared into the dark for what seemed to be forever, but in fact was only a few moments, then she closed her eyes and prayed to no god in particular that she would sleep in peace. Maybe proximity to the mountain would be enough to banish those relentless dreams.

It always started the same way. Ancient temples sprouted from jungle vines. Elaborately carved marble columns inlaid with jade, silver, and gold rose more than a hundred yards tall and glistened in Inti's harsh sunlight. As always, she was surrounded by thousands of servants, bowing subserviently—which, embarrassingly, even in her dream, she greatly enjoyed. They were chanting words she could never understand.

After staring at the temples, she suddenly noticed that she was standing in the middle of an immense koi pond. The ancient fish, large and meaty, swam about her feet as if guarding her from some underwater enemy. She saw herself reflected in the eerily calm waters, but she wasn't seeing the face of Dr. June Moone, archeologist, painter, explorer. Instead, a lean, muscular woman with stark white skin and dark black eyes stared back at her.

Outside of her dreams, June had never seen this woman who looked so similar to herself, but was obviously so different. Somehow, though, she always knew her name.

Enchantress.

Then the dream ended as it always did. The reflection reached out to touch her—or was she trying to drag June down?—and just as their fingers were about to touch…

Manuel leaned over her, pulling at her shoulder.

"Dr. Moone. Dr. Moone," he said urgently in Spanish. "You were shouting. You sounded in terrible pain. Are you all right?"

June was still in her protective cocoon, shaking the sleep away. Luis was next to his friend, looking just as worried.

"Did you see the mountain Gods?" he asked, his

eyes intense. "Were they warning you to stay away? We did try to tell you. These mountains are for believers only."

June pulled herself out of the sleeping bag and struggled to stand. The dreams always seemed to leave her weak and thirsty. She grabbed a bottle of water and drank most of it in a single gulp.

"It was the dream," she admitted. "Same one as always—and no, Luis, I didn't see any gods or demons. Just that strange woman where my reflection should have been." She thought for a moment, remembering. "You would have liked her. This time she was wearing little more than leather and chains, and that same crescent moon-shaped headpiece she'd worn before." June snorted a laugh. "Wonder what it says about me, that that's how I see my reflection?"

She rubbed her eyes and reached for another liter of water.

"It's almost dawn. I say we get started. Sooner we get there, the less stressed I'll be."

They drove through as much of the jungle as they could, then walked the rest of the way, reaching the mountain in just under seven hours. June felt the hairs on her left arm tingle as if electrified. The sensation vanished a moment later.

"Let's go this way," she said, pointing left. They looked at her curiously, and she added, "Just a feeling."

The cave entrance was an hour away. It was plainly visible, almost glowing under the intense sun. There was no way she could have missed it. She pulled the

Rover to a stop and checked her watch.

"Six hours to spare. This may turn out to be a good day after all."

Manuel and Luis followed her to the mouth of the cave.

"Please. Come with me," she insisted. Luis's smile was filled with understanding but he still shook his head no.

"We will walk with you through the outer tunnel, but when we reach the cave of teeth we must leave you to your own fortunes. But we do so praying for your safe return."

"I know better than to try to argue with you, Luis," she said, "and I thank you for all your help."

"That is easy for us to do, Dr. Moone. You showed great courage coming here to confront your nightmares. Few would have, or could have."

"Considering my dreams, I don't think there was anything else I could do."

"We want to remind you, Doctor," Manuel said, "the teeth of the cave look fierce, but they are not. They exist to lead man to truths we cannot see on our own. But on your journey, should you continue past them, you will be beyond their power to protect."

"Like I said, I don't have much of a choice."

TWO

The outer limestone tunnel was a natural jewel box, a brightly glowing rainbow of colors caught in the moving beams of their helmet lights.

They crouched to crawl under a curtain of low-hanging limestone soda straws, then wiggled through an obstacle course of stalagmite and stalactite columns that had slowly grown, then finally merged over the past million years or more.

The tunnel opened to a small cavern, tall enough, nevertheless, to let them stand. They stretched, ignored the loud sound of cracking bones, and shone their lights on the far wall.

As one, they let out a gasp.

The cave of teeth, staggering in their immensity, filled the cavern, as if waiting for the three of them to step between the yard-long fangs so the jaws could snap shut and grind their bones to meal.

Of course she knew the fangs were just stalagmites and stalactites, growing up from the ground and down from the ceiling, and still millennia away from merging and being rechristened as columns. Yet now, under their lights, the limestone drippings looked like the hungry fangs of some demon vampire, momentarily frightening, even to those who knew better.

"We must leave you now," Manuel said, his voice barely above a whisper, but still echoing through the tunnels. "Or better, you can come back with us," he suggested.

June gave him a warm hug.

"I can't," she said. "I can't live with those dreams, and I sure as hell don't want to die because of them."

"But they are just dreams. I have not known you to fear phantoms."

"Yet they feel like so much more, and I have to find out why. I know it's irrational, but I feel a compulsion that's both unavoidable and inescapable."

"Then be careful, Dr. Moone."

"Hey, like you said—just a dream. All goes well, I'll see you in a few hours."

Luis nodded and returned her smile. "We will be waiting. And we will pray for you, June Moone."

They sat down with their backs to the limestone walls and watched as their friend and employer disappeared into the distance.

For the next mile or so the cave floor was relatively easy for a professional caver to navigate. Low-hanging stalactites forced June to crawl for several hundred feet or more, but the tunnel eventually opened to a new, larger chamber.

She wanted to stop and just stare at each subsequent room. All of them were crowded with unimaginable natural wonders unseen for millennia, if ever. She walked past stunning grottos unlike any she had ever explored, alive with pristine formations untouched by man.

She glanced at her watch. It was after three in the afternoon, and she had no clue how much further her ultimate destination was, or even if she'd recognize it when she got there.

She continued on, promising herself to take more time for sightseeing on her return trek. After she found whatever she was supposed to find so she could save her life.

June had never been superstitious—not even during her teenage years, when she was the most liable to give in to irrational fears. So why was she so consumed by threats made to her by some slutted-up dream Enchantress?

Sadly, all she could come up with was that these dreams felt... different.

The tunnel ended just over two miles further along. Without warning, she found herself facing a blank wall, with no side tunnels that would allow her to continue.

Is this the wrong cave? she wondered, feeling the beginning of panic. *Have I wasted all this time?* June quickly took control of her fears. *It's not even four yet. I can get back to Manuel and Luis in less than an hour, then find another tunnel. That still gives me eight hours.*

This is doable.

This has got to be doable. Nothing can stop me now. Nothing will stop me.

As she started to turn back, the ground gave way beneath her. She scrambled, trying to grab a rock or anything for support, but instead she found herself falling into a widening shaft.

June stopped falling with a jolt when her chest reached the top of the hole. The chute was too narrow for all of her to slip through. She was stuck.

Better than falling God knows how far, she thought. *But now what?*

She couldn't see into the hole, with her own body blocking the view, but she dangled her feet, trying to find the ground below. There was nothing. The ground might be a foot away or a mile.

She didn't want to squirm, for fear it would open up the hole.

Falling to my death isn't a good idea, she thought— then, again, *What now?* She wasn't going to fail when she was this close to... *Whatever the hell is waiting for me.*

Both her arms were still free. She slowly dug one hand into the chest-level ground, seeking support. Very carefully she drilled her other hand as close as possible to her hip and legs, then into the hole. Her rope was looped around her belt. If she could reach it, she might be able to tie it to some nearby formation, and pull herself free.

Her fingers felt the cord, and she slowly wrapped them around it.

Good. She got a firm grip. Perfect. Next step, bring it into the open. She inhaled and slowly lifted her arm.

The ground around her began to shift. She stopped.

Slow, June... much slower. You do not want to fall. She waited a few minutes, pushed back her fears, then she once again lifted her arm up out of the hole.

There was the top of the rope.

She was almost home free.

Then the hole gave way, and she plunged into the blackness.

THREE

June was certain her head was going to explode. She held her temples between thumb and forefinger and gently massaged them to ease her pain. It wouldn't go away. She slowly opened her eyes. Her helmet light was still working, and she saw…

Skulls?

There were hundreds of them. Human and cave bear skulls, cemented together by crystalline deposits. How long had they been here, she wondered, but then she was hit by more important questions.

Where is here?

How long have I been here?

And how the hell did I get here? At that she remembered falling. *I'm alive. So it wasn't a long drop.*

She must have been unconscious, but for how long, she wondered. A haze still obscured her vision to some degree.

She forced herself to her feet, and felt the blood drain from her face and upper body. Her hands were cold and wet. She steadied herself until the chill faded and she could take a few steps without her legs buckling. Moving closer, she studied the skulls, frightening yet riveting.

Wickedly beautiful.

The haze dissipated, and she saw an immense altar carved from the cave walls. It was bear-shaped; a large urn was held in each paw. One was shaped like a man. The other a woman.

She was drawn to the female urn and compelled to pick it up. Then for some reason she didn't quite understand, she broke its wax seal and removed its lid.

That released the black.

Shadowy wisps flowed from the jar and spread through the chamber. Her helmet light showed trails of black fog dissipating behind it like a comet's burning trail, as its—head?—drifted toward the back of the cave. Then, in the pitch, she saw eyes.

Frightening eyes.

Animalistic eyes.

Glowing. Staring at June.

The eyes belonged to a person, barely visible until she aimed her helmet light. It was a frail woman, only partially of flesh and bone. June looked closer and saw that she was also made of smoke, and fog, and mist.

June knew who she was.

Enchantress.

She heard the woman speak, but she wasn't certain if the voice was spoken aloud, or echoing somewhere in her mind.

"We've both been waiting our entire lives for this, haven't we, June?" Enchantress asked. "Do you remember me?"

"Yes," June replied aloud. "From my dreams."

The black fog that was Enchantress drifted toward her, then reached out and held June's face in amorphous, cold hands.

"I am more than a dream, June. I am your destiny—and you are mine."

June pulled free and tried to run, making it to a tunnel, but the shadowy wisps followed and grabbed her legs, pulling them out from under her, forcing her to fall hard to the ground.

She struggled, kicking the cloudy wisps, but her feet slammed through them, like the intangible trails of smoke they were. She cried out as she fought.

"Let go of me." But they wouldn't. They pulled her back over the stone path. She turned, twisted, and tried to escape again, but they refused to let go.

"Stop fighting us, June." Still Enchantress's voice was coming from the smoke. "This has been your destiny since before you were born."

Then they were back in the chamber, and Enchantress was waiting for her. The wisps dragged June next to the witch, then dissipated back into the dark.

"It is so exciting," Enchantress continued, as if she had not been interrupted. "Worlds are going to open up for both of us, and now that I have brought you here, you must let me in."

June didn't respond, nor did she try to resist as Enchantress's face nearly touched her own.

"I must be whole again," the shadowy figure said as the smoky tendrils entered her prisoner's nose and mouth.

June Moone inhaled, and the two were one.

FOUR

It was expected to be a peaceful night.

There hadn't been any riots for more than a week. No newbie had been ushered into the exercise yard to wait for his hazing to begin. No crazy somehow conjured a shiv that he knew belonged in the gut of yet another of the certifiably insane. Even the unseasonably mild weather was cooperating. So, atypical as it was, this was turning out to be a very good night indeed.

Until explosions tore up the exercise yard. Guards positioned in Arkham Asylum's observation towers vainly searched for the source, but all they could see were patients, drugged out of their minds, numbly wandering the unexpected war zone—uncertain if the explosions were actually happening or were just some new and ridiculous hallucination, an all-too-familiar by-product of their high dosage meds.

They learned the truth the hard way.

Paramilitary thugs in gas masks and protective armor descended on ropes dropped from helicopters hovering unseen in the shadowy clouds. Even as they descended, they targeted the helpless guards, effortlessly turning them into instant corpses.

The few defenders who managed to survive ran

for cover. Entering the hospital, they ducked behind overturned beds. Inmates were still strapped into them, and they were screeching for help that wouldn't be coming.

"Shut up, you idiot," one of the guards hissed to a patient hanging from the bed, his straps starting to fray. At the top of his voice he was singing songs from an old Broadway show. "I said shut up," the guard grated. "Believe me, you don't want to let those killers know where we are."

"I did, I do," the inmate said in a voice that was barely coherent. "You think if they see me, maybe they'll take me with them? I'd like them to take me to a restaurant. You know, one that serves hamburgers and French fries and has ketchup in bottles—not in those little paper thingies that don't hold much. You think they'll take me to a restaurant?"

"They'll put a bullet in your head, you idiot," the guard muttered, still keeping his voice down. "And mine too, if you don't shut up."

"Bullet in the head? That sounds good, too, but I'd reallyreallyreally prefer a restaurant."

Finally the guard smashed his elbow into the inmate's head, knocking him unconscious. He then closed his eyes for a moment and prayed that the thugs—whoever the hell they were—hadn't heard the exchange. After a few moments, he opened his eyes again.

One of the soldiers was there, staring at him, a gun pressed to the guard's heart.

Mercifully, he never heard it fire.

The thugs moved quickly though cautiously through the halls, taking down anything that stepped in their way, not distinguishing between guards or asylum prisoners.

One of them, the commander, unhooked a radio from his belt.

"She's here somewhere," he said. "Fan out." On the move again, he held his automatic in front of him. Straight up, not turned at a ninety-degree angle. Almost looks cool in the movies, he mused, but it's a great way to break your wrist. Then he said, "And don't forget, Frost and the boss want her breathing."

The steel door to the medical wing was bolted shut from inside. Five pouches of C-4 plastic explosives removed the obstacle. Jonny Frost, easily six-foot-four, emerged from the chaos and effortlessly held up his find.

"Got her, boss," he said to a tall, muscular figure standing in the shadows. "Just where you said she'd be."

The Joker stepped out from the dark. He was tall and lean, with bright green hair, and ripped like a mixed-martial-arts fighter. Metal-capped teeth glinted in the light. He studied the beautiful young psychiatrist.

"Doctor Quinzel," he said, "how nice of you to join us. You're looking… good enough to eat. Figuratively speaking, of course. I'm strictly vegan. At least today."

Quinzel squirmed in Frost's grip, but he held firmly onto her. "Time for a little electroshock therapy," Joker said, then added, "Frost, do me a favor, will you? Dump our pretty lady on the table."

The mercenary threw Quinzel onto the exam table then strapped her into place. Joker removed his prison shirt, carefully folded it, then placed it to the side.

His extraordinarily pale skin was covered over with dozens—maybe hundreds—of insane tattoos, showing from head to foot. An eerie wide grin was inked on his right forearm while a parade of laughing "HA-HA-HA"s crept up his chest to his left arm and under his tangle of emerald hair. Dozens more were carefully placed along his side, back, and legs, filling nearly every open space.

He saw Quinzel staring at him, confused. He gestured toward the shirt.

"The government spent a helluva lot of money buying us thrift store rejects, so I'm not going to potentially dirty it with your blood. Come on. Do I look like a barbarian?"

Harleen Quinzel's eyes reflected her fear. "Please don't. Please. I did what you said. I helped you." She tried to struggle free, but the straps were designed to hold a 400-pound madman.

The Joker fell back. His eyes rolled into his head as if he simply couldn't believe what he had just heard. He shook his head to clear away his confusion, then stuck his face inches from Quinzel's own.

"You helped me?" he repeated. "You helped me? By scorching what few dead, faded memories I had into a sizzling knot?"

"That was prescribed," she pleaded. "Everything said it was the best possible cure for you."

"For my what, girl? A cure for my genius? My insanity? My ability to do bird calls? Or maybe you mean it was to help cure my bad back? You know I got that digging graves for that basketball team I kidnapped, way back when."

She stared at him, obviously confused. He leaned closer to her.

"Doctor Quinzel, do you know that for years and years they kept playing against this one other team.

26

Only this one other team, and guess what? They lost every single game. Every. Single. Game."

The Joker sighed at the thought.

"Anyway, where was I? Oh. Right. At some point don't you think even a total idiot would say, 'Maybe we should play a different team,' or better, that 'God's telling us we should quit basketball and go into business selling, I don't know, aluminum siding, maybe?' What do you think?"

"I don't know what to say," she responded. "Please don't make me. Please let me go."

"Let you go?" Joker said. He scratched his chin as if he was thinking deeply, then he gave her a huge smile. "Let you go? That is an idea, but when it was my turn to get my brains scrambled, you didn't let me go, did you?"

"I'm sorry. I was only trying to help."

Joker understood. "I know. I'm sure you thought electrifying my brains was the best way to fix all my many problems. But I've got to ask you a question, Doctor. Did it ever cross your itty-bitty brain that maybe you could spend just a little extra time and come up with a better solution than churning my gray matter into instant pudding? What do you think, dearie? Would taking a little more time have proven a better way to go?"

"Maybe. Sure. Why not?" Quinzel stammered, more than willing to agree with anything he said. "I mean, if that's what you think. I was just trying to do the right thing."

He flailed his arms, his hands waving back and forth, puppet-like, uncontrolled, as if the hinges that held them to his wrists had broken.

"Doing the right thing, huh? You tossed me into a

black hole of rage and confusion. Is that the medicine you practice, Dr. Quinzel? Is that 'doing the right thing' for all your special patients?"

He held a leather strap in one hand, and with the other traced a long, sharp pinky nail along her lips.

"Now I'm throwing you into the same black hole," he said as he stroked her face with the leather strap then rested it over her closed mouth. "Open up, doll," Joker said as he pushed the strap between her lips. "And bite hard. This is so you don't break those perfect porcelain-capped teeth when the juice hits your brain. You'll thank me later."

"You say you didn't want to hurt me," he continued as she complied, "yet you did. And I insist I don't intend to hurt you, but you know what? Sometimes hurt happens." He stepped back, then gave a wide smile and laughed his approval. "You are so going to be my Mona Lisa, and I, for one, could not be more proud."

Frost handed him the two paddles that had been sitting on the small steel instrument table. He made a show of smearing them with conductive jelly then placed them on her temples.

Quinzel knew what was coming, and his slow, deliberate moves only prolonged her horror. When he smiled at her... with that awful, gleaming, murdering smile... she screamed through the ball and leather strap.

"Forget you ever met me," he giggled, but she knew she never could.

Harleen Quinzel was in love with the man.

She convulsed as 450 volts seared through her brain. Her face contorted in impossible agony. Her teeth ground into the rubber. Joker was right—if he hadn't stuffed the ball into her mouth, her teeth would have cracked as she smashed them together.

The psychiatrist writhed in agony. She was mewling with pain, yet somehow asked for more. Pain and pleasure. More pain than pleasure. More pleasure than pain.

Until she heard the machine suddenly go dead. Her teeth stopped chewing the rubber ball, which was almost completely shredded into ragged strings, and then her body went slack. A single tear fell from her open eyes.

Goodbye, sanity.

Hello, madness, my old friend.

Joker let the last remains of her tears get sopped up in her laboratory smock then exhaled a long, satisfied sigh. He set aside the paddles and took a set of street clothes from Frost.

"Good lookin' lady, boss," his aide-de-camp said. "She really liked you."

Joker slipped on the newly pressed shirt, buttoned it then checked himself out in the med-unit mirror.

"It would never have worked," Joker replied. "She kept trying to fix me."

Frost took his Glock and screwed it into Quinzel's ear.

"Who said you were broken?"

Joker slipped on his diamond-shaped 'J' pinky ring, then he smiled… Not an ordinary smile. Not a smile to make someone laugh with him. No. This was "The Smile." The corners of his mouth slid up his face into a vast, deadly rictus, metal teeth flashing. This was a hyena's smile.

A smile that could kill.

It was a smile Frost had seen before. One that frightened the hell out of him. He holstered the Glock, then the two of them left the med lab.

Outside, the commander of Joker's paramilitary force stared down at the asylum's warden, lying on the floor, rolled up in an embarrassing fetal position, knowing full well that at any moment he was going to be killed. The force were all dressed in costumes. Weird. Bizarre. Twisted costumes. The better to frighten you with.

Panda Man, wearing a panda face mask, sported a large heart on his chest with the words "Friends forever" on it. Goat Head Priest sported an actual preserved goat's head which he wore over his black priest robes and rosary.

Crying Baby Man was dressed in a security man uniform while wearing a crying baby mask over his face. Eyeball Man was in a red janitor's outfit—almost normal except for the large eyeball mask that covered his entire head.

Finally there were Shark Heads one and two—two linebacker-sized bruisers wearing black and white shark head masks, also dressed in full black suits, with ties over white dress shirts.

Weird. Bizarre. Twisted costumes. *The better to frighten you with.*

The commander put his gun to the warden's temple.

"Bang!" he said.

He laughed as he gestured to his men that they were done. Then they all walked away, taking with them the inert form of Dr. Harleen Quinzel, leaving the warden alone and lost, whimpering on his office floor.

FIVE

Floyd Lawton, dressed in coveralls and carrying a toolbox, happily hummed his favorite television theme songs as he turned right on Kanigher Avenue, then sauntered down Courthouse Alley, past the ever-present gauntlet of Gotham City's homeless.

He gave them each a sympathetic smile, one that seemed to say "I've been there," as he tossed out fast-food coupons that promised the hungry recipients a warm meal.

They cost him nothing. He'd stolen them, and they would help thin out the crowd as the hungry hurried to get their hot but not quite so tasty Tex-Mex burritos. His generosity wasn't so much a good deed as a necessity. The fewer people watching him during his setup stage, the better it was.

For them.

He watched them scramble for the coupons. One or two managed to grab a couple. A veritable feast was in store for them. He saw a woman with a baby in one of those sling carriers try to pick up a coupon, but some guy pushed her aside and took it instead. Lawton flashed on his own daughter, Zoe, as a baby... then moved on.

Nobody said life was fair.

He had a job to do and no time to waste.

Yet he flashed on Zoe again. Damn. He reached into his pocket and took out his last two coupons and tossed them to the woman.

"Lose these, you're screwed," he said as he walked off. She grabbed them and rushed for her dinner.

Halfway up the block he stopped at the stone ledge he had scouted the day he took the job. He looked up to see the once-grand courthouse at the end of the street, then fit a thick steel plate into its pre-sized niche as planned. He tapped the "on" switch to the small camera drilled into the plate and grinned as its green light flashed.

Perfect.

Taking a monocle lens from his pocket, he propped it over one eye and checked to see if the video feed was working.

Almost perfect.

Lawton shifted the plate with a fingertip, and kept nudging it until the video feed was lined up just right. A fraction of an inch off could cost him millions.

He grinned, checked to see if anyone was watching, but as expected, the Courthouse Alley tenants were all at the fast-food place, gorging on their burritos.

Once again, perfect.

He pocketed the monocle, walked off, and resumed humming his beloved theme song playlist as he turned onto Broome Street and went into the Gardener building. As he entered, he saw a pair of U.S. marshals standing by the front desk. They gestured for him to approach. One patted him down while the other inspected his toolbox.

"What's up?" Lawton asked. "This is new."

One of the marshals checked his name against the approved list, found it, and marked it off. "Big Mafia trial. Half'a downtown's sewn up. Okay. You're good." Lawton thanked the marshal and headed for the elevator.

Fifty-two seconds later he got off at the top floor and took the stairs to the roof. He'd been worried they might have bolted shut the door, so he was prepared for that contingency, but it swung open with a push.

That's why they're civil servants, and not rich, he mused, and he chuckled.

Walking across the roof to the air-conditioning unit, he crouched next to it and removed the thin metal sheet covering its mechanism, revealing a scoped and silenced rifle wrapped in a clear plastic bag. He'd hidden it there earlier in the week, before the extra security.

Be prepared. That might have been the only thing that stayed with him from his days in the Boy Scouts.

Lawton took out his Deadshot headpiece, pulled it on, then snapped the monocle into place, giving him access to the video feed. He then removed his overalls, revealing his uniform. It wasn't necessary, but he felt more professional being properly dressed for work.

Deadshot reached into the back of the air-conditioning unit and took out a small case. A single homemade match-grade bullet rested inside. He rolled it between his fingers, loaded it into his rifle, then held the weapon as if he was born behind it.

It felt that natural.

He took his smart phone, and logged into his bank account. The balance was currently zero.

"Bastard," he growled. "Always playing games, aren't you?" He then slipped the phone into a clip on the rifle barrel and hit dial.

"Yeah?" The voice was thick and accented.

"Angelo, it's the guy you hired for your rat problem. My account's kinda thin, know what I mean? Don't wanna bounce no checks." As he spoke, Deadshot watched the street far below him. U.S. marshals were in place, screening the area. *Good luck with that, you idiots.*

Angelo's voice was light-hearted.

"No one gets paid until what needs to get done gets done."

If Deadshot felt at a disadvantage, it didn't show in his voice.

"You know the rules," he replied. "No money, no honey. Should I pack up?" The marshals turned as an armored SUV pulled onto the street. "Ah. Here's your boy now, with twenty of his new best friends. Dude is about to get a sore throat from all the singing he's gonna do."

The SUV stopped. Deadshot turned to check his smart phone then shook his head, disappointed.

"Hey. You there, Angelo? I'm still seeing only zeroes."

This time there was an edge to Angelo's reply.

"Stop being cute, man. Do your job." Below, the marshals opened the door, revealing the target—this month's mafia snitch.

Deadshot's monocle showed range, wind, ballistic curves. The camera he put in the alley was doing its job. Like always.

He dialed the range into his rifle scope.

"They're opening the door for him, Angelo. Helping him out. Yeah. He's heading for the door now which means in thirty seconds your window's closed. Forever." Deadshot let the silence grow. "Just imagine his hand on that bible."

"Okay. Okay," Angelo shouted. "There was an accounting error. We sent it."

Deadshot checked his phone screen. The balance went from zero to a cool million.

"Now double it, Angelo. You got nineteen seconds."

He looked down to the street and watched as the marshals escorted the snitch toward the courthouse door. They were surrounded by a crew of giant green-clad linebackers, all hired to protect their man. Each one of them looked like he was more than capable of taking on an army all by himself.

Angelo's voice was shrill. He stammered his response.

"We're not people you play with."

Deadshot's answer came an instant later, low and emotionless.

"Neither am I, Angelo. Ten seconds. Nine... eight..."

The phone silently lit up. His bank balance was now two million.

Deadshot fired his weapon.

His match-grade bullet struck the steel plate he'd set up in the alley. It ricocheted cleanly toward the courthouse door.

The bullet threaded through the SUV's open door. Through the tiny, temporary gap between the hulking marshals.

Into the target just as he entered the courthouse.

The snitch crumpled. Dead. The door closed behind him.

Then clueless marshals began pointing to where they thought the weapon had been fired. Everyone was frantic. Nobody agreed on the direction.

They were all off by at least half a block.

If they'd looked to the roof Deadshot had fired from,

they wouldn't have seen him there, either.

He was already gone.

Even before he could confirm the kill, he dropped his Bluetooth earpiece into a vent pipe, then rappelled down the side of the building, into the bed of a waiting pickup. He covered himself with a tarp, and the truck merged into traffic.

Perfect.

SIX

Doctor Harleen Quinzel, one of Arkham's most brilliant and dedicated psychiatrists, was no more.

Electroshock. What a wonderful way of destroying a soul, the Joker thought as he watched Quinzel's eyes roll up into their sockets and dribble pour from between her lips. He laughed uncontrollably as each hair on her arms and neck stood up on its own and began a freakish dance.

The Joker watched Harleen Quinzel disappear as each cell in her body was assaulted with electricity, a process that was intended to induce seizures as a means of providing relief from crippling psychiatric disorders such as autism, catatonia, and schizophrenia.

For those sufferers and others, properly administered electroshock treatments were accompanied by IV muscle relaxants, with each session lasting no longer than ten minutes. The Joker had received hundreds of his own such treatments.

What if those sessions instead lasted for hours? he had wondered. *Maybe even days?* And what if, instead of receiving the relaxants, they received, oh… nothing? He could only imagine the joyfully painful results as the body thrashed on the med table, breaking arms and legs and so much more.

During his own treatments he had worn a laryngeal mask over his mouth, with a tube stuck down his throat, to make certain his brain continued to receive needed oxygen. But did the brain really need oxygen, he asked himself. What would happen if he intentionally forgot the damned mask, and let the oxygen chips fall where they may, so to speak.

So he went to work to answer his questions, and he soon had the answers.

Harleen Quinzel ceased to exist, but she gave birth to a far greater insanity than even the Joker anticipated, or could hope for from the once venerable Dr. Quinzel.

Harley Quinn was very much alive, and she was more than ready to give thanks to her "Puddin'." With dyed-blonde hair tinged in pink, she was drop-dead gorgeous—in the prison vernacular, high-velocity sex on a stick. She was also as insatiable as she was insane.

More than that, Harley Quinn was the kind of psychotic the Joker had always wanted as his pet. Sure, he loved to kill. There were few things he enjoyed more. Actually, there was nothing he enjoyed more, but for Harley, killing was only the first act, and she couldn't wait to get to acts two and three, followed by an extended curtain call.

Aaaand, scene!

So when Joker plopped down into his plush VIP seat, and Harley went to join the club's go-go dancers for a little one-on-one gyration, he wasn't all that surprised that his fellow criminal conspirators wantonly stared at her. The question wasn't, "Who wouldn't stare?

The question was, who dared to?

Pretty much all the guys stared, really. Lots of the women, too, but only for a second or two. Their eyes not so innocently swept the room, only to rest on her for a moment longer than anything else. Then, if they were smart, they moved on. It was just a little peek.

He wouldn't fault them for that.

But there was a new goon in town who called himself Monster T. He stared, then he kept staring, and Joker felt him heating up from all the way across the club.

"Hey. Yes! There she is," Joker said loudly enough to be heard. "The infamous Harley Quinn. You enjoying her, pal?"

Monster T started to say yes, then realized his mistake.

"No. No way. That's your lady, Joker." Yet he couldn't help but take another look at Harley, before turning back. "I mean, you an' me, we do a helluva lotta business. I ain't messin' that up." Then he fell silent and looked at the floor, no doubt hoping that would satisfy the Joker.

The Joker stood and stared at T.

"Are you saying you don't like her?" he said. "Maybe you're saying you hate her?" Joker leaned in, and T tried to push back, but there was a wall behind him. "What do you have against her, T?"

Monster T waved his hands in protest. "C'mon, Joker," the goon stammered. "What am I gonna say, brother? There ain't no right answer."

Joker turned to Harley, who was still dancing, and whistled to her. She cartwheeled off the stage and joined them.

"Mister J?" she said, grinning.

Monster T knew what was coming next. She was gonna tear him into little pieces. Or worse.

Joker patted T on the shoulder and smiled. T flinched.

"Harley, it's been a good run 'til now, but you're my gift to this gentleman. You belong to him."

Monster T stared. What the hell game was the clown playing? Harley ground her way onto T's lap and gave an approving nod. "This guy? Cool." She brought her face close to his. "You know you're cute," she said. "So, you want me? I'm all yours, lover."

She rested her hand on his thigh. T couldn't stop sweating as his gaze went back and forth between Harley and Joker. He knew he was caught between two psychopaths, but he didn't know if they left him any sort of exit strategy.

"Joker," T said, pleading with psychopath number one. "I don't want no beef."

Joker stretched his arms and yawned. "Then accept my gift. I'm sick of her," he said as he pulled his purple .45 from his pocket and held it out. "Or better, shoot her. Push her hair right on back with a bullet. Either way, do me the favor. Please."

Harley caressed Monster T's face and gave him a series of small pecks. It felt really good, he thought, but then he shook himself back to reality. The gun hovered there in Joker's hand.

"Right between my eyes, lover," she said, poking her index finger just above her nose. "In the good ol' glabella."

Monster T had to take the gun. If he didn't, that white-skinned lunatic would surely shoot him, even with Quinn sitting in his lap for the whole club to see. So he accepted it.

"Say thank you," Joker said.

"Thank you," Monster T replied. This had to be a

joke, but they'd already taken it too far. Harley edged herself off him and stood, watching intently. T kept praying Joker would suddenly burst out laughing.

Just a joke, he'd say. Just a big, funny ha-ha joke.

The Joker wasn't even smiling.

What were they going to do to him? If he told Joker Harley was gorgeous, Joker would kill him for trying to step in on his girl. If he told Joker she wasn't gorgeous, Joker would kill him for intimating that he had lousy taste in women.

T was sweating buckets. The tension was growing. There were dozens of eyes, staring only at him.

"So," Joker said, "do you know the answer now?"

He did, and he silently nodded.

Joker laughed and gestured for him to continue. "Time for you to save yourself."

Monster T looked at the purple gun, still in his hand, and placed its barrel directly under his chin. He didn't believe in God, but he muttered a quick prayer, then squeezed the trigger and blew most of his head to hell and gone.

"Smart guy," Joker said, and he laughed. "Lotta brains."

Harley squealed with delight as she fingered some of T's smart-guyness off of her face. She leaned into Joker for a big kiss, but he pulled back.

"Don't touch me," he growled. "This is on you. You know that guy made me a lot of money. We're leaving."

"Puddin', it's not my fault I make myself look so good for you other guys can only wish an' stare 'cause they're so jealous. I mean, you should think of it as them honoring your great taste in babes—and I am your babe, aren't I, honey?"

Joker grabbed her by the arm, and Harley squealed as he dragged her from the club.

"Yeah, you are, but you keep pushing me, and one'a these days you're going to cross the line, Harley."

"Then what?" she asked.

Joker laughed. "I dunno. We'll draw ourselves a new line, and another, and probably cross them, too."

SEVEN

She crossed the line, Lawton thought. *Did she actually cross the line?*

"Say that again, honey?"

"I said Mama doesn't want me living with you because you kill people," Zoe said, and he began to sweat.

How dare she—? he thought furiously, but he said, "You shouldn't believe everything you're told, hon."

"Dad, please. I know you do bad things."

Lawton looked at his daughter, a young teenager but still a cooing baby in his eyes, and definitely the most important thing in his world.

"That's not true. Okay?"

"You don't have to worry, Dad. I still love you."

"And I love you, hon."

They continued walking as soft puffs of snow turned the gloomy Gotham City streets into a winter festival—or as close to one as Gotham City allowed. This was a beautiful night to be out, walking hand-in-hand with his daughter, the one person in the entire world he loved without reservation, but he still worried about her.

"Are you sure you're okay staying with her... in

that place? I mean, I've got resources. I'm getting us a place that's really nice."

Zoe didn't answer. Instead, she took his hand and pulled him to the corner and pointed to the multi-colored Christmas tree lit up in the apartment complex's open garden.

"Yeah, it's beautiful, hon," he said reluctantly. "But I'm concerned. Hey, I'm your dad. That's my job—but you can tell me. Is she still going out at night? Leaving you alone?"

"I'm fine, Dad. Really, and I like taking care of her. I know how to make pancakes."

"She's supposed to take care of you."

Lawton's posture slumped as Zoe took his massive hand between both of hers. This wasn't the way it was supposed to go.

"It's okay, Dad. We're all good."

He stared at her, growing up before his eyes, but her smile, so sweet and innocent, warned him to stop pushing. No matter her home life, she needed to take care of her mom. Trying to take Zoe away would only turn her against him.

"Okay. Okay, but if you ever change your mind. Ever. Call me. I'll be there before you can hang up. You understand?"

She nodded and gave him a loving smile. They continued down the street to Zoe's favorite ice-cream store. It was already a cold winter, but the girl always loved ice cream, and her favorite was peppermint, which was only available during the holiday season.

She ordered a cup with two scoops for her, then smiled at her dad and ordered his favorite—a mint-chip sundae with whipped cream and nut sprinkles. They sat at a table facing the window.

"You're doing okay at school, aren't you?"

"I'm doing fine, Dad. You don't have to search for something to talk about. We don't always have to talk, you know. Sometimes it's okay to be quiet."

"Yeah, I know, but I always want you to know if you ever have any problems there, if you ever need extra tutoring or something, you can call me. I'll find a teacher. I'll do whatever you need me to do."

"I know. I joined the band club."

"You're kidding. Really? I didn't know you played. What instrument?"

"Well, I'm not really that good, but I'm trying to play the flute. The teacher says I show promise."

"My God, hon, that's great. That's really great. When you give your first big recital or whatever it's called, let me know, because there's no way I won't be there. The flute? That's so good, hon."

"Well, I was watching this movie about a school band and the girl playing the flute made it sound so good, and I figured it was easier to carry a flute around to practice than, say, a piano. So, well, I'm playing the flute."

"You have it with you now?"

"I left it at home. Next time I'll bring it."

"I like that, Zoe," he said. "Next time. I like there being a next time."

They left the ice-cream store and headed down Barr Street toward Robbins. They continued to talk and laugh and Lawton felt happier and more content than he had in decades. It was a perfect day, but it wasn't going to stay that way.

"Floyd. You're on time. For once."

Lawton's ex-wife emerged from her car, the car he bought her in better times. She gestured for Zoe to come. The good times were over, he knew, but at least he'd had a chance to see her again.

"Zoe, go to your mom, and never forget I love you."

"I love you, too," she responded as she gave him a hug, then got into the car. "Next week?" she said, hoping.

"Next week," Lawton said. "And I'm always here. Whenever you want me."

Lawton watched the car take off. Zoe was in the back seat, waving goodbye to him. He gave a wistful smile then turned away. He took two steps then paused.

His smile was gone. The day, which had been spectacularly perfect, was over in an instant.

"Thanks for waiting for my daughter to go."

The Bat stood behind him. Dark. Menacing. Lawton never even heard him approach.

"This is nothing she should see." The voice was coarse gravel. "Besides, she'll have gray hair when you see her again."

Lawton spun even as his wrist magnums snapped into firing position. Then the demon was on him, fists slamming him in the face. He felt warm blood filling his mouth. The monster lashed out at him again, and he felt his legs slip out from under him. He fell to the ground.

The demon straddled him, punched him, but Lawton jammed his wrist magnum under the monster's chin, and fired. The slug shredded the latch of the bulletproof cowl, exposing the flesh beneath. Whatever the hell the Bat was, he was human, and Lawton's next shot would go up through the skull and split the Bat's brain in two.

The demon slammed his leg into Lawton's knee, cracking it. Lawton emptied his other magnum into the demon's armored chest.

The Bat fell back a step, but then regained his balance and drove a fist into the side of Lawton's head. He staggered. His ears were ringing and he could barely see, but he swore to himself that he'd die before he ever backed down.

Lawton reached for another gun, but the Bat smashed a boot to his hand, nearly breaking his wrist. He dropped the gun, the Bat moved to kick it away, but Lawton was ready. He grabbed a knife from a wrist holster and slashed at the Bat's exposed face. The monster fell back, avoiding the hit, but he was thrown off balance.

Leading with his shoulder, Lawton rammed the Bat in the gut and sent him tumbling back to the ground. Lawton was on him in an instant, plunging down with the knife. The Bat struggled to turn, and the knife lodged in his side, between the armor and his skin. It had to hurt like hell, but the Bat didn't even screech.

He wrapped his legs around Lawton's neck and spun him into the sidewalk.

"Stay down," the Bat said as the police sirens closed in. Before Lawton could blink his hands were cuffed and locked to a streetlamp pole. Batman was gone, and a half-dozen police cars pulled in next to him.

EIGHT

The Joker stuck his left hand out of the car's open window and let several puffs of snow come to rest on his finger. He stared at them, remembering his own childhood holidays, then licked the snow away.

"Tastes like crap. Just as I remember. Some things don't get better with age."

"C'mon, Mr. J," Harley protested. "You're driving like an old man. Pedal to the metal."

Joker growled then pushed his high-performance Italian machine to as fast as its 1,244hp, twin turbocharged V8 engine would let him.

"So what if we die," he said, and he laughed. In seconds they were a slick purple streak slamming through the Gotham City streets as if nothing would ever dare get in his way.

Harley thrust her arms out and laughed, but then she noticed Joker wasn't laughing.

"You still cross with me, Mr. J?"

Joker snarled at her and again slammed the gas pedal as far down as it could go.

"Yeah. For all those second stringers I had to kill because of you. They were decent, you know. Reliable people. Good men. Loyal men, and they're falling like dominoes."

"Well, maybe you should stop killing them? I'd hate to work for you. Your health plan sucks."

Joker leaned in and barely took the corner. Ahead of him was a local street fair. Too bad. Even as he cannoned toward them, the people scattered. He plowed into the barriers, smashed his way through food stands, then turned at the next corner and sped on.

Too bad. Nobody got flattened.

"Excuse me?" Joker suddenly said, continuing their conversation as if nothing had happened. "You're putting this on me? You provoke them with your constant need to test me. You're engineering your situations."

Harley folded her arms over her chest and gave the Joker her award-winning best pout.

"Well, I'm young. Vibrant. Alive. And I'm sure as hell not staying home at night."

Joker growled again. "You make my teeth hurt. I can't do this anymore. I'm putting this thing into a wall."

He slammed the gas down again and the car rocketed forward. *This is what life's all about*, he thought. He glanced up and saw a black shape in his rearview mirror. It was closing in on him.

The damned Batmobile.

"Forget flatlining," he said. "Buckle up." Harley laughed, removed her seatbelt and let the two halves retract into their holders.

"Hope you got insurance."

The Joker gave her a dirty look as he again slammed the gas pedal.

"Now's not the time, dear." He took another turn, and Harley almost ended up giving him a lap dance. She giggled as she wiggled back into her seat.

"Again," she demanded.

Insatiable.

The car shuddered. Something slammed on its roof. It should have been impossible at their speed, but then again, their pursuer specialized in the impossible. Sparks rained down as a blowtorch sliced the roof open.

"Puddin'?"

Batman was glaring down at them.

"I see him. I'm not blind. Hold on or you'll be flying out the window."

She clutched the seat as Joker took the next turn even faster. Somehow Batman still hung on.

"My turn," Harley said, and she laughed. Reaching for Joker's .45, she took it and fired upward into the roof.

BAM-BAM-BAM-BAM-BAM! Five rounds flatted against their pursuer's body armor. One ricocheted and shattered the front windshield.

"Let's go swimming, Harley," Joker said. "You do swim, don't you?"

"Nope. Don't even like to drink that stuff."

"Well, that sucks for you then." Joker laughed as he whipped around another turn and cannoned toward the Gotham River.

There was no way Batman could stay with the car. He whirled and fired a cable onto a fire escape. As the dark purple sports car punched through a chain-link fence and crashed into the water, the crime fighter retracted the line and swung to safety.

Harley couldn't hold on. She was thrown into the windshield and got stuck halfway through.

Batman let momentum bring him back to the river. He released the cable and gracefully arced into a dive, slicing into the water.

The car was sinking fast. Its xenon headlights cut through the murk, illuminating a clear path for him to follow. He dove deeper while reaching for a specific canister kept in his belt. He removed a small re-breather and placed it over his mouth. It wouldn't provide a lot of air, but it would last long enough.

He followed the car as it speared into the deep and buried its nose into the river mud. Then he took out his belt flashlight and aimed it at the car. Harley was out cold and drowning. Even as he grabbed her by the hair and lifted her head, he realized Joker was gone.

How the hell did that happen?

Batman pulled Harley, freeing her from the car. Her eyes snapped open and she grabbed two knives hidden in her uniform, then tried to bury them in the man who was trying to rescue her. They wrestled until he slammed his fist into her, knocking her unconscious. She'd stop resisting, and he could save her.

Gripping her firmly, he swam back to the surface. Reaching land, he lay her on her back and administered chest compressions. No response. Only one more thing to try. It was repulsive, but her only hope. Batman put his mouth to hers, this woman who had just tried to kill him.

He alternated breaths with more chest compressions.

Suddenly she wrapped her arms around him, turning CPR into a prolonged kiss. He fought and pulled away.

She coughed and looked up.

"Why the favor, Bats?" she asked.

Batman glowered at her. "Joker took something important away from me," he growled. "It's my turn."

Harley didn't reply, but she shivered.

NINE

Harley Quinn woke up in a cage in Belle Reve, thoroughly rested from her fun-filled day-long class trip with her wonderful, sexy professor, Mr. J.

She was hanging upside down—the only way she could sleep. Slowly, languidly, she unfolded and lowered herself to the ground.

Her cage was in a cell block Harley had all to herself. It wasn't that she could wander its spacious nooks and crannies—she remained locked up in her own cramped little space—but she wouldn't be bothered by the other nutcases they sealed away in this maximum-security crazy house.

Harley preferred the quiet.

So she could listen to the voices in her head.

Armed sentinels stood outside her cage, outfitted to the teeth, waiting for her to make a wrong move. Any wrong move. The last time she had, she took out four of their squad before she was brought down by a triple dose of sedatives. These guards were not going to make the same mistake.

They were armed and as brutally Neanderthal as supermax guards could be. They were also afraid of her. She might look like a pretty little snip of a girl, but she could kill a man twice her size before he could even grab his weapon.

Their commander, Captain Griggs, was a tyrannical redneck, and proud of it. He had decided to pay her a visit, and paced in front of the Neanderthals, then stopped and turned to stare at her.

"You know the rules, hotness. Stay off the bars. You sleep on the floor."

Harley walked up to the bars, grabbed them, and glared at Griggs.

"I sleep where I want," she said. "When I want. With who I want. So ha."

Griggs laughed. "This is my house, little missy. You break my rules, you pay me." He tapped the mic worn on his shirt. "Hit her."

Before Harley could react, a jolt of electricity shot through her. She let out a surprised howl of pain, and fell to the ground.

Uttering a feral growl, she picked herself up. She saw the smug look on Griggs's face, and the growl turned to a roar of rage. Without thinking she hurled herself against the bars again.

Bouncing off, she hit the floor, unconscious.

Griggs stared at Harley, lying there in her cage, then turned to Alan Dixon, his second-in-command.

"Now that's a whole lotta pretty, and a whole lotta crazy. The word batshit don't even scratch the surface."

The guards knew the routine. They pulled out their tasers, prepped them, then headed into the cell.

"Okay," Griggs said. "Let's get her done."

TEN

Floyd Lawton had to find his own ways to keep up his strength and stamina while locked away in Belle Reve— they weren't about to grant him gymnasium privileges.

Let the body go, the mind will follow, he mused. Besides, he wasn't going to be in here for long. Not even a supermax could hold him, once he decided he didn't want to be there.

Lawton rolled up his mattress, tied it tight with his bed sheet, then hung it like a punching bag. Not quite what he'd find at a fancy fitness center, but it would keep Lawton sharp and ready. For anything.

He was trapped in a concrete-and-steel cage, and the space between the bars was fitted with ballistic glass. Even if he managed to procure a weapon, Lawton couldn't shoot his way out of this place. Even so, he wasn't about to let that stop him.

WHAP-WHAP.

He hit the bag. The makeshift cord groaned as it swung back and forth. He hit it again, angry with himself that he'd allowed his daughter to see into his other life. The life he desperately wanted to keep far away from her.

WHAP-WHAP!

He kept hitting it, each punch harder than the one before.

"Yo, Floyd," Captain Griggs shouted. Lawton ignored him and hit the bag again. In his mind, Griggs's face was in front of him, on the mattress. That encouraged him to hit it even harder than before.

"I said, yo, Floyd!"

Lawton stopped, grabbed a towel, wiped the sweat from his face, and finally turned to the cell door.

"Only my friends call me Floyd."

"You ain't got no friends, Floyd," Griggs replied. He motioned to his lap dog, Dixon, who was carrying a food tray. "Besides, it's suppertime."

The guard picked a small wrapped bar from the tray and slipped it through the slot. It landed with a loud thunk.

"Nutriloaf," Griggs said. "All the vitis you need, with none of the flavor of actual food. Mmm-MMM crap!"

Belle Reve must've had a lucrative contract with whatever company produced the garbage because whatever cesspool they found it in, it was pretty much all the prisoners ever got. Lawton wouldn't have given it to a rabid dog, yet somehow it was legal to for them to feed it to the prison's long-term shut-ins.

Lawton stared up at his daily tormentor. "Know something, Griggs?" he said. "Back on the block, I'd fly to New York every Friday for a rib-eye. Wagyu beef. That's the cows they massage and feed beer. Ever had a steak worth flying cross-country for?" He grinned. "No? Bet you just fry up some frozen chuck patties, macaroni salad, and moon pies. Right?"

Griggs just stared at him.

"You think you're so smart, don't you, Lawton?"

he said, contempt dripping from his words. "Big and powerful. Well, guess what? You're here, and you're nothing here."

Lawton rested his face against the metal door and looked at Griggs through the slide window. "C'mon, big-shot. Unlock the door and take a swipe at me. Let's see what you're made of." Griggs had his army with him. They were armed and, judging from the red in their eyes, in the hunting mood, but Lawton wasn't about to give them any cause to unload their weapons in his direction. So he stepped away from the bars to let Griggs finish his little speech.

"Remember, Lawton," the asshole said, "I am your king, and tonight I'll go home. Have a cold beer. Watch some television and fool around with the old lady. While you fester in this cage like a sick dog eating the scraps I feed you. No one knows you're here, Floyd, and no one ever will. With no calls. No mail. Just your memories—and those are gonna fade away, real soon."

Lawton thought about what Griggs said, then turned and punched the bag.

"Griggs," he said, "I'll get out of here someday." The man's face appeared on the bag again. "Somehow I'll be like the holy spirit watching over you. Then I'll show you who wears the crown." He glanced at his tormentor out of the corner of his eye.

Griggs's façade cracked, just a little bit. He looked like he wanted to lash out and punch the living hell out of Floyd, but he knew better.

Instead, he spun and started to walk out. As he reached the cell door, he turned back and smiled.

"You just lost your mattress, for threatening staff," he announced. "Enjoy." He stood there, waiting for a response.

Lawton massaged his callused knuckles, then suddenly unleashed a series of blows against the wall—so hard that they cracked the cement. He looked back at Griggs with murder in his eyes.

"What?" Griggs said, but there was a catch in his voice. "Gonna take away the walls, too?" He was going to say something more when Dixon tapped him on the shoulder.

"We're needed, Captain," the toady said. "We need to go." Griggs hesitated for a moment, then nodded.

"This ain't over, killer," he said. "See you soon."

Counting on it, Lawton thought.

ELEVEN

Colonel Rick Flag took the steps three at a time. He was a big guy, large and imposing, but he moved silently, as did the two Delta operatives who shadowed him.

The colonel and his men were the best Tier One shooters in the military, as well, and they damn well knew it.

Flag paused to check the two dead cops on the stairwell floor. Broken necks. He gave his men a nod. It was time. Their target was on the next floor up. Heat scans showed that she was in the bathroom, lying down, probably taking a luxuriating bath.

Enjoy yourself for about forty-five more seconds, he thought. His men flanked him as he used the passkey to silently open the door, then entered the apartment.

Ten more seconds for her to enjoy her bubbling bliss. Without a sound he counted down on his fingers. When his pinky folded into his fist, he kicked in the bathroom door.

As expected, June Moone was in the bathtub. Thick, foamy bubbles surrounded her, and there was an ominous black septagram painted on the wall behind her. She let out a startled little scream, and stared in wide-eyed horror at Flag and his men.

"Who are you?"

Flag stared at June for much too long. His comm crackled to life, returning him to the moment.

"Ma'am," he said. "We're on the X, if you want to get in here."

Seconds later Amanda Waller entered the crowded little room. She wasn't particularly large or powerful-looking, but when she gestured the soldiers away from June, they obeyed instantly. When she turned back to the woman in the bath, she smiled.

"Miss Moone," she said. "My name is Amanda. I'm here to help you. I can free you from your burden if you do what I say."

June stared at the newcomer, and then heard sirens approaching. Were the police coming to help her, or to side with these four intruders? Three of them were armed, yet it was the woman who seemed the most frightening.

"Ma'am," the first man said to June. "No time to explain. You're coming with us. Right now."

The woman, Amanda, gave June her hand to help her up. That was when the young archeologist knew she had no choice.

The Belle Reve Prison pressure chamber was purposely kept dark. The better to see him if he tried anything.

Suddenly, a candle flame erupted, illuminating two black-as-pitch eyes set deep into a tattooed skull.

Diablo stared at the flame. It wasn't rising from some store-bought candle, but freely floating just above his open hand.

His head was pounding, sharp daggers thrust into

his brain, but he kept staring as the flames flickered back and forth...

...and ever so slowly, they took on the undulating shape of a woman, moving, swaying. He had brought her to life again, and she was beautiful. As always. Mesmerizing. As always. And so hypnotic he almost forgot his was a soul in constant pain.

As he blew out the flame, and tears streaked the terrible story told on his face, all he could do was quietly whisper.

"I am so, so sorry."

The woman disappeared into the smoke.

As always.

TWELVE

The real work of Washington, D.C., didn't take place in the light of day, but in a quiet back room, behind the leather-cushioned and mahogany-stained walls of the tried-and-true Washingtonian Steakhouse.

The important people still went there to sip fine wine and cut into a juicy filet while negotiating treaties and bills that would otherwise never see the light of day. Opened in the early 1940s, still months away from the U.S. entering the Second Great War, it was one of the very few reminders that, unlike the rest of this youth-obsessed world, some things still aged well.

Amanda Waller took another sip of her Pinot noir, then continued talking. With her in this soundproof chamber were Dexter Tolliver, the president's national security advisor, and Vice Admiral Olsen, commander of SOCOM, the United States Special Operations Command.

"It's taken some work, but I have them," she announced. "Well, most of them. The worst of the worst."

Olsen opened a bottle of the 2014 Malbec and poured a glass. Argentinian wines were his favorites.

"There are rumors, Amanda, that some of them have, ummm, abilities?"

Waller nodded. "Yes. Heard about the pyrokinetic homeboy? Some LA gangbanger gets jumped in a prison riot and incinerates half the yard." She handed Olsen her smart phone, already set for playback. "The security videos are incredible. Thirty-three dead. Filled every burn unit in So Cal. He released enough thermal energy in three seconds to melt an engine block."

She grinned as she bit into her salmon, cedar-plank barbecued with a rosemary and Dijon mustard rub.

"I have him now."

Olsen looked impressed, and handed the phone for Tolliver to watch.

"Where?"

Waller smiled as she wiped her lips with a napkin. "Let's just say I put him in a hole, and threw away the hole. We chased away our ancient fears with the light of science."

"Which means?"

"It means that maybe Superman was some kind of beacon for the rest of them to feel safe enough they could creep back from the shadows." She took the phone from Tolliver and slipped it back into its holster, then leaned in conspiratorially. "Heard about the witch?"

"The witch?" Olsen repeated. "Really?"

Waller raised her glass and took another sip, letting the silence add to her drama.

"I'm talking textbook witch. A flying, spell-casting, making-crap-disappear witch." She lowered her voice even more, and added, "I've seen things."

"And where is this witch?" Olsen asked, not expecting her to answer. He wasn't disappointed.

"In my pocket," Waller said.

Tolliver didn't look convinced. "And what's to stop

her from turning you into a frog," he said skeptically, as if going along with a joke.

Waller wasn't laughing. "There's intel in our legends, says witches have a secret buried heart. Whoever finds it can control the witch, or kill it."

"You do realize what this all sounds like, Amanda?" Olsen said. "'A heart that can be removed, yet its owner still lives?' Dexter, you're talking *Harry Potter* stuff, and it's preposterous."

Waller just smiled. She expected there'd be pushback and she had come prepared.

"It used to be that we believed we were the only intelligent life form in the entire universe. Remember? And nobody ever thought that aliens actually existed, or that they could have powers far beyond those of, well, us. And then Superman showed up. He sort of screwed the very concept of conventional wisdom."

Before anyone could reply, she put a large black Pelican case on the table. The case was made of black injection-molded waterproof and crushproof plastic, and was sealed with a biometric fingerprint lock.

"So we searched the cave where she turned up, and found this," Waller added.

"Her heart's in there?" Tolliver said incredulously. "Really?" He frowned.

Waller nodded. "Here, Dexter, see for yourself."

Waller swiped the fingerprint lock and the case opened. Enchantress's mummified heart, decorated with bear claws and bits of gold, rested in a chamber to the right of the case. In the left-hand chamber was Waller's fail-safe bomb. Given any excuse, she would press a button and it would explode, disintegrating the heart instantly.

Tolliver turned away, looking vaguely sick. He was,

she knew, far more comfortable with the intricacies of state and the duplicity of politics than supernatural mumbo-jumbo.

"Don't worry." Waller closed the case lid and smiled again at him. "You're safe, Dexter. As long as I have this, she'll do anything I ask."

"So what is it you're asking for, Amanda?" Admiral Olsen asked.

Waller didn't have to think about an answer. She knew exactly why she'd come here.

"I want to assemble a task force of the most dangerous people on the planet—something I call Task Force X."

"They're bad guys?" Olsen said, looking doubtful.

"Exactly. The worst of the worst, and if anything goes wrong, we blame them. We've got built-in deniability."

Olsen shook his head. "Amanda, let's say we're with you on this—but these people, they're villains. What makes you think you can control them?"

Waller leaned back in her plush leather chair and took another sip from her glass.

"This wine is excellent," she responded. "I'll have to order a case and have it shipped to my home."

"Amanda, please. No games."

"All right. Fine. Getting people to act against their own self-interest, for the national security of the United States, is what I do for a living, and you know how good I am at it."

"I do," Olsen replied. "But I just don't know if I'm buying this. Witches. Fire-starters. It begs the imagination. I'm pretty much a meat and potatoes guy."

Tolliver interrupted.

"And yet we might not have much of a choice.

Again, Superman. Amanda, if we want to make this happen, what we'd have to do is sell it downtown. I'll convene a stakeholder's meeting with Defense and Intelligence. You get the nod from the Chairman, and you can do anything you want." He turned to Olsen and continued. "Ever since the alien... Well, it's a whole new world out there, my friend."

"Okay, Dexter," Olsen said." If you can sell it to the boys downtown, I'll sign off on it."

Waller smiled, poured herself another glass, and silently toasted her own victory.

THIRTEEN

She knew her Puddin' would come. Maybe not today. Maybe not tomorrow, or even the month after, but when he realized how much he missed her—and he would—he'd definitely haul ass and rescue her.

So until then she was just biding her time. She was back in her Belle Reve cage, chained to a black plastic restraint chair. A spit guard was strapped tightly to her mouth. Her forehead was belted back so she couldn't move it.

It hurt like all kinds of hell, but that didn't matter. Her Puddin' was coming. She most certainly knew that.

Any time now.

Any time now.

The prison nurse hovered over her and snaked a feeding tube into her nostril. She was unable to turn her head, but then another figure stepped into view, and she saw Griggs holding up three cans of liquid nutrition. He was smiling at her.

"Looky-looky, lil' mama. Tonight it's your choice. Chocolate crap, strawberry crap, or vanilla crap."

Whistle. Whistle. *Any time now, Mr. J. I'm waiting.* Harley stared daggers at Griggs. When she was free, her first order of business would be payback. Right now, though, clenched teeth and a dirty look would have to do.

Griggs leaned closer and caressed her thigh. "Why is it always a fight with you?" he asked. "I could make it nice in here. Really nice."

Any time now, Mr. J.

Nurse Wretched, or whatever the hell her name was, connected a large syringe of the liquid nutrient to the feeding tube. She tightened its connection then squeezed the plunger. Harley shook with rage. Bubbles foamed out of her nose. She scowled at Griggs with a look so angry he involuntarily took a step back.

Any time now, Mr. J.

Floyd Lawton was trying to sleep. The nightly screams of hundreds of crazies blared through the air ducts and directly into his cell, it seemed.

Unable to sleep, he stood and paced the cell. Five steps. Turn. Five steps. Turn. Five steps… Back and forth. Back and forth. He thought about Zoe, and that he might never see her again, and he wanted to join in on the screaming. He knew better, however, than to surrender to madness. In here it was catching.

It was raining outside.

Floyd knew he wasn't crazy. He was a stone-cold killer, but only for hire. He never thought his victims were sending messages to him through his teeth, or that the only way the voices would stop was if he wore an aluminum foil headpiece. Besides, he never even heard voices, unless they came from flesh-and-blood people.

Maybe others did, but not him.

His kills were for money. Lots of money. There was

nothing personal in any of them. It was just a job—at least when he wasn't spending his days and nights behind bars.

He watched the rain drip past his cell window. He thought of Zoe as much as he could. He worried, tossed in here, away from the world, that his memories would fade like a bad dream, but he didn't want to forget his daughter.

Captain Griggs and his posse of guards sauntered along Belle Reve's pipe-lined basement corridor. Dixon, his chief tough guy, kicked a food cart aside and exposed a manhole cover beneath it. Griggs gestured toward it and two of his flunkies unscrewed the bolts which held it in place, then pulled it loose.

Griggs carried a carbine with a well-worn night-vision scope. He used it to peer into the black hole.

Two evil, glowing eyes stared back.

Dixon leaned in. "Is it true he chewed a dude's hand off?"

Gerry Moench, standing behind Dixon, waved his prosthetic hand. Dixon pulled back and looked to Griggs for help, but Griggs wasn't the helping kind.

"Time for his dinner," the captain said. "You know what to do."

Dixon sucked in air, held his breath, and grabbed a goat carcass from the cart. As he tossed it down into the hole, he let the air whoosh out.

"This garbage smells like crap," he said.

Below, in the sewer, the huge figure was locked behind bars and barbed wire. He watched the goat drop just outside the cage, into the dirty water that was flowing through the tunnel.

A large shrine made of animal bones sat to one side. A ratty couch, with rat bones scattered over it, was directly behind him. The fluorescent lights, old and flickering, barely lit this hellhole, but he didn't care.

What was there to look at, anyway?

He reached through the bars to grab the carcass and pull it toward him. He looked at the dead head, knowing he could either eat it or starve to death. So he took a bite.

Croc was close to six-and-a-half feet tall, and he probably weighed at least three hundred and fifty pounds. His skin was cracked and mottled, covered over with scales that made him look as if evolution had worked its way backward, creating the perfect hybrid of man and dinosaur. Though he looked as if he should be raging, roaring like a beast, he was calm, and quiet, and even reflective.

He had his dinner. It tasted raw and bloody, the way he liked it, so as far as he was concerned, life was good.

He took another bite, gnawed through the goat's skull, and whistled a happy tune.

FOURTEEN

June had never been to Washington, D.C. before, let alone brought into the White House Situation Room.

Yet that was where she found herself, and she was duly impressed. The room—all 5,525 square feet of it—sat in the basement of the West Wing. It had been created by President Kennedy back in 1961, to deal with then-growing Soviet threat. Overseen by the National Security Council, it was where the president and his advisors met to discuss all crises, domestic or international.

The room was narrow, but long. Its walls were embedded with large flat-screen monitors that provided secure video communications with contacts across the globe. A massive conference table filled the center of the room, from front to back. Plush leather chairs surrounded the table. The group that occupied them had come to discuss what was fast becoming a crisis that would make the Cold War seem like a kindergarten time-out.

The chairman of the Joint Chiefs sat at the head of the table, focused on his smart phone, trying to figure out how to send a text. His aide explained it to him at least a dozen times. Rick Flag sat next to Amanda

Waller, uncomfortable and fidgeting because he had been forced to dress up for this meeting. Waller's case lay closed on the table.

June Moone sat next to him as well, wearing glasses, looking shy and just a bit mousey, yet he found her distracting. Under any other circumstances...

Dexter Tolliver stood, and his eyes swept across the assembled group. Finally his gaze locked on the chairman, and he cleared his throat.

"Mr. Chairman," he began. "Do you remember al-Qaeda? A few of you might not. We certainly threw enough sigint, linguists, analysts, and drones at them. It took time, but... problem solved."

June leaned close to Flag. "Sigint?"

"Signal intelligence," he whispered back. "It's data gathering by interception of electronic signals." Tolliver continued, and he fell silent again.

"Now we have a new problem," the national security advisor stated, and he waved a hand upward, toward the ceiling. "Suppose Superman decided to rip the president out of the Oval office. Who could stop him? We have contingency plans for North Korean nukes, anthrax in our mail, fluoride in our water—but what do we do about a Kryptonian?

"Now, thus far Superman has showed himself to be a rescue-cats-from-trees kind of hero," he added. "It might be an act, but just for grins let's say he's what he says he is. What do we do if the next one turns out to be a jihadist? Then what?"

He paused for effect, then turned. "Fortunately for us, Ms. Waller has a plan. Amanda?" He gestured for her to take over.

The chairman acknowledged her with a nod. "Alright, Amanda," he said. "Who do you want us to kill?" He laughed at his own joke, and a few others joined in, if half-heartedly.

Waller gave a quick smile and stood.

"We've all heard the stories, of Samson leveling a temple with a single push—and we know of the Philistine weapon of mass destruction they called Goliath—but were they scripture, or fact?"

She paused, and scanned the room. No one spoke. None of them wanted to give voice to views that might come back and haunt them. Especially not theories that were biblical in nature. No, they didn't have the answer, but she did.

She continued.

"The question is, how did ancient societies deal with these exceptional individuals? In general, by appeasement, by coercion, and often cooperation. But this isn't the ancient world. In this day and age, what should we do?"

Their expressions remained blank. Amanda preferred it that way. First, explain the problem. Let them stew in it, then provide them with the answer. She was leading them by the nose.

"I want to build a team," she explained, "of very bad people who I think can do some good—like fight our next war, or defeat the next Superman."

The chairman crossed his arms. His body language said he wasn't buying it.

Before Waller was done, he would. She was certain of it.

"Not on my watch, Amanda," he replied. "I read your list. You're not putting these monsters back on the streets. Certainly not in our name." If he had planned to discourage her, though, he was going to be disappointed.

"General, under my plan we run them covertly," she said. "Non-attributed, strictly need to know, and if they get caught, we throw them under the bus." She looked from face to face. "Whether we want to accept it or not, the next war will be fought with these... meta-humans."

That made them pay attention. Wars were something they all understood. They wanted the best soldiers on their side, and that meant meta-humans. It was bound to happen someday. Better to get ahead of it.

"Those meta-soldiers will be ours—" she said firmly, "—or the advantage will be theirs. We're not the only ones kicking over rocks, looking for these extraordinary people. You must know that. And ours isn't the only belief system they'd fight for."

"But you can't control them," the chairman protested. "Nobody can." He sounded adamant, but his voice was low. He was teetering. She had him. Yet she didn't answer directly. Instead, she turned to the only one in the room who could prove her case.

"Doctor Moone." The young woman looked anxious. Waller nodded to her. "Now, Doctor."

June stood and took off her glasses. She placed her hands on the table, gulped anxiously, then whispered one word. Softly, and to herself.

"Enchantress."

It took three long seconds.

New fingers sprouted from her wrist as her old ones were sucked back into the skin. The top of her hand became her palm, then spun back into a normal hand again, only now tattooed. Her torso twisted around itself as parts of her face bulged out, while other parts sunk inward.

Gasps rose as the chiefs stared in disbelief, and she transformed in front of them. Transformed into something that might not even be human.

Within moments, June Moone was gone.

Replaced by something very different. Something ancient.

A crescent moon headpiece fit over her thick black hair, which hung dark and loose, almost like vines. Her clothing was animal skins decorated with leather, chains, jade, and even stone. She peered around the table, her dark eyes staring at each of the so-called leaders of America.

"Fantastic," she laughed. "A meeting. Let's do something fun. Perhaps get a drink?"

Waller stepped in front of her.

"I'd like you to meet Enchantress," she said firmly. "Everything we know about her is in your briefing packs. She walked this Earth a long time ago—maybe as far back as the beginning, and she'll likely be here when we're long gone."

"So," the chairman interrupted. "This meeting is now a magic show?"

Waller smiled, and didn't even try to hide her contempt.

"General, the issues we face strike at the core of our beliefs. Our science. Magic or not, this lady can do some pretty incredible things."

The chairman frowned, but she had his attention.

"Like what?" he asked. Waller smiled again, but this time it was sincere. He'd asked the right question, and at exactly the right time.

She had him.

"Go get it, girl," she said.

Enchantress's eyes followed Waller's hand to the box

containing her desiccated heart. She forced a tight little smile. Then—snap—she disappeared. The chiefs stared at one another, not certain what they had just seen.

Five seconds passed. Ten. Twenty.

"That's all you've got?" the chairman said, breaking the silence. "I've seen David Copperfield do a helluva lot better."

"Wait for it, sir," Amanda responded, a bit of annoyance creeping into her voice. "It's coming."

SNAP!

Enchantress reappeared, unleashing a mild shockwave that scattered papers across the room. She dropped a thick binder on the table. A binder secured with Iranian seals. Written in Farsi.

Waller slid the binder to the chairman.

"Sir, how about a little something from the Weapons Ministry vault in Tehran?"

Cautiously, he opened the binder and leafed through the papers. His eyes widened in surprise.

"We've been chasing these plans for years." The chairman slid the binder to General Conway, who rifled through it one page at a time.

"Thank you, Enchantress," Waller said. "We'd like Dr. Moone back now."

But Enchantress wasn't paying attention.

Conway paused momentarily on a photograph.

It was the remaining jar from the cave.

Waller saw it, too. She quickly swiped the lock and opened the case. Without attracting attention, she shoved her pen inside.

Instantly Enchantress snapped around and stared at her. Then her skin began to retract, squeezing her face, strangling her with her own flesh. She tried to resist, but the pain was too great.

"Enchantress," she whispered.

In an instant June Moone had returned. She looked up to Waller, pleading with her eyes.

"Please don't make me bring her back."

Rick Flag pushed a glass of water to her.

"It'll be okay. I promise."

Waller shook her head dismissively. "There's no reason to be worried. I control her, as I will all the others to come. You and the rest of the world will never have to fear metas ever again."

Tolliver stood up again, a broad, victorious smile coiled across his face.

"Mr. Chairman, sir. I move that we authorize Amanda Waller to establish Task Force X under the A.R.G.U.S. program." Immediately all eyes turned to the chairman.

A moment later, he nodded his assent.

Waller, too, was grinning. She had won.

She always won.

Under the table, Rick Flag took June's hand in his.

FIFTEEN

With its landing gear extended, descending at a constant three degrees, the KC-135 Stratotanker began its approach to the Belle Reve runway, less than five miles away.

The facility was pretty much in the middle of nowhere, surrounded by a vast bayou of cypress trees and swampland. Only a long causeway connected it to the rest of the world, but the drawbridge was raised, isolating it further.

The aircraft was coming in low at an approach speed of 100 knots. It buzzed over patrol boats bristling with machine guns, manned by alert guards.

The prison looked like an Iraq firebase with its missile launchers, plastic barriers, camouflage netting, and patrolling Humvees. Nobody was getting in uninvited.

Even more important, nobody was getting out.

Captain Griggs watched as the Stratotanker hit the tarmac. Moments later it taxied to a halt. Waller, Flag, and Moone made their way down the ramp. He put on a big fake smile and closed the gap to shake hands with the colonel.

"Welcome to Belle Reve Special Security Barracks,"

he said. Flag ignored his hand and nodded toward Waller.

"Kiss her ass," he suggested. "She's in charge."

Without hesitation, Griggs turned to Waller and extended his hand again.

"Ma'am, welcome. We're here to assist you in any way."

"Where are they?" she said.

Griggs felt his face flush. Didn't any of these people believe in damned pleasantries?

"We'll get you in there, ma'am." He glanced at the .45 strapped to Flag's legs, and the carbine strapped to his chest. This was his chance to even the score.

"Sir, you have to surrender your hog leg and rifle. No weapons past that line."

Flag nodded toward the airmen unloading cases of firearms from the Stratotanker.

"I'm bringing in a lot more than this." He tapped his .45 and walked past Griggs as if he wasn't even there.

The table hastily set up in the outdoor shooting range was covered over with sub-machine guns, rifles, pistols, plenty of scary black plastic, and stacks of loaded magazines. There was enough ammo to begin and end a revolution. Yet Waller and Flag were impatiently waiting for the real weapons to be unloaded from the KC-135.

Moments later the first one arrived.

Floyd Lawton—Deadshot—was escorted into the garage by an army of armed guards, accompanied by a very worried Captain Griggs. He was shackled from head to toe.

"Unlock him," Flag snapped. "C'mon. Lose the restraints."

* * *

Griggs looked him, then at the gun show of weapons filling the room, then turned back to Flag.

"You know what this man can do?"

Flag scowled. "I'm here to find out."

Griggs wanted to protest, but he was smart enough to know it would only get him into trouble. With half of Washington breathing down his ass, whatever was going on, it was big—way above his pay grade. He was trolling in some very dangerous waters, and if he wanted to make it out again, he would have to be especially careful.

Doing his best to ignore Lawton glaring at him, Griggs unlocked the assassin's shackles and chains.

"So, what is this?" Lawton drawled. "Cheerleading tryouts?"

Flag checked out the table crowded with weapons. "What gave it away, Lawton? The fifty grand in Gucci weapons?" The colonel picked one up, checked it out, then dropped it back on the table. "Have at it, Lawton. Not that I'm expecting much. I've seen legends crumble."

"Have we met?" Lawton asked, not sounding particularly interested. "Do we know each other? Because you're sure acting like it."

Flag checked out the Sig Sauer P220.

"I hunt people like you for a living," Flag said as Lawton studied the table. "Mind showing us if you can run that iron or not?"

Lawton finished a quick survey of the weapons. He looked up and smiled. Six catwalk guards were aiming their carbines at him. He knew he could easily take out five of them if he tried, but it was possible that last one might cause him some trouble. He turned and eyed the distant steel targets that had been set up.

Hell. My dog could hit them, he thought.

His fingers drifted over the banquet of weapons. He still wasn't sure what was going on, which made him wonder if these were even real. Flag and company sure as hell wouldn't let an assassin called "Deadshot" anywhere within a thousand yards of these babies.

He didn't have to look to know Griggs was jumping out of his skin.

Good. Let him suffer.

Flag's hand rested on his sidearm, fingers drumming the holster. He watched Lawton pick up a combat-tuned .45 pistol, savoring its heft. He slid a full mag into the grip, then sealed it with a satisfying *SNAP*. He thumbed the slide release. It clicked shut on a fresh round.

The .45 felt real. Felt heavy enough. He still couldn't believe they would trust him with a working weapon.

Or maybe they're just nuts. That would explain it. Casually he aimed the gun at Griggs. Instantly a half-dozen riflemen had their weapons ready for the kill. They didn't even have to wait for orders. Flag waved for them to chill. As one they lowered their rifles.

What the damned hell is going on?

"Everyone calm down," Flag shouted, loud enough for all to hear. "I'd like to end the day with the same number of holes I had when it started."

Lawton hefted the .45 and shook his head. "So, the firing pin's filed down, right? Or the mag's fulla dummy rounds? Bet I pull the trigger and nothing happens. Can I be trusted? Is that the real question here?"

Griggs was turning gray with fear.

Waller walked over to Lawton and locked eyes.

"Yeah," she said. "You're exactly right. Why would we put a loaded gun in the hands of an infamous hitman? We gotta be insane, right? Just pull the damned trigger."

Lawton just stared back, then finally lowered the .45. He could hear Griggs exhale.

BAM-BAM-BAM-BAM-BAM-BAM!

There was a continuous roar as Deadshot opened fire on the distant targets with inhuman speed and accuracy. He reloaded with a blur. Again and again. Hitting the targets, dead center each time.

A pall of blue smoke filled the area. Empty shells piled up, mag after mag.

It was all damned real.

With practiced ease, Deadshot grabbed weapon after weapon, feeding mags, sending rounds down range. Hit after hit. A jackhammer roar of gunfire and steel impacts. Finally he stopped. He didn't have to shoot again to prove whatever the hell point they needed him to prove.

Flag checked out one of the steel targets. Directly in its center was a single red-hot hole, counterpunched from continuous hits on the exact same point.

Deadshot turned to Waller as he put down the Colt M16, 5.56mm automatic.

"Now you know what you're buying," he said. "Lemme tell you the price. One, I want outta here. Two, I want custody of my little girl. Her mom can get, like, one supervised visit a month. She is with her mom, right?

"Three's a rent-free condo for us in Gotham City, the rich part with, like, doormen. And four, you cover my daughter's education. Full ride. The best private schools, and get her in a good college. Like Harvard, or Yale. And if she gets bad grades, you're gonna down low that crap and make sure she graduates.

"That's my price." He looked at Waller and Flag, who were staring back at him.

"Y'all must got good memories. I don't see no one writing this down."

Flag grinned. "Hey, look around, pal. You're in no position to make demands."

Deadshot was staring at Waller. "I'm not talking to you, soldier boy. I'm talking to your boss."

Flag looked again at the steel targets, each one sporting a single hole.

"You can shoot. I have to give you that." He turned back to Lawton. "But the folks who think big thoughts for a living think you can do the job of a professional. Like me. And that, Lawton, you cannot do."

Deadshot was still staring at Waller, trying to provoke her answer.

"I can show you professional. How about a professional beatdown?"

Flag smiled. "I would very much enjoy that," he said, and Lawton smiled. After all this talk crap, a fight was exactly what he needed.

He tensed, ready to begin, and the colonel followed suit. They stood there, motionless, each waiting for the other to move.

"Colonel. That's enough," Waller said.

Hell.

Waller gestured, and her guards replaced the restraints and escorted him away. Still not quite certain what had just happened, Lawton was escorted back to his cage. The steel door opened and he stepped inside.

While he'd been out shooting tin cans, Waller's boys

had been busy. A new, professional-grade punching bag was hanging from the ceiling. Boxing gloves sat on a thick new mattress. Next to a steaming steak dinner.

He stared at it as if it was a mirage, then the aroma reached his nose. He impaled the ribeye on a fork—actual stainless steel, none of the plastic crap—and tasted it.

No. This was real.

That meant Waller had made her decision about him even before they let him pick his weapon of choice.

Damn.

SIXTEEN

Croc counted his pushups with machine-like efficiency...
941, 942, 943... He was good for a few hundred more.

He stopped and sniffed. Croc detected a rat, a few
hundred yards away. Just behind the steel bars.

"I know you're there," he said, pausing in his daily
exercise routine. "I smelled you long before you got
here."

Rick Flag had been watching from the front tunnel,
hiding in the shadows so as not to be seen. A wasted
effort.

Croc was a lot taller than he, covered over with
scaled skin so thick ordinary bullets wouldn't even
begin to pierce it. He looked as if he could easily bench
press a pickup truck if he wanted. His appearance was
different, though—changed from the photos in his
file. That meant he was still mutating, becoming more
reptilian with every passing year.

"You're gettin' awfully close," Croc said, and
he growled—a low, menacing sound that vibrated
through the air. "Ain't you scared?"

"Is there a reason I should be?"

"Beside the fact I like to bite off the heads of federal
agents? And that you stink like every one of 'em I've

ever known and chewed on? Nah."

Croc walked over to the bars and stuck his head against them. Flag stepped up on the other side, coming within snapping-off distance.

"Why'd they put you down here?" Flag asked.

Croc's mouth contorted into what might generously be construed as a smile.

"I asked," he said. Before Flag could follow up, Croc snorted and lumbered back into the shadows.

The room was dark and cold and Joker lay on the floor, arms spread wide, drunk and miserable. A circle of knives and guns surrounded him. Beyond that was still another circle with more guns and knives and hatchets and blades just waiting for him to pick his favorite then take it to his neck and slice all the way through.

He didn't think he'd ever miss her. After all, she offered him nothing beyond total subservience and unconditional love. Traits he was absolutely certain could easily be replaced by adopting some mangy, flea-bitten shelter dog.

But finding another sex-starved, mallet-wielding psychopath didn't turn out to be quite that easy. Even though he had wanted to take a drill to her head every time she called him Puddin' or Mr. J, he actually craved that now.

Where are you, you Looney Tune? Your Puddin' wants you.

Joker was lying in the center of the room, hidden in shadow. He reached for a long knife but let it go as Frost walked in. His idiot major domo was breathing hard and couldn't wait to tell his boss what he'd learned.

"Boss, I got some information," Frost said, carefully stepping over the nearest corpse. "It cost. It cost big."

"I don't care," Joker said as Frost pulled up a chair across from him.

"Wanted you to know that."

"Just tell me. Where is she?"

Frost knew this was where everything could go south. If he presented the information the wrong way, Frost would be joining the rest of these prematurely retired Mafioso.

"It's complex, boss. Because it's not just her. *Everyone* is disappearing."

"Everyone?" Joker repeated. He didn't like where this was going. Frost was treading deep water now.

"But I got answers and even a possible suggestion. I mean if you want to take it."

Frost waited. This could turn on a dime and still give change. But Joker just lay on the floor and stared up at the ceiling. Obviously, Frost thought, he wasn't going to kill him. He breathed a silent sigh of relief and continued.

"So like I say, it's not just her. There's some new law. Federal, not city or state. It comes down to this: if you're a bad enough bad guy, they stamp terrorist on your jacket and send you to this new secret court."

"You are getting on my nerves, Frost. You said you had answers. I'm not hearing them."

"I was coming right to it, boss. I couldn't find anything about the court itself. You know, it's all top secret, but by spreading some cash to the right people, I'm close to getting some real info."

"How close, Frost?"

"Real close, boss. I swear on my life."

Joker slowly looked up, eyes glistening with black hope. The fire in his madness was still burning.

"Oh, please," he said. "If you're going to swear, swear on something that matters."

SEVENTEEN

They finished an early dinner, then June left the compound and made her way into Midway City. Her life had changed so suddenly that she hadn't had time to think about any of what happened, let alone make plans on how to deal with it all. She found herself overwhelmed, and desperately needed some alone time.

How do you deal with the devil, when she can control your every thought?

June drew in a breath of crisp air, and looked up at the thick blood-red clouds that blanketed the city. Gunfire erupted in the distance, and a barrage of explosions sounded even closer. It was deceptively calm where she stood, in the city center, but it sounded as if there was a war raging, and not too far away. No one had told her what it was about, though.

How do you deal with the devil, when she can control your every action?

June was fighting her own war, too. A monster lived inside her. One who wanted to control or destroy anyone who got in its way. June didn't believe she could control it. Yet wasn't control precisely why Waller and Flag brought her with them?

How do you deal with the devil, when she can control your every breath?

Waller was just plain scary, but Flag...

June wasn't sure what to make of Flag. If she'd ever had a type, he wasn't remotely it. He was crude and clumsily distant. She supposed it was understandable why he wouldn't let any of the inmates get close. Showing those killers any sign of weakness could lead to disaster.

Flag didn't allow himself to get close to any of the SEALs under his command, either. Was there anyone he cared about? Anyone around for whom he could act human?

Maybe he was just a soldier with a mission, and nothing more. Perhaps that was all there was to him.

And yet, she felt... something.

Was it transference? June fought that possibility. She refused to accept the idea that she might be weak enough to fall for someone, just because he was in a position of authority. Like the patient who falls in love with her doctor. "I love you for saving me."

Flag wasn't saving her.

He was using her.

And yet...

What might he feel? Did he see her as someone for whom he cared, or was she just his current assignment? Maybe even his latest weapon. A gun he'd aim at his enemies, then replace when needed with an even bigger one.

Enchantress was the biggest gun anyone could own.

She stopped in her wandering and looked around. The debris extended in all directions, as far as the eye could see. The soldiers guarding the hotel told her that this mountain of concrete and shattered glass had once been a world-class museum. She could just about see parts of crushed dinosaur bones and diorama displays, mixed in with the rest of the trashed landscape.

A tunnel had connected the planetarium to the museum, a late add-on built in the last decades of the twentieth century. Next to it were the remains of a shopping mall. Elite designer brands, once sought after and treasured, were now irretrievable under tons of steel and stone.

So much for "diamonds are forever."

She continued on, not yet ready to return to her room, not nearly tired enough to put aside the day and go to sleep. June wasn't certain she'd ever again have a good night's sleep.

She paused by the chest-high fence that traced the path of the Midway City River. Still untouched, the waterway seemed to stand apart.

The river walk was a place people visited to get away from the rest of the world, even if only for a while. It was quiet and lined with trees and hedges that gave the illusion that the world didn't exist beyond the foliage and the high stone walls.

There were eclectic shops where visitors could buy small gifts, jewelry, clothing, or even get a tattoo if that was what they wanted. There were nearly a dozen restaurants scattered along the walk, as well, from American fast food to Mexican, Thai, Persian, Indian, and more, and places to enjoy several dozen flavors of ice cream and gelato for dessert.

None of them were open now, of course, but they calmed June because they reminded her of the way things had been. The walk went on for another couple of miles before circling back.

It was peaceful, but June was more than aware that it was a deceptive calm. Midway City was ground zero for a war she still didn't understand, and she was Patient Zero.

She, or Enchantress.

"Hey," a voice said, interrupting her reverie. "Looks like we both needed to get away," Rick Flag continued as he approached.

"This seemed to be a time-out. I figured I'd grab a few minutes while I could." He glanced in the direction of the violence, which seemed to have abated for the moment. "Everything's gone to hell and back out there. I expect I'll get a ping any second now, telling me to haul ass."

June remained silent, still confounded by him. Thinking back to their first meeting, with her stuck in a bathtub, she fought the urge to be embarrassed, but...

Inexplicably, she felt something when she looked at him. He was talking to her, but she wasn't sure he cared if she listened.

"I want to make sure you stay behind," he said. "We can't risk anything happening to you. If you get killed, Enchantress might be freed. I don't think anyone knows."

Shop talk, she realized. It's all about the job. Is there anything else to him?

"This walk is better than I thought it would be," she said, changing the subject. She pointed to a line of stores that stretched across the other side of the river. Most of them were still intact, but all were shuttered.

"I always wanted to check it out," she added as they slowly headed toward one of the stone bridges that crossed the waterway.

* * *

"Nice," Flag agreed, "but you should check out San Antonio's river walk some day. It's better, and bigger, too." He looked at her, trying not to stare, but that was becoming harder to do.

Keep it professional, soldier, he told himself.

"June, if you don't mind," he began. "I have so many questions about Enchantress…"

For some reason she looked exasperated, but she nodded.

"Colonel, you can't possibly have as many as I do. Ever since the cave I've been asking myself a hundred new questions every day. I've not been able to answer any of them."

"I still have to ask," he responded.

That's it, she mused, and she could feel herself becoming angry. *All I am to him is business. Nothing more.* But if he could tell she was irritated, he didn't show it.

"Are you one person or two?" he asked, and there was a barely concealed excitement to his words. "Is she living inside you? Oh, God, this is so damn bizarre that I don't even have a clue how to phrase it."

June laughed at that.

"Relax," she said, and the anger dissipated. "It confuses the hell out of me, too. I've had these dreams, and she's been in them for so long now. The last few months, they seemed to keep coming back every night. Every damn night."

"How did you two… meet?"

This is an interrogation, then. Okay, she told herself. *Keep it professional.*

"First in the dreams," she replied. "Ultimately they led me to that cave. That's where I first saw her in person."

"You saw her? So there are two of you? Two distinct bodies?" Flag asked.

"I think... but then there weren't. This will sound insane, but in the cave it didn't look as if she was all flesh and blood. She seemed to partially be, I don't know, smoke.

"Each time I summon her by calling out her name, I become her. Then if she says her name, she becomes me again. It's like there are two brains living in one body, only the body keeps changing, too. Like I said, I don't understand it, but it scares me more than anyone can know."

"When she's her, when you're gone, where do you go? Are you conscious? Do you know what's happening?"

June thought about that for a moment. "It's like I see what she's seeing," she said. "I hear what she's saying, but it's also like I'm not there—even though I am." She paused.

"You okay?" Flag asked.

"Rick, I don't want to talk about her any more. I really don't. I'm sorry. It hurts too much." Standing at the apex of the stone bridge, she stared at the moon's reflection rippling in the water below.

"I came here because it lets me forget. I know it's just for a little, but it's enough. Having to talk about all this just brings me right back. I need a break."

"I'm sorry," he said. "I should have waited for later." He stared down at that same reflection, breathing in the cool air. She put her hand on his.

For support? Or for something else?

He didn't know.

"Please understand," she said. He kept his hand there, under hers. For a long time they stood in silence, enjoying the brisk, clear night, knowing it would change very soon now.

Then she turned to face him, tears filling her eyes.

"When I become her I never know if I'll be her forever. I don't know what she's going to have me do. I don't know who I am, and it scares the hell out of me and I don't know what that makes me."

"It doesn't change you, I know at least that much," he responded. "You're not her. She's just using you, and I'm going to be with you until we find some way, any way, to stop her."

He turned his hand and cupped hers with it. She didn't move away. He felt nervous, the same kind of nervousness he'd had back in junior high school, with Marsha Lane. He laughed aloud, and she looked confused.

"Is something wrong?" she asked.

He looked at her and smiled. "Nothing's wrong. We're not even in the same neighborhood as wrong."

Then he kissed her.

She kissed him back.

No. This night wasn't at all going to be anything like junior high.

EIGHTEEN

The prison yard was on fire. Orange jumpsuits raced crazily in all directions. Guards no longer tried to keep order—they just wanted out.

Another explosion erupted in the yard, spreading the fire even faster.

Burning inmates were screaming in agony before they fell to the ground, charred and dead. Others ran in fear, in a mad, impossible attempt to outrace the flames. They all wanted to find a way out of this sudden hell.

Almost all of them failed terribly.

The prison fire department barely put out one fire when another explosion rocked the yard. Then two more. The destruction was everywhere and nobody was exempt. Not the firefighters. Not the guards. Not the prisoners.

Diablo stood in the center of the inferno, arms outstretched in victory. A king's fiery crown rested on his head, a look of pleasure on his face as the flames danced over him.

Two guards ran toward a truck already crowded with inmates. He let the duo reach it and clamber aboard. Once they were safely inside, and the truck began to move toward the steel gates, Diablo unleashed a series of fireballs. Mercifully, there was no time for any of them to scream.

"This is my hell," he shouted over the chaos, "and nobody's gettin' out."

Diablo was on his own here in the center of the inferno.

Some of the guards and prisoners were still writhing in the fires as Flag lowered the tablet, horrified by the violence. He stared at Diablo, sitting alone in his pressure chamber.

"You did this," he said. "You killed them all. You burned them, and stood there while they were screaming in agony."

"I know. I didn't need to see it again. I'll never forget."

Flag turned to Waller. "Why the hell wasn't he executed, and be done with? Why keep anything with that much goddamn power alive?"

"I wanted him alive… as a precaution," she replied.

"For what? What could possibly be so bad you'd risk working with him?"

Waller smiled, but remained silent. Flag would have to learn why on his own. He stared again at the tablet, the scene paused, frozen in a moment of time. Flames surrounded the people. He saw them screaming, saw them dying, until he couldn't look any longer. He handed the tablet back to Waller.

He had to focus on the mission.

"That isn't me anymore," Diablo said.

Waller studied him then gave a brief smile. "Sure looks like you, though. Would definitely pass recognition software—but just for my edification, if it isn't you, who is it then?"

"That guy's dead," Diablo said, turning away. "He's gone. Now please, leave me alone."

"And yet," Waller pressed, "you *say* you're dead, but you're still here, while all those you killed remain dead and buried. Which is why you were brought to Belle Reve, your hell away from hell."

"And I deserve nothing less."

Diablo walked to the rear of the chamber and sat, his back to Waller and Flag. He had worked so hard and for so long to forget his past, to shove it away where it could no longer affect him, but seeing the video, taken so very long ago, brought it all rushing back.

He knew in his heart that he wasn't that killer anymore, but what did it matter, when the hell he had once caused would never go away? Wasn't it enough that he was being punished for his past? Must it continue to be dredged up day after day, month after month, year after year?

Someone always made sure he wouldn't forget, as if he ever could. Today it was Colonel Flag. He was probably a good guy in his head, too.

"Diablo, look," Flag said. "You wanna die in here? I don't think so. You got a real shot at walking the block again. Having a cold beer, a nice meal. A woman."

Diablo laughed to himself but still didn't face his tormentors.

"Is that what I want, or what you think I want?" he countered. "You're not the first to ask, and you won't be the last."

"Ask what?" Flag wanted to know.

Perhaps if he talked to them now, maybe they would go away and leave him alone with his unwanted memories. After a moment he stood and walked back to the chamber door to stare at Flag and Waller staring at him.

"You want to recruit me as a soldier," he said, certain he was right. "Like all the others, you want to ask me if I'll be your one-man army. You want me to use my, umm, abilities as I've done in the past, but now in your name, for your cause, under your, shall we say, direction.

"Really," he continued, "this is all about your needs and wants. Not mine." He paused, knowing he had already lost them, but he continued anyway. *May as well get it out there to these Washington big shots*. He doubted it would sink in, but just maybe it would stop the next Rick Flag or Amanda Waller from coming here and bothering him.

"I'm a man, Colonel," he said. "Not a weapon, and I swear I'll die in peace before I raise my fists again. I've done enough harm."

Flag heard the words but he wasn't listening to the meaning.

"Diablo, you have to understand what we're facing here. What the world is facing."

"The world's always facing one kind of hell or another, Colonel. But you know the good thing about being locked up in this crematorium for the rest of my life? Nothing that happens out there has any affect on what goes on in here."

Diablo fanned his hands and a word was spelled out in flame.

"Bye."

By the time the flames had faded, Diablo had returned to his chair at the far end of his chamber.

His back to them. Not happy. He knew he'd never be happy again, but he supposed he was content.

Flag looked to Waller as they walked away, unsuccessful.

"Your gangbanger's now a hippy, Waller," he said. "This whole trip was a bust."

"We need him," Waller insisted. "There are ways. There are always ways."

"Maybe there shouldn't be," he replied. "Not for everyone. Maybe we should just leave him alone to wallow in his own guilt. For God's sake, Waller, the man doesn't want to kill. We should be holding a party for him, not a wake."

"He doesn't necessarily get what he wants, Flag," she said without looking at him. "But me, I always get what I want. That is what I do."

Flag looked back to see Diablo alone at the far end of the chamber, his shoulders slumped.

"Looks to me like we've got ourselves one of those classic standoffs you always hear about—unstoppable force, meet the immovable object."

Waller laughed. "I prefer Archimedes. 'Give me a lever long enough and a fulcrum on which to place it, and I shall move the world.'" She walked away from Flag without waiting for a reply.

As she did, Flag got a text and hurried to the medical office, entering the records room. June was there as she said she'd be. He locked the door as she wrapped her arms around him and pressed closer.

"I've been a nervous wreck," she said.

Flag gave her a long, soft kiss.

"I'm here," he said, "and I'll stay here until you ask me to go."

"Then I guess you're not going anywhere. Just having you here makes me feel better. This is the first time since this all began that I feel, I don't know, maybe 'calm' is the word. That I've felt the way I think I should always feel." She peered at him intently. "I'd want you to stay until it was all over, but I know you can't. Not until it really is over. Until she's no longer part of me."

They kissed again, held each other even longer, then separated, went to their corners, and resumed the work of reviewing prisoner dossiers.

He separated the dossiers into two piles—one of files that might be of some interest, while the other with files he ruled out.

"Rick, am I the reason you just don't walk away from her? You know, Waller?" June asked. "I can see how much you hate her."

But it was so much more complicated than simply hating her.

"Nobody walks away from Waller," he said. "It just isn't done. I know what you're going through, June, but we have to play her game, and hope it works."

June paused, and put down the dossier she was holding.

"I'm sorry, Rick, but I don't think so," she said. "You can't possibly have any idea. Can you imagine someone whispering vileness in your head all the damned time? Twenty-four-seven. Grabbing the steering wheel of your life and drunk driving through everything you've worked for?"

Her eyes were wide as she shook her head. "Nobody can understand. Not really. I've lost it all to her. I've lost everything."

He reached for her to take her hand, but she pulled it away.

"June, I'm not the enemy," he protested. "I've seen what you're up against."

"And I hear that voice every second of every day," June countered. "What if Waller can't make it go away? What if I can never get free?"

Flag was determined not to leave it at that. "If Waller says she can help you, she can help you."

June laughed, and it was a real laugh that broke the tension.

"Good God, Rick—you're such a company man."

He again reached to take her hands. This time she let him.

"I'm not saying trust her," he said, though he looked nervous as he did so. "I don't, but she's pragmatist. As long as you've got something she wants, she'll do everything she can."

June wasn't quite so certain. "She may want to, she may even expect to, but Waller thinks because she has that... thing... that heart locked in that box, Enchantress will be her servant." She scoffed. "But it's the other way around. Waller is Enchantress's servant, and the witch is planning something. Big, and very bad."

"You're connected to her. Does that let you inside her thoughts? Do you know what she's planning?"

"No," she replied, "and you have no idea how thrilled I am that I don't. From just what I've seen, that's someplace I know I don't want to go." June became silent. Her eyes took on a faraway look, but then she focused again. "I think she's testing us," June said. "Testing me. Waiting to—" She stopped abruptly and turned away. "I didn't want to talk about this. I can't deal with it now. Can we please get the hell out of here?"

Flag pulled her close and kissed her.

"I'm here," he said. "You're safe with me." She smiled and kissed him back.

The door behind them burst open.

Waller entered.

"I sure hope you two are using protection. Don't want you spawning the antichrist, do we?"

Flag frowned at her. "Stop it, Amanda. Just stop." She shrugged a *Fine. Whatever.* "We need to talk." Her look said, *in private*.

"June, give us a minute, please," Flag said.

Looking and smiling at Waller, she gave Flag a quick kiss. She walked past Waller, through the door, and shut it behind her. Flag glared at Waller.

"I won't even comment on what you just said," he growled. "Respectfully, ma'am, I'm up to here. Have you noticed that we're in a prison? These are criminals. Psychotic, anti-social freaks."

"We've been through this. You lost."

"Yeah, but this makes no sense. Lemme hit the Tier One units. I'll build you a team of pipe-hitters who'll do anything you can dream up. You need real soldiers…" He looked toward the door, and the prison that lay beyond. "…not scumbags."

Waller let him finish, then took her turn.

"Colonel Flag, have you ever heard that back in World War Two, the U.S. Navy made a deal with the Mafia to protect our ships on the waterfront."

Flag couldn't care less.

"Maybe you should buy a new calendar," he responded. "This isn't World War Two."

She wasn't fazed. "What you don't get is," she

said, "this is World War Three."

"What are you really up to?"

She leaned against the wall and gave a long pause, peering at him the entire time.

"You want the big picture?"

"No, I like being fed a steady stream of crap and kept in the dark, like a mushroom."

"Unfortunately, it's need-to-know," she said, shutting it down. "All you need to know is that you work for me. You don't question my orders. You execute them."

Flag took out his cell phone and held it up.

"That can change with a phone call," he said. "I know people, too."

Waller set her own cell on the table then crossed her arms, openly challenging him.

"You know that without you minding her, your lady friend will have to stay here. Strapped to a board in a drug-induced coma."

Flag laughed.

"My God, Amanda, I gotta be five kinds of asshole. They warned me about you. Only I didn't believe the stories."

Waller crossed to the outer door then paused, looking back.

"Nobody does," she said, then added, "Oh, by the way, we're going operational."

NINETEEN

Captain Griggs couldn't wait for the weekend. His job at Belle Reve Maximum Security prison meant his weekdays were spent trying to corral the worst of the worst, and there was never any satisfaction in that. But Friday nights, and Saturdays, and Sundays—those were his to enjoy, and there was nothing better than driving down to the casino, drinking as much 190-proof grain alcohol as he could, and winning at blackjack like the big boss he was.

Or maybe winning a little.

Anything but losing.

Which was exactly what Griggs was doing.

The casino was a neon eyesore, frequented by shady thugs and Belle Reve guards. Slutty cocktail waitresses sashayed their asses through the place, driving up tips any way they could. The cops wouldn't close down this place. They were among its best customers.

He'd lost next week's pay when he signaled the dealer for another card. Damned nine of clubs. Lester, the dealer—Griggs seemed to remember that might have been his name—scooped up his newest pile of chips. Griggs thought the house was tilting in that scumbag's direction.

"Lester, slide me another ten K. You know I'm good for it." The 190-proof liquor told him it was going to turn around, but Lester didn't know any such thing.

"No can do, Griggs. Sorry, pal."

"C'mon, Les. How long have I been coming here? Have I ever not paid off my losses? And haven't I always given you a tip, win or lose?"

Lester didn't say a thing.

Two big, scary bruisers, sporting big fake smiles, swept in and strongly suggested that Griggs accompany them. They squeezed his upper arms until he thought he was going to pass out.

"Okay. Okay," he said. "I'll go talk to the big man. He'll tell you I'm good."

The bruisers pushed him into the kitchen and pointed to the folding chair sitting in front of the counter. There was a comfortable-looking leather recliner there as well, but Griggs knew that wasn't for him.

He took his seat and waited.

A few minutes passed before a half-dozen—they had to be gangsters—entered, followed by the casino boss. Griggs greeted him with a wide, friendly smile.

"Hey, man, am I glad to see you. I know I'm a little behind. You know how it is. A run of bad decks. I just asked for an advance, and suddenly I'm here." He looked for some sort of response, and didn't get any. "So what's the problem with a little upfront? I mean, ten thousand? I've paid you back a helluva lot more than that."

"Griggs, this is real," the casino boss said, his voice barely above a murmur. "You got any idea I had'a stop these guys from burning down your house. With your kids in it."

Griggs didn't know how to respond—didn't dare say anything, for fear of getting it wrong. This wasn't just a meet 'n' greet. He sobered up best he could.

"I'm sorry, sir," he apologized, and he meant it. The man leaned back in his leather-cushioned recliner.

"Everybody's sorry when push comes to shove. Now you're sorry, but unlike all the others, you're lucky."

Griggs wasn't sure he understood. "I'm lucky? Sir… how am I lucky?"

"You're lucky you got friends. Like Mister J."

Griggs was still trying to figure out what was being said when a hand came to rest on his shoulder. Griggs didn't have to turn around to know who it was. There was a pinky ring with a diamond "J" on it. That was clue enough.

Joker.

The ring's owner leaned into Griggs, grinning maniacally. Frost handed the casino boss a satchel filled with cash.

"You'll find it all here, but Griggs here can count it." The man who spoke was well over six feet tall. Griggs looked up at him, wondering what the hell he was talking about.

"No, sir," he said finally. "I trust you a hundred ten percent."

"Just a hundred ten percent? That the best you got?"

Griggs felt like he was seconds away from a stroke. He wasn't sure what to say, but saying the wrong thing would get him a one-way trip to the wood chipper.

The big man grinned and laughed.

"Just playing with you, Griggs. Relax."

Joker turned to his aide. "Mister Frost, what have I told you about playing with the help? Next time just take out his heart and crush it."

"Got you, boss," Frost said.

Joker turned to Griggs and talked to him like Griggs was his new best friend.

"It's okay. You're with me now. I've got plans for us, boy. You have suddenly become my…" He turned to Frost. "What was it he became again? You know, the mobster's all-round guy?

"Consigliere, sir? And yes."

"Right. My consigliere. Thank you, Frost. Griggs is like my consigliere."

Griggs swallowed hard and tried to keep his face as unreadable as possible. As far as he was concerned the worst thing in the world was to be the Joker's friend. That crazy clown was, as his father used to say, "fickle as a feather in a Kansas tornado."

As Joker held out his ring, Griggs deflated. Accepting his total defeat, he kissed the diamond J.

Griggs had been sold, and bought, and there was nothing he could do about it.

TWENTY

Rick Flag stood by the hotel window and watched June smiling as she dreamed. She was amazingly beautiful, and smart and sweet, but he still wasn't certain why she had chosen him. He definitely wasn't in her league.

Flag was a soldier. His job was to kill people who threatened the United States. He wasn't the sentimental sort, and that made him better at his job. He could have sex with a foreign spy, put a bullet in her head while they were doing it, then move on without remorse.

Yet he didn't want to leave June's side.

Ever.

He heard her calling his name and he walked to the bed, thinking she was awake. She was still sleeping, though.

Then a frown replaced her contented smile. Her voice grew deeper, with a very definite dark edge. She was no longer saying his name, but she was calling out to another.

"Enchantress."

The word slipped from her lips. She repeated it.

"Enchantress."

An instant later she changed. Transformed from the beautiful archeologist to something darker and deadlier. Flag grabbed his gun, and reached for his cell phone.

"Don't you dare call Waller," Enchantress said. Flag couldn't tell where the voice originated. He froze. "If you do…"

Suddenly leaning over the bed, it was June he was seeing. He took her hand and checked for a pulse.

There wasn't any. She was dead.

She was intubated, and there were IVs in her arm. Electrocardiogram stickers were everywhere, the detritus of a heroic life-saving attempt by the hospital staff.

Without knowing why, Flag was screaming. He didn't want to leave her—not after having just found her. Not after she so completely changed his life.

A grim-faced nurse unplugged her.

She was gone.

Again he screamed.

This time the scream brought him back to reality. He was in their hotel room. There were no signs of any life-saving equipment.

June was gone, too. Replaced by Enchantress.

This time her eyes were open. Flag aimed his Glock at her face. She ignored it. Maybe she just didn't give a damn.

"What was that?" he demanded. "What did you do to me?"

Enchantress held a finger to her lips.

"That was a preview," she said. "Tell anyone, especially Waller, and I will be back. For the main act."

She was gone in an instant.

Flag still had no idea if any of what he'd seen was real.

Amanda Waller was in the bedroom of her Virginia home, out cold, sleeping off an empty wine bottle. A loaded pistol lay on her nightstand.

Enchantress watched her as Flag had watched June. She remained perfectly still, and saw the case—the one with her heart in it, lying on the floor by Waller's bed.

Waller's phone lay on the bedside table.

Will Flag disobey, and call?

Minutes passed.

The phone remained asleep. Like Waller.

She moved toward the case, and a red light flicked on. Instantly she froze again.

Abruptly she knew exactly what she was seeing. It was the access to Waller's secure office. So she disappeared from the bedroom…

…and reappeared in a very cramped space. A secure phone and a sheath of documents sat on the desk. The top one was labeled "Top Secret." She flipped through the briefing pack from the White House meeting June had attended. There was a boring minute-by-minute summary of the meeting. Nothing of importance.

She flipped the page, and stopped dead.

There, in front of her, was a photograph of the second jar from the skull cave altar. At a glance she knew it as the male counterpart to the one that granted her life. It was enticing.

She stared at it, transfixed, and touched the image as if daring it to become a three-dimensional reality, instead of a two-dimensional facsimile. But then, for just an instant, she shuddered as if sensing something. She slowly looked up, almost afraid of what she'd see.

Yet there was no reason to fear it.

The male jar sat on a shelf, right in front of her.

TWENTY-ONE

Gerard Davis used his foot to push down the lever in the subway station toilet. No way he'd ever touch that diseased filth with his bare hands. Then he stepped out of the stall, all the while breathing only through his mouth.

Gerard didn't enjoy taking the subway home. It was dirty and ugly, and he would have placed a large bet that their facilities hadn't been cleaned since the Truman administration.

As he rose through the ranks at work, he allowed himself to believe that one day he'd be given a company car, and perhaps a driver to take him to work in the city's midtown, then drive him back to its western suburbs where he lived with his wife Adrienne, a painter, and their two kids, Julie and Gene.

Most recently he got the raise, but he did not get the car, or the driver, or enough money to pay for either of those perks himself.

When he became a vice president, though—in a maximum of five more years—his subway days would finally be behind him. It couldn't happen soon enough.

The soap dispenser didn't work, but then it never did. Still he washed his hands in the dribbling cold water and shook them dry. He checked the mirror to see if he was acceptable, but where he only should have seen his reflection, there was a woman standing next to him.

In the men's room.

The woman bounced his head off the wall. In her free hand was a pottery jar of some sort.

As Davis slumped to the ground, barely conscious, Enchantress cracked the jar's ancient wax seal. Black, inky tendrils emerged, snaked through the bathroom, and into Gerard Davis's nose.

His pupils dilated. His expression changed from confusion to confidence, and malice. Possessed, he was no longer businessman Gerard Davis.

He was Incubus.

Incubus peered at the woman by his side, and understanding dawned. He and Enchantress collapsed into each other's arms like the survivors of a shipwreck.

"Brother," she said, her voice rich with emotion. "We are free."

Incubus took in a deep breath. He ignored the pungent vinegar that so disgusted his body's former owner.

"Thank you, my sweetest sister." He looked around him, unimpressed by his surroundings. "What is this world?"

"The same hateful sphere," she replied, "only later. Much later."

Incubus stared at his hands, trying to find the power that had always been there.

"We're so weak now," he said.

"And they are strong, but I will never be trapped again. I swear on the stars I'll kill them all first." She paused, daunted in her moment of victory. "Brother, I am their slave."

"Their slave?" he said, confusion in his words. "But they worshipped us."

Enchantress shook her head sadly. "We have become denied. They forget the old ways. They're machine people now. Clock people. But I will build a machine such as they cannot imagine, and grind their cities and mountains into dream smoke."

Incubus peered at his sister, once so vital and filled with life. She looked weak now. Used, and very tired.

"What of God?" he asked. "Will he stand for that?"

Enchantress shook her head again. "They have forgotten God, too, and he them." A look of anger flashed in her eyes. "So who can they send against me? Their machines? Well, I now have you, brother. Feed on them. You have time now to rebuild your strength. I will rejoin you once I slip my bonds."

Incubus reached out for her, but as he did she disappeared. There was so much he wanted to ask. She had lived in this mad world for a long time, and she knew how to survive it, but he was new here and he needed her counsel.

Overwhelmed with his rebirth, Incubus felt lost. So much had changed since last he breathed the perfumed air of his youth. Yet he knew, as always, he would make do in this new world. Once his sister returned to his side, they would rule this land together, as they once ruled the planet.

Enchantress reappeared in the hotel room to find Rick Flag sitting on the bed, gun in hand, its red laser targeting the center of her forehead.

"Hi," he said casually. "I'm here to see June again." An edge entered his voice. "Bring her back now. Right now."

"Or what?" she demanded. "You'll shoot me?" She laughed at a threat even he knew was futile. "You realize if you do, you'll also kill her. That's certainly not what she'd like you to do to her."

Enchantress put her hand on his gun and gently nudged it down. "You're not shooting anyone today," she continued. "Besides, soldier, she's mine. She's been mine. I only let you have a taste."

Flag knew his threat was a bluff, and she'd called him on it. She looked at him oddly, smiled, then wrapped her arms around him and kissed his cheek. He tried to pull away but felt a compulsion growing inside him. She was June, even if she wasn't.

She drew her skirt back, revealing tattooed thighs. He tried to turn away, but wasn't able to.

She was controlling him.

"I want June," he said again, but there was a catch in his voice. She kissed the side of his face, moving down to his neck. "Return her to me. I want her now."

Enchantress hesitated, and he thought she seemed to be weakening. June was somewhere inside her—he would bet his life on it—and she was resisting as best she could.

"June. If you hear me, whatever you're doing is working. Fight her, and don't stop fighting." Despite his words, though, Flag felt helpless. Nothing in his past had remotely prepared him to take on a fight like this. He was fighting to save a woman he had only known for a handful of weeks. He was fighting to save the life of a stranger he was certain he now loved.

"I want June," he said again, and he gathered himself. "Now!"

Enchantress felt her control over June slipping, and she accepted that she had no choice. As long as they possessed the heart, she could never realize her full power.

"Enchantress."

The word spilled from her, and saying her name forced her to relinquish control.

For now. But soon, very soon...

June woke, and knew instantly what had occurred. She and Flag held each other for a long time.

"She's trying to take over my mind," she finally said, her voice weak but gaining strength with each word.

"I know," Flag said. "Waller warned me. We're in a war, June—a different kind of war, but if we work together we'll be able to beat her. We will be able to free you."

June wasn't sure she believed it.

"You can't know what it's like," she said. "She takes control over every thought I have, and when she does, when she digs in, it feels as if my head is about to explode."

"We will fix this," he replied, and he looked her straight in the eye. "I will make it go away."

"No, Rick—please listen," she responded. "The pain is so terrible, I'm afraid dying might be the only thing I can do to make it end. My dying might be the only way to stop her."

Rick shook his head. "You're right," he admitted. "I don't know how bad it is, but I do know that you can fight through it. That's what soldiers do. There's too much at stake to just give up. Believe in me. Believe in yourself. We can fight her."

"Maybe you can, but I'm not a soldier. Yes, I know how important this is, but I also know that once she gets back her full strength, she'll have the powers of a god. I can't fight gods, Rick. I'm going to lose unless we get her out of me. Forever. Killing me will kill her, too."

"Don't ask me to do that."

"Then tell Waller to. She won't let sentiment get in the way of saving the world."

He paused, as if considering her words.

"Not until we've exhausted every other option. Can we put a pin in it? Please? Just for now?"

June held him as tightly as she could.

"She lives in my head, and she's evil. She's beyond evil. If you have to choose between me or her, you have to stop her. If you can't, Waller will."

"That's not going to happen on my watch."

"Rick, it's like you said. You're a soldier fighting a war." An expression of calm settled on her features. "When the time comes, you will do what you have to."

TWENTY-TWO

"Gerard Davis" stood on the crowded subway platform. He shut his eyes, taking in just its smells.

This world, he thought, *is foul.* Its incessant noise offended him. The humans were, if possible, even more annoying than he remembered. His sister was correct. She understood that this Earth needed to change back to the way it was, thousands of years earlier. When the humans worshipped her... and him.

As God intended.

He stood silently and ignored the growing buzz surrounding him. People saw him and instinctively backed away, as if there was something off with him. Something very wrong.

A transit cop saw him standing, facing ahead, not blinking. Not moving.

"Sir, you okay?" the cop asked. "Can you breathe? Are you on something?" No response. The cop tapped his comm, powering it on.

"This is twenty-one. Send medical to my location."

A doctor pushed through the crowd. He took Gerard's wrist.

"I'm a physician," he said. "He doesn't have a pulse."

"How is that possible?" the cop asked.

The doctor didn't allow himself to be distracted. "He didn't answer when you spoke to him, did he?"

The cop shook his head. "No."

"Okay, help me shake him," the doctor instructed. "Just a little. Enough to tell if he's unconscious." They grasped him firmly, and shook. Gerard Davis simply ignored them. His mind was in another place, at another time. A better time.

They laid him on his back on the subway platform. The doctor leaned over him, still searching for any sign of life.

"He's breathing abnormally," he said anxiously. "Okay, I'm starting compressions now." He placed one palm on the center of Davis's chest, his other over that, then pushed down with a fast, forceful movement. He lifted his hands for just a moment, then lowered them back to perform a second compression.

Still no reaction.

The doctor moved to repeat his actions when the prone figure suddenly convulsed. His limbs jerked as his neck and chest twisted impossibly, spinning as if there were no skeleton under the flesh. His body began warping before the eyes of the onlookers. His hands shot up and grasped the doctor in an iron grip.

His flesh unfolded. The doctor tried to fall back, to get away, but the figure wouldn't let go, and the doctor began to transform as well. His arms bent back and collapsed in chaos, as if he had ten separate elbows.

The cop let out a bellow and tried to pull the doctor away, only to be caught in the insane transformation. His body folded and distorted in ways the human body was never meant to go. The three of them collapsed into each other and somehow, impossibly, they merged, becoming a single mass—continuously churning, folding, unfolding, rotating.

At first transfixed, the onlookers were jolted into action when one of them screamed. Then more of them were screaming, and scrambling to escape. Utter terror swept through the crowd as they shoved and stumbled to get away, climbing over one another in the attempt.

If the thing even noticed, it did not care. It kept folding and unfolding and twisting into knots. A fleshy extension snaked out from the mass—not quite an arm but functioning in much the same way. It reached into the crowd and latched onto another man, dragging him bellowing into the hideous mass.

It continued to grow and it continued to fold and unfold. It shook and oozed, surging and moving. It dragged in others and it grew, reforming into something almost human.

The new form of God.

Incubus.

The thing rolled onto the tracks, extended a crystalline appendage to the third rail and absorbed its electrical current. With the sudden surge the Incubus grew. Bigger. More powerful.

A lattice of glowing energy enveloped him. Red, green, and blue fractal fire sparked from his body, which itself was still writhing and twisting beyond human capability. Finally he stood, and his combined mass was larger than the sum of his components. He exuded power and energy.

His sister had told him to grow stronger. She was, as always, right. He felt so much better now.

There was a sound and he turned, only to be blinded by the headlights of an approaching train. A hand grew and extended from his chest and slammed into the train with a burst of magical energy. The leading subway car, with all of its passengers, instantly exploded with light, then just as quickly it imploded, the energy spiraling inward.

Incubus saw the light, and it was good.

June looked out the hotel window. The distant sky was beginning to glow. Dawn was approaching, but it seemed to take forever. Flag sat in the hotel chair.

She was supposed to be asleep in the bed, but both of them had spent the night staring at each other.

"You can't watch me forever," June said.

Flag shrugged. "I'd like to try."

A soft chime brought them back to reality. His phone buzzed with a new text. He swiped the screen and read his updated orders.

Crap.

"Recall message," he said. "Gotta go."

Before he could move, though, June received the same text.

"Looks like we're going together," she said.

TWENTY-THREE

Griggs loved it when it all went to hell.

When the guards armored up, carrying riot shields and gas masks, and thudded down the hall, it meant that Belle Reve's army—his army—had a situation to deal with. It also meant that whatever they had to do would pretty much be swept under the rug.

Civil rights are hereby suspended, he mused with glee. *There are heads to crack and bones to break.* Griggs was in seventh heaven.

"We hit 'em hard and fast," he shouted to his boys. "We can do anything we want to keep the peace. We're in charge here." Dixon gave him a thumbs up, and whooped as they gleefully moved in.

Floyd Lawton heard the commotion outside, and prepared himself for the fun and games. This happened right on schedule, pretty much every other month, when the guards could no longer scratch their own itches. They needed a release of some sort, and taking out their frustrations on the prison population was their favorite way to go.

He heard Griggs shout from the hallway.

It wouldn't be more than a minute or two.

His cell door flew open and guards wearing gas masks and plastic-knuckled gloves moved in, carrying riot shields. He was swarmed with boots and fists. Lawton knew he could try to resist, but sooner or later he'd be overwhelmed. Better to let them tire themselves out.

His time would come. Sooner, rather than later.

They dragged him to the restraint chair and shackled him in. Griggs was first.

"Time to pay for the room service, Deadshot." He slammed Lawton in the face with the butt of his pistol. Then again, and again. Before long the prisoner's eyes were nearly swollen shut, but he just grinned.

"That all you got, bitch?"

Griggs sneered and punched him again, only harder. That one actually hurt, but Lawton still grinned defiantly. Then a black hood was pulled down over his head.

"Just getting started," Griggs laughed.

Diablo heard a strange noise he hadn't heard before. He paced the pressure chamber, eyeing the walls for any sign of a malfunction. Anything that might make it possible for him to escape.

That was the one thing he wouldn't do.

Diablo sighed. He knew he belonged here. Behind bars, in prison, where he'd be rendered harmless, and the rest of humanity would be safe. He knew he deserved all the punishment he endured, and perhaps more.

Bring it on, boys, he thought wordlessly. *Bring everything you've got.* But then he figured out the reason for the sound. Water was gushing through the pipes. The pressure chamber began to flood. It was designed to fill up in seconds, if flames were detected—but Diablo wasn't trying to escape.

He hadn't done a thing.

Instinctively he generated sheets of flame, hoping to evaporate the water, but it didn't work. His flames died out, and the level continued to rise. Water filled his lungs. It would only be a matter of seconds before he drowned.

Then he relaxed, and stopped fighting.

He should have remembered.

Outside the chamber, a gloved fist hit the dump switch, and the pressure chamber spilled its guts. Griggs enjoyed this, Diablo knew. Bringing the animals to the edge, then pulling them away. Then starting it all over again.

"Hey! They're killers," he would say. "They deserve everything they get. And if one accidentally kicks the bucket, so what? Crap happens."

Diablo fell to the floor, coughing uncontrollably. Before he could even begin to recover, though, guards in firefighting gear stormed the chamber and injected him with sedatives. He went down for the count.

Do whatever you want to, boys, he thought as he lost consciousness. *I'm fair game.*

Griggs gave the order. Dixon and two others dragged Diablo to one of the Gitmo stretchers—the one with the big wheels—and he was strapped into it. They checked the restraints carefully.

"Give him a few minutes to recover," the captain said. "Then let's party."

* * *

The riot squad used a cutting torch to sever the iron bars separating the Belle Reve sewer tunnel from the rest of the facility. The guards accompanying the squad had their tranquilizer guns ready. Croc wasn't going to get within twenty-five yards of them unless they wanted him to.

The guards passed the bone shrines Croc had set up, tied together with viscera and tendons. Two of the newbies threw up on the spot. One of them walked along the edge of the water channel, opaque with filth and slime.

"Captain, if that thing's ahead of us, why aren't we going the other way?" he asked nervously. "I mean, like as fast as our feet can carry us?"

"Miller, just shut up and do what I tell you," Griggs snapped. They walked another quarter mile through the darkness, their flashlights barely lighting their immediate area, let alone the path ahead.

Miller paused to wipe his brow. This place not only stunk, it was hot as hell, and humid, too. He wiped his face again, then shoved his handkerchief in his back pocket and took another step.

Into a slick patch of slime.

His boot slipped and he fell into the river of slime that ran down the center of the tunnel.

Dixon rushed to the edge and reached out to grab the kid, but the newbie was already under water. A moment later his helmet bobbed to the surface, followed by his body. Before they could try to reach him, his armor exploded.

Damned Croc, Griggs thought furiously. He shook his head and looked to the others. "Prime your tranq guns. We gotta put the bastard to sleep."

"You saw him. He's a monster. Why can't we just kill him?"

"Hey. I don't like it any more 'n you, but they made it clear. We don't do exactly what they said, we lose our jobs. 'A course, they said nothin' about not hurtin' him bad. So feel free. Have your fun." He added, "I sure as hell will."

Griggs's men held their tranquilizer guns and waited for the monster to come up for a breath. Nothing happened. It felt like it took forever. Then they saw the top ridges of Croc's head breach the surface.

They had a place to aim.

"Now!" Griggs shouted.

As one they fired their guns. A dozen tranq darts slammed into Croc, and he roared in pain. Screaming, he lumbered toward them, intending to rip them apart. He pushed closer. Closer. They fired a second round.

He stopped screaming as he fell unconscious into the sludge. A dozen flashlight beams immediately danced along his back, checking him out. "He playing possum, Griggs?" Dixon drawled.

"That's what we're gonna find out," Griggs replied. He pulled out a tranquilizer gun and shot an ox-dropping dose into the monster's back.

Raging in pain, Croc sprung to life and groped for the dart. He thrashed around frantically, then his eyes rolled back into his head and he collapsed, face down in the sludge.

Guards with ropes and chains jumped into the water to secure their prize.

"They can't win," Griggs said, and he laughed.

TWENTY-FOUR

She counted down the seconds, as she had been for the past two days. One second at a time. Sixty times a minute. Thirty-six hundred times an hour. Eighty-six thousand four hundred times a day.

She knew they'd be coming.

On time, just as promised, and now it was Harley's turn. She reached into her mouth and carefully pulled out a long jailhouse knife, the culmination of the world's greatest sword-swallowing act. She drew it out slowly. Cautiously. Each second was torture to her—normally she wasn't someone who believed in taking her time.

Harley Quinn liked to act the instant she got an idea.

Like now.

Still, the woman who had been Harleen Quinzel understood, better than most, the concept of delayed gratification. Pull the blade out fast—like she really, really wanted—and the odds were she'd give herself a fatal tonsillectomy. Now Mr. J might want her to go through life without saying a word, but Harley didn't much like the idea.

Just as the blade's tip cleared her lips, she heard footsteps approaching. Right on time. The riot squad stopped in front of her cage, their weapons aimed and ready. She gave them her sweetest 'You got me, copper' smile and raised her hands in submission.

"I'm cooperating," she said innocently. "Look—it's me being cool. See? Harmless."

Cautiously they opened the cell. Without saying a word, they fired their tasers.

She was ready.

Harley spun out of the way of most, but two or three slammed her in the back. This gave her time to twist and pull the shiv from its hiding place in her sleeve. In a single, elegant dance, she whirled and stabbed the closest guard. She recognized him.

Milo, she thought. *Perfect. I didn't like the way he leered at me. Only Mr. J gets to do that.* He gurgled, clutched his throat, and dropped to the ground while she giggled.

Another group stepped up and tasered her.

This time she couldn't dodge.

They strapped her to the restraint chair and immobilized her arms, legs, chest, and neck. A gag was tied around her mouth. She liked that. It was something Mr. J might do.

They wheeled her down a long corridor that took her to the Belle Reve airstrip. Outside she recognized many of the faces lining the path—guards with whom Harleen Quinzel had worked, and others she got to know better as Harley. Mixed in with the guards were soldiers. Armed. Grim. That was new. She'd never seen any of them before.

There was a big plane waiting out there, and a military helicopter hovering overhead. As they moved toward it, some distance away Griggs came running from the prison. She wished he'd been the one to get the shiv, and not poor, dead Milo.

Before he could reach the group, though, they stopped in front of a group of medics. They grabbed her head and held it in place, while one of them held a medical wand to her spine. Another opened the Pelican case he was carrying, a "Van Criss Labs" label on its side, while yet another removed an injector gun from it and held it up to her neck.

She tried to resist, but whatever it was, he injected it into her with pinpoint precision. Harley screamed through her gag. She'd never felt anything quite that painful before, and it was no fun at all.

She swore she'd die rather than go through that again.

The medic operating the portable wand checked some readings and gave a thumbs up. A bandage was placed over the wound on her neck, signaling the guards to wheel her toward the plane again.

Griggs ran toward the C-17 Globemaster, but found his way blocked when a different crew of soldiers wheeled yet another restraint chair toward the special forces medics. Deadshot was strapped into this one.

The prison captain cursed his luck. He had to get past the guards, but his way was still blocked. He had to get past the guards, so he'd have to bide his time, and wait for an opening. It had better come fast, though. He had to do what Joker had ordered him to do.

Otherwise… well, he didn't even want to consider the alternative.

Deadshot struggled, but couldn't move an inch in

any direction. These guys were pros. One of them held up an injection gun. Disappointingly, Lawton didn't scream, but his whole body shuddered. Griggs just stared at him.

One day I'm going to put a bullet right between that bastard's eyes. But today wasn't that day. The guards wheeled him away.

Diablo was next. He was already unconscious when he was wheeled into place, fire-retardant blankets wrapped around him. That was a good idea, Griggs mused. If the man was conscious, and decided to play games, he could pretty much incinerate everything within a five-mile radius. He'd done it before.

There was an IV strapped to his arm. A heart monitor was in place. If he began to stir they'd know it immediately, and additional sedatives would be pumped into his system. He was brought to the medic holding the injector.

The man was recognizably nervous as he placed it to Diablo's neck. He activated the injector. Diablo shook for a moment, then settled back into blissful unconsciousness. The medic let out a sigh of relief as he was wheeled away.

Not two minutes later Croc was brought into position. Unlike the others he was chained upright into a small forklift. No restraint chair could possibly hold him. He roared as the medic approached, but the chains holding him were made of unforgiving and unbreakable promethium-infused steel. The medic placed the injector to Croc's neck, near his spine, and fired it.

Croc bellowed in pain, but the chains held. Then

the medic scanned him, checked the results, gave a thumbs up, and the monster was taken away. The medic collapsed into a folding chair and reached for a cold bottle of water.

Griggs knew how he felt, but he had bigger fish to fry.

Better the fish than him.

He watched from behind the barriers, pissed off that his best prisoners were being taken away from him, and no one knew the hell why. Truth to tell, he didn't care about most of them, but he desperately needed to get to Harley.

The guards pushed her restraint chair toward the jet's ramp and waited there. If Griggs delayed any longer he'd never have another chance. He rushed over just as they started up the ramp. Leaning in close, he whispered in her ear.

"You're being transferred," he hissed. "I don't know where." He pressed something in her hand. "It's from Mr. J. Take it. He wanted you to have it."

It was a tiny cell phone with a jeweled letter J on it. Tears welled up in her eyes. Walking alongside her chair, Griggs gave her his best warm, hopeful, bullshit smile.

"Please tell him I was good to you."

Harley grinned at him. "You are so screwed," she hissed back, and she laughed.

Griggs stopped in his tracks and his face turned white with fear. He wanted to apologize for all the crap he'd pulled, and beg her for a break, but the guards wheeled Harley up the ramp into the Globemaster's cargo hold. A dozen armed military personnel stood ready to receive her. They all looked dour, so she grinned at them with her sunniest, happiest smile.

"I love field trips. Hope you boys do, too."

* * *

Harley's chair was chained to a wall alongside the others who were already inside. The guards took their seats and strapped themselves in. The ramp was pulled into the plane and the hatch was sealed behind it. A moment later they lifted off the runway and roared into the sky.

Harley looked at the others and laughed.

"So this is the freak flight, huh?" she said brightly. "Well, I dunno 'bout you, but I'm happy to have the company."

She leaned her head back and closed her eyes. A moment later she opened them again.

"Hey. You know if we get snacks on this flight? I am starving."

TWENTY-FIVE

The van that pulled up to the guard shack gate was driven by a large panda. He lowered the van window and looked at the guard.

"This is Van Criss Labs, right?"

The guard answered slowly. "Ummm, yes," he said. "And you're...?"

"From Grant's Gifts. I gotta deliver a gift basket to a Doctor Van Criss," the panda said, checking his notepad. "They said they wanted it delivered by a panda. We get asked that a lot. In-joke, I guess. Go figure."

The guard smiled and nodded. They'd had stranger deliveries. He checked the computer list for today's guests.

"Sorry. You're not on the access list. I can't let you in."

"Yeah," the panda said. "I sorta figured that could happen. I mean, this is a surprise gift, so your Criss guy wouldn't've known to put our name in. No prob. Hey, you mind if I leave it with you? I mean, I'm way behind."

"Sure," the guard said, shrugging. The panda handed him an overflowing basket then made him sign for it. When he got back the guard's autograph, he rolled his window shut.

The basket exploded in the guard's face.

The Joker opened the van's back door and leapt out. He was carrying a good-sized ball-peen hammer. He pushed his way into the shack and used it to finish off the semi-conscious guard.

Tie off all loose ends when you can, and they won't unravel later. He read that somewhere. He thought it might have been in a bubble-gum comic. Joker tapped the button on the shack's computer, and the gate slowly swung open. He looked down at the dead guard and smiled his rictus grin.

"Never trust a gift panda driving a van," he said. "Words to live—or in your case—die by."

The alarms started blaring the moment he shot his way into the building. He could have ripped a security badge off the dead guard, then walked the halls without triggering the company klaxons, but then he'd have had to search for guards to kill. This way they came to him.

Besides, Joker realized, his personal thugs would have set off the alarms anyway, once they stepped inside and shot at everything they saw. These guys didn't believe in subtlety. It's why he hired them in the first place.

Joker took a gun from a dead guard, thanked him for it, then used it to kill several more security goons. He was living evidence that they weren't very good at their jobs. Panda Man used a silenced assault rifle to take out several other guards, scientists, and technicians, while the thugs cleared the rest of the way toward their ultimate target.

The assembly vault stood at the rear of the lab. Dr. Van Criss watched the chaos through the vault's bulletproof glass and over the monitors positioned throughout the large room.

"What the hell is going on?" he shouted. Frost suddenly stepped into view, but he wasn't offering answers. He was, however, carrying an oversized carbine which he fired at the glass. One shot.

Two.

Three.

He looked at the window and ran his finger over a tiny divot, the sad result of some pretty extensive firepower. Inside the vault, Van Criss looked confident.

"Why are you in my way?" Joker said, pushing Frost aside. "This is what I get for allowing my underlings to do my job for me. Move. Vamoose."

Frost stepped back as Joker held up a tablet for the doctor to see. On its screen was a live video feed of a woman. Her mouth was duct-taped shut and a very nasty-looking gun was pressed to her head.

"You like movies, Doctor?"

Van Criss rushed to the switch that opened the vault door. "Please don't hurt her," he begged. "I'll do whatever you say."

Joker nodded enthusiastically. "I know."

He entered the vault. Van Criss stared at his feet. The Joker was barefoot.

He padded around the room, searching various shelves and cabinets before finding the object of his desire lying on a steel table in the back of the vault. He held up the nanite injector gun.

"This is it, isn't it?" he asked menacingly. "What you used on them."

"I don't know what you're talking about," Dr. Van Criss responded. "Who was it used on? What do you mean?"

"Look at me, Doctor. Do I look like the kind of guy who likes sitting around and explaining crap?" He let out an exaggerated sigh. "Good help is so hard to find these days." He placed the injector to the doctor's neck and before Van Criss could respond, Joker squeezed its trigger. "I'll just have to do this all by myself."

Dr. Van Criss fell to the ground, screaming in agony.

Joker looked at the injector and grinned.

"Yep. This is it."

PART TWO
THE WAR

TWENTY-SIX

Colonel Rick Flag, exhausted from battle, wished the damn war was already over.

He stood on the helicopter skid as they approached the Midway City Airport. In the distance he could see large columns of smoke staining the clouds gray.

How much of Midway has already been destroyed? he wondered. He glanced at the news channel streaming over his cell phone. Getting up-to-the-minute intel from reporters on the ground was always faster than waiting for it through "official" channels.

Government bureaucracy. Still immobilizing America after more than two centuries.

"War has come to our country," the on-air reporter said. "A good part of our city has already been overrun, and we have yet to see the face of our enemy." She paused for dramatic effect before continuing. "Too many have died, and experts fear this is just the beginning. Let's go to Walter Goodwin, standing outside of city hall, for further details. Walter…"

Flag shoved the phone back into its holster and marveled at the makeshift base the military had hastily set up. It looked as if it had been there for years, not hours. The tarmac was littered with inflatable tents. Air

Force gunships sat on the ground. Weapons were being loaded onto them while the ground crews pumped fuel. Everywhere Flag looked, armed choppers lifted off and disappeared into the cloud-shrouded city.

For them the war was just beginning. Flag was pretty certain he would never see any of those men and women again.

He watched as soldiers were carried on stretchers to portable hospital units that hadn't been there four hours earlier. Medics were rushed in from nearby medical facilities to patch up the wounded so they could be sent right back into the fray. Their injuries had barely been stitched together, let alone healed.

His chopper landed and Flag stepped off the skid and crossed the strip toward the building where his twenty-three-man SEAL platoon waited for him. He passed a blacked-out window and noticed his haggard reflection. He looked as if he'd been through hell, and hadn't yet made it back.

He entered the complex to see his men. They looked just as drained as he was. Four soldiers, however— Kowalski, Gomez, Grey, and Nate—were different from the rest. They were muscular, oozing with confidence, covered with armor and ass-kicking weapons.

Fresh meat for the fight.

He'd never worked with any of them, but he knew they were SEALs, the best of the best, and unlike Flag's so-called team, they'd follow orders. Without question.

Their leader, Lieutenant Edwards, went by the nickname GQ, and his combat record read as impressive. Besides being an Academy grad, and having a PhD from Stanford, GQ had been awarded a trunkload of medals. It spoke volumes that he wasn't showing off by wearing any of them now.

But Flag had been in the military for most of his adult life. On paper the man sounded perfect. Over the years Flag had run across a lot of corpses who did, as well. He would reserve final judgment until after their first skirmish.

GQ gave a big smile and saluted Flag with crisp precision.

"First fight I've been able to drive to," he said

Flag nodded. "Let's hope it's not a regular thing."

GQ leaned over and dropped his voice to a whisper. "So what's in there, Rick? People are scared. I heard a squad of Rangers fast-roped off their helo, then shot themselves."

There was the sound of an aircraft, and Flag turned away answering him. The C-17 had landed, with Waller's recruits from the inner circle of hell. It was rolling to a stop.

Damn, he thought. *This is so wrong.* Then aloud, and to no one in particular, "They're here."

GQ knew just enough to return with dangerous snark.

"I'm calling it now," he said. "This is gonna be a total goat rope. How'd you get sucked into this?"

"I don't like this any more than you do, Lieutenant." Flag couldn't turn back to answer Edwards to his face—not without betraying the depth of his own doubts. "But once we're on the objective, these assholes are mildly interesting. 'Sides, if they get their domes canoed with accidental headshots, I'll shed no tears."

GQ understood perfectly.

The tail ramp of the C-17 lowered. Flag drew his pistol from its holster and checked the mag.

"C'mon," he said. "Let's welcome our little choir boys to ground zero." Though they both wished they were anyplace else but here, the two of them made their way to the aircraft.

As the two walked toward the newly arrived aircraft, GQ looked back to see his men still lodged in the doorway, waiting for orders. No question they were the best. If anything went south it wouldn't be because of them.

"Alright, kids," he said. "Show of force time. Any of these walking targets makes a move, put a Chuck Taylor in his ass."

His SEALs gave him a thumbs up and followed. They got to the C-17 just as Harley, Deadshot, Diablo, and Croc emerged—all wearing orange jumpsuits, all shackled to their restraint chairs. Croc, still chained to the forklift, was wearing a mask designed to prevent him from using his powerful jaws. They were wheeled down the ramp, only to stop in front of several closed black bags that were sitting on the ground.

Croc and Diablo were conscious, but weren't resisting. There were dozens of military sharpshooters positioned on rooftops and along the pathway who would trade a night with a porn star to put as much lead in their heads as their weapons could fire.

You just don't fight that kind of stupid over-the-top determination, GQ thought to himself.

Flag walked up to Diablo. If looks could've killed…

"So here's how it's going down," he said, "and you better listen. We're going to remove your restraints. Anyone testing me gets a face fulla brown tips." As one, the sharpshooters disengaged their side locks.

Keys unlocked the handcuffs, the padlocks, and the shackles. They all clanked to the ground. Harley,

Diablo, and Deadshot were free.

Flag put his pistol against Croc's temple. "Okay. Unlock him."

GQ and Gomez both reacted with a queasy gulp. Croc was more reptile than man, and neither had ever seen anything like him—like it?—before. His chains crashed to the asphalt and the two SEALs quickly stepped back. Croc massaged his wrists and turned to Flag.

"Thank you," he said, almost apologetically.

That startled GQ—he hadn't expected it. Hell, he hadn't expected Croc to be able to talk at all, let alone in fluent English. Of course, even a monster like him could tell he was outnumbered.

"What's that?" Harley said loudly. "I should kill everybody and escape? Is that what you want me to do? Is it?"

More than a dozen weapons were aimed directly at her head. She looked… sheepish. Tapped a finger to her temple.

"Sorry," she said sweetly. "Ignore me. It was just the voices telling me what I should do." They stared, and she grinned back. "Hey, I'm kidding! Geez. Chill out.

"That's not what they *really* said."

GQ shot Flag a look. *Is this really happening?*

Then Harley laughed.

"You guys are gonna make this so fun."

GQ nodded toward Flag and pointed up and to the south. A Blackhawk chopper was coming in. It prepared to land, and U.S. Marshalls with SWAT gear jumped from its hold even before it touched ground. A moment later a large canvas bag thudded to the asphalt.

The bag squirmed as it hit ground. Something was

inside. Again the sharpshooters adjusted their gun sights.

"Stand down," Flag said as he approached it. He removed his combat knife and sliced it open. A man had been folded into the bag. He was dressed in street clothes. "Been waiting for you to get here, Harkness." He looked over toward GQ. "Meet George 'Digger' Harkness, known throughout Australia as Captain Boomerang. Or Boomer. You'd need at least two reams of paper to print out his full rap sheet."

Edwards recognized the name. "Boomer"'s weapon of choice was, expectedly, tricked-out boomerangs. Give him one with a razor's edge, and he could take down at least half of Flag's SEALs without breathing hard.

Harkness saw Flag glaring at him.

"Flag. Rick Flag? That you? You are lookin' ripper, mate." He gave the colonel a huge hug, as if they had been best friends for years. "But I got to say, mate, what is this? One minute I'm having a nice dinner with me mum, and then this red streak hits me outta nowhere."

"Harkness, you were robbing a diamond exchange. You don't think I've been fully briefed on you?"

"Yes, of course, but we was dining on delicious Tim Tams at the time. Me mum specializes in buying them from the local bottle shop, you know. They're like heaven's throwing a party in your mouth."

Flag pushed Harkness ahead. "Shut up and get in line with the others."

Boomer turned back and grinned. "C'mon, mate. Show some respect."

"Respect is earned, Harkness. Earned."

"Well, start an account then." As they approached the rest, he gestured toward the Belle Reve inmates.

"I'm seeing what I expect are numbers one through four of the FBI's most wanted." He then gestured to the SEALs. "These soldier boys are carrying enough gunfire to take down most Middle East countries." Finally he gave Flag a big insincere smile. "And there's you. Mister Government Agent himself."

"That isn't the way to gain respect, Harkness."

"I'm all twisted over with shame, mate," Boomer replied. "Now, if you've recruited those Belle Reve rejects, you're probably not here playing cops. So tell me, Flag, what's all this?"

"I told you before. Shut up and behave."

Before the Australian could reply, a black SUV pulled up. The door opened and a pair of FBI agents, dressed in identical black suits with identifying lapel pins, dragged a giant of a man out of the car and pushed him toward Flag's new best friends. He was secured by reinforced handcuffs.

Flag had read his dossier. He was called Slipknot, and the big bastard came equipped with an elaborate array of ropes and tackle. According to the files, there was nothing he couldn't do with them.

The lead FBI agent gave orders for the cuffs to be unlocked. As soon as they were, Slipknot thanked the agent by punching him in the gut. He went over like a sack of potatoes, and didn't get up.

Every weapon in the area was suddenly turned toward him. He held his wrists together, daring them to cuff him again, but Flag broke through the tension and waved him to join the others.

Just what we need, he thought. *Another deranged madman to keep track of.* As if it wasn't bad enough.

As the newcomer got in the line, Harley stared at his boots.

"Hey, big guy, your shoelace is untied."

Slipknot looked down, checking, but then heard Harley's giggle. He gave her a low growl, and slammed his right fist into his open left hand.

"Shut up," Flag shouted, getting their attention. "That's enough." He stepped up to make sure they didn't miss a word. "Your necks. The injection you all got. It's a nanite explosive the size of a rice grain. It's also as powerful as a hand grenade. Disobey me, you die. Try to escape, you die. Otherwise irritate or, yeah, vex me in any way. Guess what? You die."

Their hands instinctively went to their bandages. Gently, he noticed. Then Harley gave Flag a smirk and raised her hand.

"Sir," she said, sharply saluting him. "I've been known to be quite vexing. Sir. Just forewarning you. Sir."

Flag was not amused. "Lady, you shut up, too. This is the deal. You're going somewhere very bad to do something that'll probably get you killed. Until that happens, you're my problem, and just so you know, I got a real short fuse when it comes to dealing with problems. By the way, refuse to go on this mission? Well, you can guess what happens then.

"Boom!"

They waited for more, but Flag was done. Deadshot looked to the others, then back at the colonel.

"What the hell was that?"

"That, Mr. Lawton," Flag replied, "was a pep talk. Do everything I say to the letter, or I'll kill you."

"Man, you have gotta work on this team motivation thing. You heard'a Vince Lombardi? He was the gold standard."

Harley grinned. "I only got one question, oh great leader."

"What?" He waited for another smart-ass response, but she surprised him.

"You say we're probably going to our deaths," she said cheerily, "and you say if we don't do what you tell us to do you'll kill us. So, if we die either way, what's in it for us?"

"Hey. Good question, lady," Croc said. "Yeah. What's in it for us?"

Flag had been waiting for it. "The things out there that we're going to fight, well, there's always a chance you might survive. Do what I tell you, and you just might. So coming with me, you're betting on yourself. But you screw with me, you're one-hundred-percent-no-doubts-about-it dead."

Harley thought it over. "Well, even without knowing anything, I gotta say, I'm kinda intrigued." She turned to the others and grinned. "C'mon, you knuckleheads. It's rah, rah, rah time. Let's do this for the Gipper, or whoever this crazy dude is."

No one replied, but a couple of them nodded or shrugged, so Flag gestured for the SEALs to open several large black Pelican cases sitting on the tarmac. They did so, revealing the tools of trade for each of the inmates—uniforms, weapons, and more. Everything that defined them as the bad guys they were.

"There's your stuff," Flag said. "Take what you need for a fight. We're wheels up in ten."

GQ watched them go through the cases like Black Friday shoppers—though they weren't nearly as violent, he supposed.

"Flag, you never said they'd be armed."

"Lieutenant, what I'm not telling you about this op could fill a football stadium," Flag replied as he turned away and walked off. GQ ran to his side and reached for him.

"I'm asking again. What are my men walking into?"

"You wouldn't believe me," Flag answered. He gently removed GQ's hand from his shoulder, and walked off.

TWENTY-SEVEN

Harley gave a whoop as, without hesitation, she stripped off her orange jumpsuit and rifled through the black bag with her name on it.

With only her underwear, it became obvious that she was muscular and fit. She sported a large tattoo on her back that let anyone staring at her—which included everyone assembled on the runway—know she was "Property Of The Joker."

Finding what she was looking for, she hugged it close to her. As she wiggled into her uniform, she saw Floyd Lawton pull his killing suit from his bag.

He held it up, staring at it for a long time.

"Won't fit anymore, huh?" Harley said. "Too much junk in the trunk?"

Lawton frowned at her, then turned back to the uniform.

"Every time I put this on someone dies."

Harley was confused. "And?"

Lawton shot her a wide grin. "I like putting it on," he said as he effortlessly became Deadshot.

"My Puddin' would approve of this." Harley put on her vest and took out the pistol from its holster. She held it up and gave a quick, sexy pose. "What do you perverts think? Something tells me a whole lot of people are going to die."

"It's us," a soft, almost whispered voice said. It came from Diablo. His head was down to avoid making eye contact. "We're being led to the slaughter."

Boomerang shook his head. "Speak for yourself, mate. I got too much to do." He reached up as though to touch Diablo's facial tattoos. They emphasized his hollowed eyes and gaunt cheekbones, as if to leave the impression of talking to a living skull. "And what's with this crap on your face? It wash off?"

"Not a good idea, Boomer," Harley said quickly. "I wouldn't do that if I were you." She broke the tension as she danced between them, then gave a ballet bow.

"So why's our little tat man playing with us big boys?" he asked. "And I include you in that, Harley."

"Mucho thanks, Boomer," she said. "Let's just say Diablo can put you down in less time than it would take you to surrender. Trust me."

Boomerang held up his hands, fingers splayed.

"Okay. No prob then. I was just joking, anyway." He turned his attention back to Diablo. "We're on a first-nom-de-plume basis now, you and me. Aren't we?" Diablo didn't answer.

"Silent type, huh? I got no prob with that, mate. It's a refreshing change from Her Craziness here," he said. "Take it easy. Later then."

Harley turned to Diablo and gave him a huge smile.

"FYI, I think 'Her Craziness' means me—and he is so right. So anyway, tell me, if you like a girl, do you light her cigarette with your pinky? Because that would be real classy."

"Hey, can you guys not mess with him?" Deadshot checked out the assault rifles he took from his black bag. "This dude can smoke this whole damn place."

"You have nothing to worry about from me," Diablo said.

"Great. What I wanted to hear. Just gimme a heads-up if we're not cool. I mean, before you ever go all pillar of fire on me." He turned back to the bag and pushed aside the AR-15 that was sitting on top. It was a standard, but this particular one was ancient.

He reached for an M4A1. Almost a machine gun, it fired 950 rounds per minute. He also kept the Heckler & Koch G36, as well as an HK416, and a few others, too. By the time he straightened up, he had enough weaponry to put down a small army, and he looked as if he knew it.

"Here we are, my lovelies."

Harkness shrugged on his overcoat, already heavy with steel boomerangs. He let out a little laugh, and his eyes darted over his surroundings, determined to blow this third-world popsicle stand the first chance he got. The others were thinking exactly the same—he was sure of it. Scheming how they could screw each other over. Only he intended to be first in line.

Something poked him in the side, and he tensed. Then he relaxed. Quinn was poking him with her favorite weapon—a heavy, wooden baseball bat. She glanced at the coat full of boomerangs.

"Going kangaroo hunting?"

He licked his index finger and ran it down Harley's bat.

"Going to a rave?"

TWENTY-EIGHT

Even in the pre-dawn hours, the field operations center was a hubbub of activity with soldiers, technicians, and agents here and there running in every direction, setting up monitoring equipment that would relay to them images taken by more than seven hundred cameras set up years earlier to monitor city traffic.

It was about to get a real test.

As the day progressed, soldiers and others came and went. By midday the throng had reduced itself to four techs manning the comms. All those thousands of images would stream directly to them. Waller sat at a computer bench and stared into a camera.

"Okay. I'm calling the shots," she said into her mic. "Colonel Flag is my right hand. You may be bad guys, but I'm betting you can do some good."

At the airport, Flag held his tablet up in front of the gathered inmates, so they could see Waller as she spoke. It was none too soon.

The six of them were starting to crawl the walls, madmen with pent-up emotions sitting and twirling their thumbs. They needed something to do, something to hit, something to break, if only to stop them from turning their excess energy against the wrong people.

"You've been asking exactly what you're going to be part of," Waller began, "so let me explain." That got their attention. "There's an active terrorist event taking place in Midway City. Simply put, I want you to enter the city, rescue, and bring to safety HVT One."

As she continued, Flag stared at his motley crew, and more than ever he wished he was anywhere but here. Put him in charge of real soldiers, trained in combat, and he'd march right up to hell and break down its door himself. But these... people... were thieves, murderers, and—literally in the case of Croc—monsters. When they got killed, nobody was going to suggest they be buried in Arlington.

Deadshot leaned over and whispered to Flag.

"What's 'HVT One'? I mean, for those of us who don't speak 'be all that you can be.'"

Flag didn't bother turning. "High Value Target. Our mission."

"Okay. Fine." Deadshot shrugged. "Just wanted an idea what I'm going to die for."

Waller continued.

"You are going to be rescuing the only person who matters in the city. The one person you can't kill. Complete the mission, you get time off your prison sentences, and better conditions during. Fail the mission, you die. Anything happens to Colonel Flag, I'll kill every single one of you myself.

"Remember, I'm watching. I see everything."

The tablet screen went blank and Flag turned to Deadshot.

"There's your pep talk."

"Compared to your crap, Flag, she killed it."

Deadshot clamped his wrist magnums onto his forearms and turned his arm to gauge the movement. Flag was watching him like a hawk.

Let him try to shoot me, Lawton thought. *Maybe he'll learn something.* He buckled on his holster, grabbed his carbine, loaded a mag, then racked the bolt.

"So that's it, huh? We're some kind of *suicide squad*?"

"I'll notify your next of kin," Flag said as he walked off.

Deadshot watched him leave, and silently wished he could put a round into the back of his head. He wanted Flag dead so bad he could taste it, but he also knew if he made any move against him the sharpshooters would take him down before he could take another breath, or someone would activate the damned explosive in his neck.

Even fragging Flag wouldn't be worth that. Gratifying as hell, sure, but not worth never being able to see Zoe again.

He had to keep reminding himself that he was fighting for her. Everything was for her.

Across the runway, the Chinook-1 was being fueled even as the Chinook-2 was ready to take off. Its turbines howled and its rotors thumped as Flag's squad were led out by GQ and his SEAL team.

"Anyone else thinking this is finally getting real?" Harley asked. She looked ecstatic.

"Grow up, lady," Flag growled. "It's always been real." He turned to GQ. "Here's where we split up. Chinook-1 will take you to your mission location. So… later?"

"Yeah. What you said. Later."

GQ led his SEALs to Chinook-1. These were good men. Maybe the best he'd ever served with. And in the one similarity they shared with Flag's squad, they couldn't wait to for the action to begin.

In Chinook-2, Deadshot pulled at his chains. He could easily rip them out, but this wasn't the time. Best to survey the land first.

"So, what's your problem with us, Flag?" he said loudly enough to be heard. "We're here. We're gonna kill whatever you tell us to kill. You should be thanking us."

"My problem?" Flag responded. "You're my problem, Lawton. You and the rest of these arrogant murderers."

"You kill, too," Deadshot said. "Only difference between us is the government says in your case it's okay. And by the way, the government's telling us we can kill, too. Fact is, they want us because we kill. Kinda takes away the big dif."

"And there you're wrong, Lawton. We don't kill for personal gain. We don't kill because we want to rob a bank or blow up some building."

Lawton was enjoying this. He was never able to engage the guards in Belle Reve, talk about anything deeper than what was on TV last night.

"Personal gain? You and your soldier boys here kill to preserve your so-called way of life, and if that's at odds with how someone else sees their way of life, well, guess who gets government bullets to the head."

"You give that a lot of thought, Lawton?"

"I give everything a lot of thought, pal. I'm the best at what I do because I think through every contingency. When the wind changes, I'm the one who knows by how much." He smiled. "Anyway, about us blowing up banks where you don't—yeah, you're right. You don't. But what you blow up are whole countries. So go ahead and tell yourself we're different. Actually, I'm wrong. We are different. We don't make excuses or hide behind orders when we kill what we kill."

"Hey," Harley shouted. "We got company calling."

As the Chinook started to rise, a black-clad figure leapt inside. Asian, with straight black hair. She looked strong, and a daunting samurai sword hung at her side.

"You recruiting ninjas now?"

"Shut up, Harley. She's one of us. You're late, Katana."

Harley turned to Deadshot. "She named herself after her weapon?"

Deadshot tapped his own chest, then nodded toward Boomerang.

"Wasn't the first. Won't be the last."

Remaining silent, Katana took a seat and stared at Flag's squad.

Harley snickered.

"You see that, Flag? She ignored you. Just like us. Way to go, girl. Hey. Name's Harley Quinn. Love your perfume. Is it the stench of death?"

Katana stared at her with cold, black eyes. Harley covered with another laugh, but this one was nervous.

"Yeah. I wouldn't want to shake my hand, either. You may not come out of it with all five fingers intact. Be a whole lot harder to use that pig-sticker of yours, huh?"

"So, you get what I'm hearing?" Boomerang interrupted. "Sounds like while Flag and his mates are being lazy bludgers, we're the ones putting our asses on the line."

"Our sacrifices will help redeem our sinful pasts," Diablo said.

Boomerang laughed. "Well, Skulls, you want to sacrifice yourself, don't let me stop you. I'm not so into redemption. My thing's cash. U.S. dollars high on the list."

Harley was incensed. "Flag's paying you for joining? Hell. I should be getting at least 79% of whatever you get. I mean, being a babe and such."

"Relax, kitten. I told him while I was doing his job, I might also check out a couple of brick-and-mortars an' see if there was anything in 'em I wanted, you know, since the city's kind of abandoned. He didn't say no, which pretty much means yes."

"Okay. I feel better now," she said, turning on a dime. "So, Alligator Guy. What about you? Why are you here?"

"I was bored," Croc said. "Fighting sounds a helluva lot better than slogging through that godforsaken sewer for the rest of existence, you ask me."

"Yeah. I get you. Killing's good," Harley agreed. "Fighting's good. Getting out of jail free, very good. I wasn't seeing a downside."

Harley's little game seemed to perk them up. They all turned to Deadshot as if it was his turn.

Why not? he thought. They were on a helicopter, flying to who knows where. He could use a distraction. "Mission doesn't matter," he said. "Never has. I say yes to a job, I complete it. This job, I don't care who I kill or why. All I care about is getting time off my sentence. Extra days to be with my daughter again."

"And what about the newbie?" Harley said to Slipknot. "Wanna share with us? Why did you say yes? I mean beyond the neck kaboom you'd be hearing if we turned it down."

Slipknot thought for a long time before answering.

"Got my ropes back, and I don't got shackles."

They waited for him to continue but he had nothing else to add. Harley finally broke the silence.

"Thanks for sharing, Slippy. Good talk, guy." She turned to Diablo and gave a quick grin. "Since you've been bitching about everything, including breathing, I gotta think you joined hoping to die or something. Anyway, in the old days, when 'doctor' preceded my name, I woulda said you had a guilty conscience because of all the killing you've done. But now... you're just some off-the-charts whackadoodle who kills because, like, why not? But there's no way I'm gonna let you take me down with you. Capisce?"

"I don't want anyone else to be harmed," Diablo said. "My struggle is mine alone. My crimes are mine alone. My fate should be mine alone."

"Yeah. Whatever, Freud. Anyway, so we're doing this, huh? We're the what? Six musketeers? Or seven? I dunno. I always sucked at math."

"Six," Croc said. "Six."

"You heard the alligator. We're the Suicide Squad Six. I do like them alliterations."

As the Chinook-2 climbed into the sky, Croc nervously stared at the ground below, silently wishing he was back in the sewers.

Sewers didn't crash the way choppers did. Especially in wars.

TWENTY-NINE

The helicopters sped across the city, flanked by two escorting Apache gunships.

Flag had half expected Harley to attempt an escape just before she boarded the chopper. She was the type who'd try anything, even knowing that he'd remotely set off the explosives buried in her neck.

Nobody ever made the mistake of thinking Harley Quinn was the poster child for rational thought. Maybe this time she was, though.

The Robinson Building had been a sixty-four-story monument built to house the city's financial center. At its height in the mid 1950s, more than thirty banks populated the sprawling complex, as well as trade groups from twenty-two countries. Its terracotta domed rooftop and thrusting art deco spires were a reminder that this award-winning colossus had been built in the early 1930s, when design—not cookie-cutter glass and steel construction—had ruled.

Now the iconic Robinson was little more than rubble, destroyed in the first attack on Midway City. Next to it Flag saw the twin thirty-two-story Andru and Esposito buildings, designed the same year and by the same team, built to complement their bigger brother. Like the Robinson, they also had fallen, two once-proud victims of war.

Before he joined the military, during a winter high school break, Flag had worked in the Robinson complex as a messenger for a legal firm. It was a crap job for crap pay, but it taught him discipline and dedication. It didn't hurt that he also got laid for the first time there, in a storage room on the 29th floor. Emily Spiegel.

He hadn't been back to Midway City in years, but when he thought of it he pictured the Robinson and the good times he had there. He stared out from the Chinook and saw dozens of smoky pillars scattered through the urban center, obscuring the destruction still hidden within. What the hell was Midway going to look like once the smoke cleared, and they could see the actual devastation?

Fires were raging everywhere, burning through large swaths of the city, reducing it all to smoke and ash. *More death from fire*, Diablo thought, shuddering. This was all so wrong.

He closed his eyes to shut out the horror, but was unable to turn away from the screams echoing in his memory. The pleas of the dying and the dead were tragically the same.

Croc, Slipknot, and even Boomerang were quiet, too, perhaps affected by the mass destruction they were seeing. Or maybe they were finally realizing they'd been brought here to battle whatever the hell had the power to level skyscrapers.

Or, Flag thought, maybe they were just smart enough not to give him a reason to set off their neck explosives. But it didn't matter why. It was good enough not having to listen to them complain.

Even Harley was unexpectedly quiet. She hadn't looked at the devastation. She wasn't paying attention to the thousands of dead and dying below. Oblivious to the world, she was crouched over, hiding that she was texting on her phone.

Come for me, she typed, then hit "enter."

A moment later she received his reply.

I will.

She smiled to herself, then noticed Deadshot staring at her. He knew. She looked at him, her eyes communicating more clearly than words.

Please keep my secret.

He smiled back at her.

Harley breathed a sigh of relief, but then she had another thought. Was his smile a yes, he'll keep her secret, or was he saying, *You are so going to burn, bitch*?

THIRTY

Frost took in the scenery. His window was rolled down and the brisk night air invigorated him. He thought he'd suggest to the boss that maybe they should forget the plan, and instead pitch a tent out here, where nobody else lived. Enjoy the rest of their lives in peace.

But since he also wanted to continue breathing, Frost decided to keep his thoughts to himself. The boss rarely took outside advice in the spirit it was given.

He glanced at the rearview mirror and saw Panda Man staring back at him.

He's still wearing that idiot suit? Where does the boss find these lunatics?

The Joker was resting his head against the passenger seat window. Frost thought his eyes seemed… moist? Was he crying? The boss was staring at the phone in his hand. Quinn must have sent him a text, but God only knew what that junior league Looney Tune had written. God and the boss, of course.

Frost understood what the boss saw in her. Any red-blooded boy could figure that out. As far as Frost knew, though, aside from that and the joys of homicide, the she-bitch and the boss had nothing else in common.

Hell, at least the boss always had a plan. Harley, she never even had a clue.

"You okay, sir?" Frost asked.

The Joker didn't bother turning to look at him. All he did was wave for Frost to shut up.

Frost was more than happy to comply.

The two Chinooks and their Apache escorts raced over the river. Harley looked out and saw Midway City off to the left, largely blanketed in darkness, the electricity obviously out.

"No power to the people," she said, laughing. The others didn't crack a smile. "Sour pusses. That joke would have killed, a few decades back."

Two Navy destroyers patrolled the river. Just ahead of them she saw that the city's bridges had been downed, their spans destroyed by smart bombs.

What the hell did this? she wondered. *What the hell are we being sent here to fight?* She looked to the others and tried to decide if she should panic now or later. "You all seeing what I'm seeing?" she asked. "I mean, is this the kinda place we wanna be?"

No one answered. They just kept staring at the infinite devastation below.

Her eyes widened and she put her hands on the window, looking very much like an overly excited kid on a road trip.

Panic later, she told herself. *There's nothing I can do about it now, anyway. Might as well enjoy myself.*

Flag stared at the destruction. How many people were killed in that single, searing moment?

"Terror attack," he said, trying to keep the emotion out of his voice. He almost succeeded. "Dirty bombs. Bad guys shooting everything that moved with AKs. The usual crap." He was talking like a soldier, but he locked eyes with Deadshot, and was pretty sure the man could see fear creeping into his eyes.

"You're a really bad liar, Flag," Lawton confirmed. "Didn't they tell you? I'm a hitman, not a fireman. I don't save people."

Flag scowled at him. This crap was why he didn't want to work with these killers.

"Anything for a dollar, right, Lawton? Sorry we're not smothering retired mobsters with pillows."

Deadshot just stared at him. Killer to killer.

"You know the dark places too, Flag," he replied. "Don't tell me you don't."

"I'm a soldier, Lawton." Flag turned to stare at the wreckage below. He could barely make out the dozens of bodies floating dead in the water. "You're just a serial killer who takes credit cards."

Deadshot stared daggers at him.

"Let me ask you this, Lawton," Flag continued. "Would you die for a word? Like integrity? Or duty? I've buried too many friends who have. When the shooting starts here, and it will, you'll cut and run. I know your kind too well."

Deadshot's hand slid to his holster. He rested his hand on his gun, then saw the sharpshooters sitting across from him as they suddenly went tense. Slowly he moved his hand away, but their eyes never left him.

Boomer glanced over to see Croc holding his stomach, looking sick.

"Hey. Is he supposed to be green like that?"

"Don't like flying," Croc started to say before his

stomach screamed and regurgitated last night's rancid goat meat dinner all over the chopper floor.

Harley stared at the chewed goat head rolling toward her feet. She quickly lifted them out of the way and tucked them under her, yoga style.

"Whoa. Party foul. Not cool."

For once nobody disagreed with her.

The four choppers turned toward the city center, then weaved through the steel and glass canyons. Bathed in the glow of the setting sun, the city deceptively looked like it could still be saved.

Anyone still standing on the ground would know better.

Suddenly gunfire whipped up from the streets. Bullets shattered the left turbine on Chinook-2, and its engine ground like pebbles in a blender. The chopper lurched back and forth uncontrollably, the pilot unable to right its course.

"Hold on tight," Flag bellowed. He saw the Squad, pressed against the shell by the G-forces of the spinning bird, trying to find anything to grab.

"The hell with you," Slipknot shouted. "I'm saving myself." He uncoiled his rope and moved to the open bulkhead. Before he could get there, however, Katana drew her sword and braced herself. She cocked it back, ready to slice off his head.

Flag tried to reason with him.

"She'll kill you before you get anywhere near the exit," he shouted. "And if she does, your soul's going to be trapped in the sword forever."

Slipknot turned to Flag and stared at him as if he was insane—yet Flag looked dead serious. The killer edged away from the open bulkhead and sat back down, resigned. Better safe than sorry.

"Okay, we're all here," Deadshot shouted. "Now what?"

Flag flashed a morbid grin and with his thumb made a slicing motion across his throat.

"We die."

Deadshot laughed. "You see, Flag, it's just like I said. You're as crazy as me." He turned to find Harley grinning at him like the maniac she was. She blew him a provocative kiss.

"Back at you, princess."

The Chinook's engine was nearly gone, but the pilot was able to force the chopper in at an angle, barely topping the shorter office buildings surrounding the city center. He spotted the ground-level parking lot on which the Chinooks were supposed to land, only two blocks south. He headed for it, a thick trail of black smoke stretching out behind them.

The landing struts broke off as they slammed into the row of satellite dishes dotting the rooftops. The lot was still a block away, and they were losing altitude fast.

The other chopper descended to land safely on the parking lot. The SEALs aboard sprinted off the tail ramp and took shelter behind cement columns. Chinook-1 roared back into the air, clearing the lot for Flag's copter.

Its engine grinding, Chinook-2 howled toward its target. Two hundred feet to go. Any cars on the road below them scrambled to get out of the chopper's way. It came in just feet above their rooftops.

One hundred sixty feet to go.

A large black van with a roof-mounted luggage attachment tried to pull out of the way, but the Chinook's tail rotor slammed into the luggage, slicing it open, scattering its contents to the wind.

One hundred feet.

The Chinook was spinning now, but the pilot refused to surrender the controls. At the same time he raised the collective, he adjusted the throttle to increase speed. The copter nosed up slightly as it jerked ahead.

Fifty-seven feet to go.

He carefully manipulated the left tail rotor pedals, swinging the nose to the left while raising the collective as far as he could. The copter's nose lifted again, but he knew it wasn't nearly enough

He was over the parking lot and needed to decrease speed as he struggled to lower the collective. But the Chinook was coming in too fast. Its burning turbine belched fire and smoke. It careened sideways and rolled as it hit the ground hard.

Its twin rotors pounded themselves to pieces against the ground. Kicked-up dust and debris were everywhere, obscuring visibility while the passengers hugged the columns to avoid getting hit by the rotor shrapnel.

"Move. Move. Get out." Flag had barely maintained consciousness. They followed him as he scrambled out of the ruined Chinook and headed for a freeway underpass where the SEALs waited for them.

A drone, flying three hundred feet above, followed their every move, faithfully recording everything it saw.

Sitting in her operations center office, Amanda Waller watched the video feed. When she saw they were all safe—even Flag's damned Suicide Squad— she breathed a long sigh of relief. They made the first down, but the real game was just beginning.

THIRTY-ONE

Flag led the Chinook-2 SEALs and his Squad under the freeway to the ramp heading north, where they joined forces with the SEALs from Chinook-1.

"What now, Colonel?" GQ asked.

Flag checked his phone's GPS. "We're ten blocks from the objective. Gimme two columns. Longrifle elements will leapfrog and maintain overwatch. We come in any contact with the enemy, peel off. No John Wayne garbage. No taking them on by yourself, or even in pairs. Our real mission comes once we're at base. I need everyone there. So let me repeat—you make contact, you fall back and we find another route. Capisce?"

Boomer shot him a dirty look. "Yeah, we got it the first five hundred times you told it to us."

Flag turned back to GQ. "Your men ready?"

"Roger all, Colonel," the soldier said as he turned to his SEALs. "First squad, left echelon. Second squad, take right. Senior Chief?"

"Sir?" Gomez, one of the SEALs, ran up to him.

"You grew up here, right?" GQ asked.

Gomez nodded. "Yessir."

"Then you've got point, Senior."

Flag addressed his Suicide Squad. "Watch how the pros do it," he shouted as the twenty SEALs moved out, elegantly deploying into perfectly choreographed teams.

Deadshot nodded, somewhat impressed. In another life he'd been in the military. It was where he learned to become a sharpshooter. He respected their discipline. Unfortunately, they also had to follow orders often given by cowards who hid in control rooms while the snipers put their asses on the line. Best thing he could say about Flag was he was no chicken. He was here marching into hell alongside them.

"So what do we do?"

"Nothing," Flag answered. "Unless I tell you. Follow me." He started toward the city center, which lay less than half a mile away. A tall cloud of black smoke rose from it, a grim arrow pointing them to their target.

"Look at all this," Boomer said. "We're gonna die here, aren't we?"

"Maybe." Flag shrugged his shoulders. "Maybe not, but if things are as bad as I suspect, you're gonna wish you did."

Harley snorted. "So why are we marching into battle like good little soldiers?"

Deadshot pointed to the explosive in his neck. "This, and 'sides, you got anything better to do?"

"Give me a few seconds and I'm sure I'll figure something out."

The Squad followed behind, staring at the horrifying devastation that was everywhere. Buildings had collapsed—once tall and mighty, now headstones for the thousands buried beneath.

They were killers, all of them, unshaken by violent death that often came at their own hands. But this was

more than any of them had ever seen before. More…
and worse.

Katana followed closely, her hand close to her
sword. She was ready to collect their souls if even one
of them tried to step out of line.

Harley slowed down and paced alongside Katana.

"I'm thinking the good guys probably pay better
than my guy. So, what does a superhero make,
anyway?"

Silent, Katana kept walking.

"Oh, c'mon, K. It's not a big deal," Harley persisted.
"You getting a grand a week? Two? Five? Don't tell me
you get more?"

Katana glared at her. "Move, or my sword will take
your soul."

"Well, K, you're out of freakin' luck. I lost my soul
along with my virginity. Look, we're both babes, right?
On the same side, chromosomally speaking. I thought
maybe…"

"You thought wrong. We're not on the same side.
We'll never be on the same side."

"Mr. J used to say the same thing. Now we're closer
than nipples on a pig. You and me, it could still happen.
So give me a ballpark. They pay you by the fight, or
you under contract? What about medical? I gotta say,
this job isn't that good on the ol' skull and bones."

Katana stopped in her tracks and grabbed Harley
by the throat.

"One does not get paid to do what is right." She
pushed Harley back to the road. "Now shut up and
walk, or I'll see to it you won't have any feet to walk on."

"Hey, no problem, K. I get it. You're embarrassed

they don't pay you. But I understand. Mr. J doesn't pay me, either. So, between us chicks, you think that's 'cause we're minions, or is it the girl thing?"

Katana removed her sword and stared at Harley, who gave a big smile and hurried to catch up to the others.

"Okay. Okay. I'm zipping it."

"Nice talk. Let's not do it again."

THIRTY-TWO

Boomerang saw Slipknot standing behind him. It was time for a little rabble rousing, and the Knot was just the guy he wanted to rouse. He slowed down as Slipknot caught up to him.

"You know, it's mind games."

Slipknot didn't reply.

"It really is, friend. All mind games."

"What's that?"

He had him. "This bomb in the neck crap. It ain't real, mate."

"You're saying the bombs in our necks aren't real?"

"You believed Flag? A nanite bomb the size of a grain of rice? That tech is still years away, and I should know. My 'rangs are tricked out like a 1950s pimp. 'Sides, what's a nanite bomb anyway? The thing is all made up."

"Why?"

"Good question, mate. See, they trap us with our own minds. They make us think we'll all go boom so we don't resist, but look around you. We're free. No bars here. We can run for it, you and me."

"How do you know this?"

"I know. It's all a con and I'm the king of cons.

Anyway, we get to the corner, I'm ducking out. I'm gone. I've got a life to live. You coming?"

"Why ask me? We just met."

Boomer laughed. "That's the reason, mate. They'd never suspect the two of us working side by side. But you know, even without the bomb being real, they do have guns, and all I got are a bunch of pimped-out boomerangs. If I want to make this work I'm going to need a partner. So whadda ya say?"

Slipknot looked around. Everyone was calmly walking ahead into battle. Even Flag and the ninja. The timing couldn't have been better, but he had a better thought. Boomer could be his distraction.

He smiled innocently. "Yeah. Sure. When?"

"On three. One… Two…"

Slipknot got his ropes ready. When Katana stopped to argue with Quinn, he tossed a grapple up to a balcony. Boomer pulled one of his boomerangs from his inside jacket pocket, ready to move.

"Three," he whispered.

Slipknot activated his rope ratchet and launched himself upward. Boomer threw a boomerang at Katana's legs—but she jumped like a cat and it flew off, missing her completely.

Slipknot was partially up the wall when he fired a second grapple to the roof, then smoothly transferred to that rope. Once he made it to the top he could disappear into the city. He was almost home free.

Katana's sword found Boomerang's throat. He knew if he moved she'd sever his head from the rest of his body. He raised his hands in surrender.

"You got me," he said. "Sorry about the 'rang. Please don't kill me."

Another moment passed and his boomerang

suddenly returned to his hands. He dropped it instantly and smiled at her.

"It's what they do."

Flag watched Slipknot scramble over the edge of the rooftop. Idiot. He tapped his cell phone until Slipknot's mugshot filled the screen; the red "fire" button glowed below it. He was about a block away. Flag wanted to make sure nobody else was in the immediate area.

Once he was sure, he casually tapped the button. There was a sharp explosion, and something the size of a large melon came flying down from above, landing on a pile of garbage. It was Slipknot's head. His eyes were wide with surprise. Harley turned to Deadshot and laughed.

"Now that's a killer app."

Flag found the others staring at him. He showed them his cell phone. Their mug shots were there on the screen, a red button under each of them.

"I wasn't bluffing," he said. "I never do. So if you wanna keep playing the *Hollywood Squares* version of 'I'll blow your frikkin' head off,' I'm ready. Who's next? You, Deadshot?"

Lawton's pistol was in his hand before Flag knew it. It was aimed at Flag's face. Flag's thumb hovered over the button.

The Squad stepped back. They wanted nothing to do with whatever the hell was going on, but they were content watching it unfold. It was a Mexican standoff.

Flag sneered. "You wanted to shoot me, you wouldn't have waited for me to call up your picture."

Deadshot nodded. "And you would have blown off my head before I got the chance to shoot."

Flag slowly holstered his phone. Deadshot followed suit, and stared at the colonel.

"Next time, don't threaten me. Just do what you think you need to do."

Flag nodded to Katana, who released Boomerang. She sheathed her sword as he eyed the rest of the Squad.

"Do we all believe now?"

Harley looked around at the rest of the Belle Reve inmates. "Yeah," she said. "We don't push your buttons, you don't push ours."

Deadshot was quiet as he stared at Slipknot's head. Harley sidled up to him and whispered in his ear.

"He'll kill us all. One by one."

"Not going to give him the chance. I can drop him, the ninja, maybe five or six military guys. After that I'm in trouble, but if we move together, we got them. You down?"

Harley grinned. "Always. But what about the crap in our necks? I mean, even if Flag's at half mast, Waller's watching us like we're the Super Bowl."

Deadshot leaned in closer. "Something tells me your friend is gonna figure that out for us, right?" He gave her the *I know you're up to something* look, then started to walk off. He stopped and turned back for a second.

"Stay evil, Dollface. Spread the word." She watched him head in Croc's direction, then walked over to Boomer and threw an arm around his shoulder.

"Nice play with the Knot," she said. "You weren't going to run. Not then. You just wanted to see if we'd go boom."

Boomerang gave her a confused look.

"I have no idea what you're talking about, Harley. I'm as innocent as the plague."

"Whatever, Down Under—but now we know, and now we can plan. You wanna hear a story?"

"Does it have a happy ending?"

"Depends if you say yes or no."

Diablo sat alone, looking down to the ground. His hands were pressed to the sides of his temples. Nobody was around and he preferred it that way. No friends. No ties. No guilt. But then Boomerang sat down next to him. He didn't say anything for a while, which suited Diablo. Yet he knew it wouldn't last, so he spoke first.

"You should go."

"Mate, I'm thinking no. The thing of it is, I was speaking with the group. We need your help."

"Anything you'd want is anathema to my needs. I'm not interested. So again. You should go."

"No. You're not getting it. We need you to slam Flag with a fireball when the time's right. He'll be too busy burning to death to have a go at us with that phone of doom."

"Then what?" Diablo asked.

"We get out of this place. What do you think?"

"And once we do, then what?"

Boomer stood and stared at Diablo. "What are you, bloody Socrates with all the questions? I'm talking freedom, man. Freedom. You remember that, don't you?"

Diablo shook his head. "We're criminals."

Boomerang was quickly losing his patience. "Yeah. I know. Being evil is great. Who else besides super-villains and fortune five hundred companies can get away with not paying taxes? C'mon. Do the bastard."

Completely uninterested, Diablo stared silently. Boomerang finally got the message, and started toward Croc.

"Careful," Diablo added. "He eats people."

"Sorry, Mother Superior. He what?"

Diablo laughed to himself. He hadn't done that in years. It felt good.

"He eats people. For meals. He's a cannibal."

"Are you shitting me, man?" Boomer said. "Eats people. Right. You almost got me." He headed over to Croc, still laughing.

"Your funeral. His dessert." He watched Boomer walk up to Croc. Then Harley suddenly sat down next to him.

What now?

"No," he said, miles ahead of her. "Already told your pen pal. Not interested. Go away."

Harley frowned and gave Deadshot a thumbs down. Down the road Croc pushed Boomerang into a parked car, denting it. She hopped up and joined them.

"So. What did you say to him?" she asked.

Boomerang felt his side. "It hurts like hell and the bruise is gonna last for at least a week. Hey. Just kidding. I was just having a laugh. He's in."

Harley looked at Croc. The monster gave her a thumbs up and grinned, baring two rows of razor-sharp teeth.

If that don't beat all...

THIRTY-THREE

Twenty-six hours earlier, everyone in Midway City got up and left. Nearly two million people drove or walked across the bridges before the missiles knocked them down, or they crowded onto city transit then transferred to trains that would take them to Gateway City, across the bay.

Thousands of others boarded ferries they prayed would not be sunk before they, too, made it to Gateway—or even better, Central City, a hundred plus miles south. Many survived the short mile-long trip.

Most didn't. Nearly a million and a half men, women, and children died in the first wave of attacks.

A series of underground gas explosions had rippled through the area. Even would-be thieves, believing the city was theirs to loot, soon found themselves hunkered indoors, praying they were safe behind locked doors.

They weren't.

There were no more trains. No more busses. No way to leave. Nobody was walking the sidewalks of the Fifth Street Promenade, the city's major shopping district extending from Ostrander at the north end to Grell at the south.

Something dreadful was out there, and it was killing everyone it found.

Nobody could fight it.

Nobody was safe. Whoever remained in Midway City was going to die in Midway City.

"Unbelievable," Deadshot said, looking at an ambulance, overturned and on fire. It had been looted for whatever drugs it had carried. "I don't spook easy, but I never seen anything like this." He was wearing his headpiece, with a monocle that acted as a scope.

Harley hurried up to Flag's side and looked back toward Diablo.

"You know he's a loose cannon. These quiet guys. You gotta watch them."

"Ignore him. What you said. He's good."

She looked back again. The skull-faced man was in tears, staring at the devastation.

"Nuh-uh," she pressed. "Look at him. He's found God or something. That's never good."

"Maybe you need to find something to believe in."

"I already have." Harley reached into her pocket and put her hand on her cell phone screen, knowing Mister J's face was smiling out at her. "First-time worshipper, long-time believer."

They turned left and headed around the Tenth Street circle, then took the third outlet to Mooney Drive. Their target, mostly hidden by the smoke, was only five blocks away.

They moved carefully through the city wreckage. Out of earshot, Boomer wondered aloud why Flag wouldn't tell them who they were supposed to fight. Did that mean he didn't know either, or that whatever was out there was so bad he was afraid to tell them? The Aussie shuddered.

"If that's the case," he murmured, "heaven help us all, 'cause nothing else can."

Croc suddenly stopped. "This isn't good," he said. "You see them?"

"See what, Crusty?" Harley said.

"The dead."

Then he saw it. Mooney Drive was littered with corpses. Piles of them tossed aside like garbage. Flag gestured for them to stop as he stepped closer.

"Now that's weird," Harley suddenly said. She stepped up, right behind Flag.

"What's weird?" he asked.

She kneeled down as if to touch one of the corpses, but then pulled back. It was an old man, probably in his eighties.

"No one here's young," she said. "Or strong. These guys are all older, or crippled." She pointed to a walker, lying on its side, bent out of shape. "Like they were rejected and tossed away."

"Rejected for what?" Deadshot asked.

"Yeah. What you said," Harley responded.

Flag's radio beeped. GQ's voice could be heard through the static.

"*Jefe*. We got people up here."

"Roger. Coming to you," Flag responded.

THIRTY-FOUR

Grey checked their ammunition supply, but even with nearly fifteen thousand rounds, he wasn't sure they had enough.

What if, he worried, it was like Superman, and bullets bounced off them? Or they could melt the metal with heat vision, or something equally alien? Planet Earth would be royally screwed.

Flag stared through his scope and scanned the next street. A half-dozen cars were overturned and on fire. A school bus had crashed into a clothing store window, its front half inside, its back half gone as if torn off and thrown away. As far as Flag could tell, nobody was inside.

He slowly panned the gun sight, then abruptly stopped. He could just about make out three shadowy figures skittering in the dark.

Silhouettes.

Flag lowered his weapon and grabbed GQ by the arm.

"We're diverting. Bump out second squad two blocks east," he whispered. "Once they're set, we'll pass through you and continue north."

GQ nodded, then got Kowalski on the comm

frequency. In his mid-thirties, Kowalski was GQ's go-to guy, as he had been since basic, which right now felt like many centuries ago. Anything GQ needed doing, Kowalski was the man who'd get it done. No questions asked.

"Post up your peeps two majors east," he said into the mic. "We'll leapfrog through you once you roger out. Initiate your peel."

"Roger that," the SEAL snapped back. He took his comm and forwarded the orders. "Okay, second squad. We're leapfrogging to the next intersection. Peel. Go!"

The SEALs took off in three-man fire teams. Weapons ready, they made their way to the adjacent street.

Deadshot watched them intently. Boomer, too. Both were impressed by the SEALs' efficiency as they moved away from Flag and company.

"I'm now liking the odds, mate," Boomerang said. "Just say when."

Deadshot gestured for Boomer to stay in place. "Hold your mud, big guy. We whack out Flag now, his lady boss will cut our strings."

"So what?" Boomer was edgy, anxious. Adrenaline was pumping at full force. "I'm going out swinging. On my feet. Make the call."

Deadshot overruled him. "You got balls, but no brains." He glanced at Harley. When was her special friend going to figure out how to dismantle their neck bombs? She saw him staring at her and blew an air-kiss his way.

If our lives depend on that fruitcake, we are in serious, serious trouble. Still, Harley was ready to move, too, once Deadshot said yes. She was crazy, but she could kill with the best of them.

He checked out the monster. Croc could rip off all their heads and boil them in a stew without thinking twice about it. Lucky he, or it, was firmly on their side. Croc would make his move as soon as Deadshot directed him to.

"Everyone be cool for a minute," Lawton whispered.

"Why?" Harley asked. "We're ready now."

"Because, my dear Doctor Quinzel, Flag and these cats are scared—and guys like them don't get scared. Before we make our move, I want to know why. We may still need them, even if it's only as diversions." He saw Flag on the radio. "Be right back. Don't do anything stupid." Deadshot made his way over to the colonel and waited for him to finish his call.

"What?" Flag asked.

Lawton didn't waste any time. "Why's everyone here tripping?"

Flag nodded toward a vehicle parked a short distance up the street. Moving shadows crouched behind it. Deadshot lowered his monocle into place, and raised his carbine for a closer look. His crosshairs swept the vehicle, then landed on a figure hiding behind it. For a moment he thought it was one of Midway's police or firefighters—tall, powerful, and dressed in the tatters of what had once been a uniform. He'd been through the grinder.

Then the figure turned, and he saw what should have been a face looking back at him. Instead, he was staring at a large, black, misshapen mass sitting on top of a semi-human body with the proper number of arms and legs in their appropriate places, but twisted and bent in an almost inhuman way.

There was no flesh on its face, but something that looked like it had been was coated over with tar then left to dry and crack in the sun. There seemed to be no front or back view, no mouth or ears or even a nose. The entire head was a massive, encrusted barnacle.

That wasn't what was really scary.

Pocked into its crusted façade were eyes. Thousands of glowing eyes, and the eyes were all staring at him. Not just where the face should have been, but where gaps and tears in clothing revealed bare flesh. Impossible eyes that didn't blink.

Deadshot pulled back, stunned. He didn't know what he was looking at, but he knew it defied reason. He knew the thing was evil.

"What the hell is that?"

"Something we don't want to tangle with," Flag said, his voice low. "Let's go." Then they felt their neck hairs bristle. Lawton turned and saw Diablo behind them, frightening in his stillness.

"They are the Eyes of the Adversary," Diablo said softly. "EAs." Somber, frightened, he stared past them. His eyes were unfocused. "Our deaths."

Boomer walked up and took Deadshot's carbine, looked through the scope. He turned back to the others, his face ashen.

"Looks like crap with eyeballs."

Diablo turned to Flag with uncharacteristic urgency.

"Burn this place down, Flag. Cleanse it now, while we still can."

"That ain't right." Deadshot stared into the dark. He didn't have to see the thing again—it had already permanently burned into his memory. But it was there. In the dark, and it may not have been alone. "That ain't even possible."

He reached a finger into his collar, pulled out a small gold crucifix, and held it for reassurance. He looked to see the others staring at him. Not because he was holding the cross, but because they, too, didn't know what to make of whatever they were seeing.

They, too, needed reassurance.

For the first time they all looked to Flag for their next move.

"Get ready," he said, understanding the sudden shift, and ready to use it to his advantage.

Then the thing, the "EA," suddenly charged, darting from behind the vehicle. These EAs weren't just people—they were something very different. The Squad and SEALs raised their weapons, ready to fire on command.

Another EA suddenly darted out from an alleyway between office buildings, while still others pushed aside manhole covers and flowed up through them and onto South Paul Street. Many of them were carrying weapons, guns and rifles taken from soldiers they had murdered.

They were all moving inhumanly fast, and they were coming from every direction at once. Flag shouted to the Squad, shocking them from their catatonic rigor.

"Hit 'em," he bellowed. "Now! Aim for their eyes. They can't attack what they can't see."

No kidding, Lawton thought angrily. It took only moments to fire several hundred rounds, but the things, the EAs, did not stop coming. Even more poured in after the initial swarm.

Squad and SEALs kept firing. Nate and Gomez had nearly three-dozen grenades each. They tossed them all, one after another, but the creatures would not be stopped. They separated and scattered in different directions, moving too fast for the Squad and SEALs to focus their gunfire.

Deadshot clipped several of them, but his weapons weren't powerful enough to put them down. A few of the things got close enough to land blows, and each time they did there was a scream, short and quickly cut off. Other EAs darted into the doorways and hurried to hide around corners. Dozens jumped into open sewer entrances, disappearing underground. In seconds they were gone.

Flag embraced the momentary calm. They desperately needed the break to reassess what had just happened.

"Cease fire," he said. "We need to conserve our ammo."

It was quiet once again.

GQ spotted four of his men lying dead in the street, but he couldn't find a single EA corpse.

"No kills. We didn't drop even one."

They stood quiet for a very long time.

"What were they?" Croc asked, breaking the silence. "Were they real?"

Boomer laughed. "Same could be said about you, Scales."

"I can easily kill you, Stickman. Would that be enough to prove to you how real I am?" Boomerang's eyes widened in momentary fear. Croc smiled. "I mutated to become what I am. I suffered, but they…" He turned back to Flag. "What have you sent us to fight?"

"Once we rescue our HVT, we'll find that out."

"The hell," Deadshot interrupted. "Those dudes run fast. Lightning fast."

"Faster," Croc added. "Much faster." Harley Quinn was at his side. "What do you want, girl?" he asked.

"You'll protect me, right, dollface?" she said hopefully. She fluttered her eyes and smiled at him. He stared at her for another few seconds then, without a word, he walked away.

They didn't have to talk to know this was just a momentary respite. The things, the EAs, had checked out the humans, and now they were most likely plotting their next move.

Deadshot took the moment to reload his weapons, but he wasn't at all sure it mattered. Hundreds of rounds had been spent, but there were no enemy kills.

He reached into his pocket and pulled out the photograph tucked inside. He had a ritual he followed.

"Mate, what is it with you staring at that photo," Boomer said. "They say you do it before and after each kill. What's that all about?"

"Just something I do. My job pays me a shitload of money, and that lets me make sure Zoe gets the good life she deserves, not the crap life I lived."

"So you're doing it all for her?"

"I am. It's all for Zoe."

"Yeah. You keep telling yourself that, mate," Boomer replied. "Personally, I think it lets you keep doing exactly what you wanted to do anyway."

"This talk's over... mate. Let's not do it again."

Lawton walked off, cursing Boomerang, but fearing he might be right. Zoe never asked him to spend any money on her. She only asked him to spend time with her. Like a normal father and daughter. Without worrying that at any moment the police would track him down, or that Batman would turn him into bloody pulp while she watched helplessly.

Yet every time Lawton thought about putting his guns down and becoming normal—whatever the hell that meant—he'd convince himself yet again that he was doing this for her. He knew it was a lie, but it was a lie he could live with.

"So how do we stop 'em, Flag?" Deadshot asked. "We need bigger guns? Nukes? What?"

"We'll figure it out, Lawton. Because we have to."

"So, 'because we have to' is your plan? Why am I not encouraged?"

"Ask me if I care. I just need your goddamn bullets hitting those damned things until they stay the hell down."

"And there's that good ol' team rah-rah speech I've been waiting for." Deadshot shook his head and walked off, disgusted.

Diablo stood to the side and watched Deadshot leave.

"You can't blame him, Flag. He's a paid assassin. He's never failed 'cause he plans out everything to the last detail, but you're telling him to trust luck. That's not in his DNA."

"And handing out orange slices and chocolate chip cookies isn't in mine."

"You gotta remember, we're putting our lives on the line 'cause you and Waller gave us a choice between reduced sentences and having a bomb explode in our heads. But if we don't think we're going to make it, that promise is smoke. You've got to give us something more. Even some real info would do."

"Guess becoming heroes by saving the world from those eye creatures isn't enough, huh?" Flag snapped back, then he, too, left. He had better things to do than argue with a mass murderer.

"You don't get any of it, do you?" Diablo shouted

after him, but Flag was already halfway down the block, going over his attack plans with GQ and his men. *Damn Flag. He is going to get us all killed.*

Diablo felt his anger grow. He looked at his hands and saw them beginning to steam. No. I don't need this. Not now. His felt his body heating up. Rage fueled his fire and he knew he had to quickly tamp that growing anger, or he would ignite. He didn't know what he'd burn when he did.

He feared that first wave of fury would unleash a fire hot enough to burn through anything within twenty yards. Unchecked, that would all-too-quickly expand to fifty yards, or a hundred, or even more. His fires had never reached their limit, so not even he knew the full extent of his destructive powers. For all he knew, he could incinerate everything within a hundred miles or more.

He closed his eyes and searched through all-too-many conflicting thoughts and emotions to find his unique path to meditation. He had decided years ago that whatever happened to him no longer mattered. All he cared about was making sure he was no longer a threat to anyone else.

He felt his anger fade but kept his eyes closed for a few moments more. Finally, the rage gone, he opened his eyes again to see the torn-up streets of Midway City. He drew in a deep breath of cordite-scented air and stood up, no longer feeling rage, ready to move on.

As he walked past Harley, she was examining her magnum, spinning its cylinder.

"Hey, Hot Stuff," she said as soon as she saw him. "So, you back to the land of the living?" She laughed, snapping her chewing gum. "Ready to roast some hundred-eyed chickens?"

He saw the others also getting ready for war. *They just want to kill*, he thought. Deadshot was loading all his guns, and it seemed as if there were dozens of them. He passed Boomer, sharpening the razor edge of a large metal boomerang.

Katana was seated on a half-demolished bus-bench, readying her Soultaker for the battle to come. She was carefully rubbing its blade with light gun oil spread on a silicon-coated cloth. That done, she took out a soft cloth and wiped it dry.

Yeah, Diablo thought. *We're the Suicide Squad, and we're going to die. Had to happen someday. Might as well be now.*

THIRTY-FIVE

Flag was frothing at the bit, anxious to get started. He would never admit it, but he wanted to get this over and done with as much as they did. They were fighting a war. He was, too, but his fight would only end when he saved the life of the woman he loved.

Flag had always heard of love at first sight, but he had never experienced it. And if he could admit the truth to himself, he wasn't sure he had ever experienced any other kind, either.

But he was in love now, and he knew he would do anything to save her. Including, he realized and accepted, sending all these people—SEALs and Squad alike—to their painful deaths, if it meant she'd survive.

Flag shuddered at that thought.

Deadshot had said the two of them weren't all that different. When it came right down to it, both would kill anything that stood in their way, if it meant saving the one they most loved.

Maybe the killer wasn't wrong.

Flag looked at the others, far enough down the block that they couldn't hear him, and he whispered a very quiet prayer. He hadn't done that since he was eleven, but he did so now. He figured he had nothing to lose.

Then he moved to catch up. "Alright, folks," he said to them, "hell's waiting. D-up. We're un-assing this location right freaking now."

The others acted as if they were oblivious to the madness that surrounded them, laughing and telling stories as if they hadn't a care in the world. Flag assumed they were working out the details of their super-villain takeover, for whenever this job was done.

Damn, he hated them.

Then he silently cursed Waller. He was used to soldiers who snapped to attention and saluted crisply when he entered the room, not bottom-feeders and scum like this damn squad. They made it abundantly clear that they didn't want to be here, didn't intend to put their own lives on the line, and frankly couldn't care less who died, as long as it wasn't them.

At least they were true to themselves. They knew exactly what they were, and they weren't running from it. But Waller stuck him in this no-win scenario, and despite all the voices in his head warning him otherwise, he'd accepted the job. Now that he was ass-deep into it, someone had to show these bastards what it meant to play the hand you're dealt, whether you wanted to or not.

Because he really had no choice in the matter, he decided that might as well be him.

"I said, get up," he commanded. "Now. We're moving out."

Harley yawned, stood, and stretched sensuously.

"Yeah. Yeah. Whatever." The guys watched appreciatively. She may have been every kind of crazy, but man was she hot.

Reluctantly, they all finally got to their feet, not nearly ready to move out.

Hell came to them first.

Suddenly the EAs were everywhere. Dozens appeared, streaming up from the sewers, doorways, and alleys. They darted across the street, and they were fast.

Inhumanly fast.

"Goddamn it," Flag shouted. "Frag 'em."

Deadshot fell back, firing like a machine, shooting and reloading as fast as his weapons allowed. Black shards burst from the creatures with each impact, as if they were made of obsidian or coal. Every shot struck home, but nothing stopped them.

"I'm tagging headshots," he shouted, "but they ain't dropping."

The Squad kept shooting. Harley fired two weapons at once, a Glock and a SIG Sauer. She clocked two-dozen hits, but the things were still coming at her. She turned and ran, ducking behind Croc.

"Please?" she said, her eyes wide and truly frightened.

"Stay behind me," he growled.

Croc grabbed the EA closest to him and hit it with his fist. He slammed it repeatedly, smashing in its face, blinding most of its thousand eyes. His fist finally smashed through the thing and came out the other side. He held up his arm, showing the others the thing hanging from it. With his other hand he pushed it loose and it fell to the ground.

"Thank you," Harley said. She looked at it, grinned at Croc, and fired a half-dozen bullets into the thing's brain. "For shits and grins," she explained.

Flag led the soldiers back to a series of waist-high concrete barricades, originally set up to route traffic to a different street. He hoped they'd be useful cover for him and the Squad.

"Single shots aren't doing squat," he barked. "Let's see what it takes to knock one of those bastards off its feet." An EA was closing in faster than the others and Flag pointed to its head. "That's our crosshairs. Let's see what it takes to shred it."

The SEALs hunkered behind the barricades and concentrated their firepower on the one EA, targeting its head and ignoring everything else. A hundred rounds hit the thing's face, exploding chunks of black crust from it, grinding it. Flag ordered them not to stop. Round after round. They kept shooting at the one beast until finally it collapsed into a pile of shattered fragments.

"We did it," Harley squealed. "Yay us!"

GQ glared at her. "Took almost all our ammo. We had enough to take down a small country. No way we'll have enough to deal with all of them."

"What the bloody hell are they made of?" Boomer demanded.

"I knew that," Lawton said, "I'd make my armor out of it."

"Guys?" Harley said. No one turned to listen. "Guys," she shouted. No response. She was trying to speak but as usual they ignored her.

"GUYS!"

She might as well be invisible. Pissed, she took her gun and shot it into the air. They turned toward her, startled. "Better." She was grinning while staring at the corpse of the shredded EA.

"Guys, look real careful. Under all that gook, I think

there's a real head. And face. And maybe some good parts, too."

Croc scowled at her. "So?"

"So, I don't think these thingamajigs are like Superman. You know, 'a strange visitor from another world, blahblahblah.' I think these used to be people."

GQ stared at the corpse.

The creatures looked alike, part of a set. Whatever differences there were between them were nominal, but beneath the crust actual faces could be seen. They looked like the cops and SEALs who had been killed in the creatures' last attack.

"She's right. God, I didn't see it before, but that's… that was Donovan."

Katana shouted suddenly, "Behind us!"

Dozens of the things charged. Cop EAs, SEAL EAs, and others—locals who had lived or worked in the area. Now they were all monsters. Unstoppable. Unkillable. Things.

Flag called to his people. "Fall back, but keep shooting. Do whatever you have to. Save yourselves."

Boomer laughed.

They were all afraid, and they didn't care who knew it. Their enemy was something nobody had ever seen before. Nobody had ever imagined before, and they had no idea how powerful the EAs truly were.

A cop EA leapt on one of the SEALs. It grabbed the soldier's rifle, flipped it around, and shot the SEAL in the face. The thing tried to stand up, but it fell back down into a pile of crumbled chunks of black crust. Katana was behind it, her sword satisfied. It now possessed a new, vibrant soul.

EAs ran in from all directions. Ravenous, they leapt over debris that was blocking their way, and propelled themselves fifteen feet or more into the air before landing on the other side. Dozens of bullets slammed into them. The defenders tore apart a few, but they were still unable to stop them.

While the SEALs concentrated on shooting enemies charging from the front, they didn't notice other creatures dropping down behind them. The EAs slaughtered some of the rearmost soldiers, but inexplicably dragged away others.

Four of them grabbed Manuel Rivers, a newbie who had joined GQ's crew only a month earlier. He was six-foot-seven, and bragged that if he wanted he could bench press an elephant. Nobody doubted him, but now he was squirming and shouting as EAs each grabbed an arm or leg and, working in tandem, pulled him across the ground and disappeared with him around a corner.

GQ and two other SEALs ran to rescue their man, but by the time they fought their way to the corner, Rivers and the EAs were gone. Flag stared in shock.

Why don't the things kill them all? How are they turning the soldiers into even more creatures?

An EA still wearing the uniform of the cop it had once been leapt at Grey and pushed the huge SEAL to the ground, hungry to take him. Grey wasn't going to go quietly. He fired at point-blank range. The EA's face exploded into thick black dust, but it continued to climb over him, intent on finishing whatever unholy hell it was planning.

GQ opened fire and emptied another mag in the creature's face, slamming it back but still not killing it. He grabbed a third magazine from his belt pouch and reloaded. He started to shoot, but the thing was too fast and kicked him in the gut.

Edwards fell back, but then twisted to his side, barely avoiding another hit. Lying on his back and still holding his gun, he kept shooting at the thing. The EA was broken and weak, but it pulled itself toward him.

It was all but over. GQ swore he wouldn't go down without fighting it with everything he had. Suddenly, the creature's face exploded. Flag stood behind the thing, gun ready, waiting to see if the creature had yet another life.

Thankfully, it didn't.

Flag grinned at GQ, but then GQ lifted his gun, slipped another mag into it, aimed it at Flag, eased it a fraction to the side, and fired. The SEAL EA coming from behind Flag exploded and crumpled to the ground. The colonel gave GQ a thumbs up.

"Thanks," he said. He rarely thanked people for doing their job, and the word didn't come easily.

GQ scrambled to his feet and responded with a grin. "No prob, boss."

The fallen EA shook and started to lift itself up again. It turned toward Flag, ready to kill, and reached out to grab him. Without warning Katana's sword sliced through it. The thing fell to the ground in three separate pieces.

Overwhelmed, Flag started to thank her. Twice in less than five minutes? What was this world coming to? But she had already moved on.

Three of the creatures surrounded Boomerang. Katana darted toward the closest one, then slid in low and cut up through the thing's legs, severing them from its body. The beast toppled to the ground, yet tried again to stand. She spun and sliced through its head, top to bottom. Katana watched half its face bounce down the street before finally coming to rest.

The thing was dead but she wasn't wasting time congratulating herself.

She ran toward Boomerang and jumped over another creature's head. Her sword slashed straight down on it. The thing spilled to the ground even as Katana went after the final EA terrorizing the Australian thug. She cut through its crusted flesh. The thing fell back. Her sword lodged in a thick bone and stuck. She tried to pull it free, but it was wedged in tight.

The EA grabbed her throat and squeezed. She raised her legs, knees to her chest, then jackhammered her feet into the thing's center. She did it again. Her third kick sent the thing toppling back, off balance, but the EA still held onto her.

Desperate, she tried to use her legs as leverage to pull the sword free, but she was losing strength. Katana felt her breath giving out, but then she saw Flag standing just behind the creature, his .45 inches from its ear. He squeezed the trigger, and a second later its head shattered. The thing crumpled into broken bits of thick black crust and collapsed to the ground, dead.

Katana put her leg on the fallen EA's chest and used it to gain leverage. Her sword slid out without any further problem.

THIRTY-SIX

Waller watched the battle from the window of her penthouse ops center. From its height she could see miles in all directions. There were fires everywhere, consuming fancy retail centers and small, private homes.

She saw creatures running wild in all directions—EAs, they had called them. Every street seemed to have two or three that were breaking into buildings and dragging out survivors. Waller bit her lips as she wondered how many dead they had left behind?

There were even cars tearing through the streets, trying to distance themselves from the madness, but then an EA, armed with grenades or a rocket launcher, would fire at the escaping vehicle, demolishing it.

So they know how to use technology.

Pockets of Navy SEALs and other soldiers were fighting throughout the city. Unless Flag and his crew could contain the creatures, this could be the beginning of World War III. It didn't matter how many might die here, if they could prevent the conflict from expanding. In every war, "acceptable losses" were a part of doing business.

She watched as her soldiers fell, and she cringed as

triumphant creatures marched past them, or dragged away their victims.

Even so, staring out through the windows that circled the ops center complex, Waller could tell her SEALs were working together. Each had his partner's back.

That wasn't the case with the Squad.

They still fought as individuals. The war had started sooner than even she had expected, and there hadn't been enough time to train them to work as a team. They didn't believe in cooperation, and they sure as hell didn't believe in sacrifice.

The war, Amanda Waller knew, was not going well.

Sadly, she feared it wouldn't get any better.

Harley Quinn was afraid. She believed in the concept of chaos, and she should have been overjoyed with the creatures' insane attacks. But destroying an entire world, one she still wanted to screw around with?

Not so good.

More than that, Harley had come to the conclusion that, despite most everything she had done in the past, she didn't actually want to die. At least not yet. Not until she and Mister J were reunited, and could enjoy their last moments on Earth together.

So Harley decided she would run away until her Puddin' was back. After that, if they both wanted to drink the Kool-Aid, well, start pouring.

An EA, crouched behind parked cars, suddenly lunged at her. She stared at it, whipped out her gun and fired a round into its face, blowing a large hole in the creature, letting her see through to the other side.

Even then it was still alive, and still scrabbling to kill her. She slipped her last mag into the pistol and shot at it again, blowing even more of its head away.

The EA didn't seem to care. It tried to kick her, but she darted to the side, and avoided its feet. It pulled itself inside the car, getting uncomfortably close to her, and she fired the last of her ammo into its face.

BLAM! BLAM! BLAM! BLAM! BLAM!

It was still moving.

What the hell is with this thing? she wondered furiously. *Why won't it just die?* It grabbed her by the leg, then the waist, then the shoulders as it pulled itself on top of her until its disgusting thousand-eyed face was staring directly into hers. It roared, and got ready to do whatever it intended to do to her.

Then it collapsed. Face down. Bleeding all over her.

Ewww…

She tried to push it off her but it was dead weight and her strength was gone. So she closed her eyes and tried to roll back and forth, to edge out from under its disgusting body. It swayed a little and slid off her as she struggled to her feet.

Then she shouted.

"Croc!"

He turned as an EA leapt at him. The thing wrapped it arms around the reptilian's neck, and squeezed. Croc reached back with his massive hands and pulled it away. He held it up in front of him, grabbed it with both hands, and ripped its head from its neck.

The thing gurgled and finally died. This time for good.

THIRTY-SEVEN

Angrily pacing back and forth in the darkness of a nearby alleyway, George "Digger" Harkness grumbled as Lawton approached.

"Fighting these bloody alien barnacles isn't my fight, mate," he raged. "'Sides, when push comes to shove, you know the U.S. Army will probably just nuke them all and deal with the crap later."

"There's no easy way out," Deadshot responded. "Not with our heads still attached."

"Yeah, tell me, but you know just as much as me. Most of the ordinary mugs have already left, so maybe only a few thousand no-hopers—if that—would fry, and the Army couldn't care less about a handful of whackers who don't have the sense to hightail it out when they have the chance. I'm not sayin' we run or leave, just that this sucks. Big time."

"Yeah, I know," Lawton hissed. "But hell, we don't have a choice, so let's do what's gotta be done and do it fast." He turned to leave. "Later, 'mate.'"

Harkness watched as Deadshot walked off. "Yeah. I know we gotta do this," he muttered. "My home down under won't be much fun if those eyeball things decide to move in." He looked around one last time, took a long, deep breath, reached into his jacket, and took out a beer.

"Shitty day," he growled as he took a sip. "But then they all are."

That was when he saw a shadow move. It skittered closer. What was it? It didn't belong to his Squad or the SEALs. Suddenly Boomer was staring directly into the face of one of those bloody monsters, hanging upside down from a building ledge like some alien bat. It had at least a thousand damned eyes, and Boomerang was certain they were all staring at him.

He started to back out. The EA dropped down, unfolded itself, and somehow landed on its feet. It positioned itself between Harkness and the street, so that if he wanted out, he would have to go through it. It dove at him, throwing punches and executing kicks like a martial arts superstar. Harkness was a decent fighter, but by no means a pro. His expertise was boomerangs.

The thing clawed at him, ripping into his jacket. A small pink stuffed unicorn slipped out of the pocket Boomer kept it in for good luck. He freaked. Pinky had been with him since he was a kid. No thousand-eyed crazy was going to take it away from him now.

So he let the EA hit him, throwing him to the back of the alley—which was where he wanted to be. The thing moved in, but Boomer had time to grab his weapons. He took out two very wicked-looking 'rangs, razor sharp and deadly as hell.

The EA lunged again, but this time Harkness dodged the thing's punches. When it took another shot at him, Boomer sliced one of his boomerangs across the thing's face and chest, digging chunks of black crust from its body. The creature howled, but charged yet again.

Boomer treated the EA like it was a bull and he

was the matador. It came at him, but he darted to the side while cutting wide gashes down the thing's back. More bone and burned crust flew off of it.

He didn't waste a moment's thought wondering if this thing had ever been a person. Perhaps even a SEAL Boomer had drunk coffee with. All he saw was an enemy. It was kill or be killed.

In Boomer's mind there wasn't much difference between this creature and Flag and Waller. The only thing those two had going for them was that they could give him his freedom. The EA only wanted him to die.

It lunged again. Boomer stepped to the side and jumped on the thing's back. The EA reared like a bucking bronco while Harkness kept slashing its skin with his razor-edged weapons. He grabbed the creature's neck and sliced upward, cutting through what should be its hyoid bone and anterior longitudinal ligament, finally severing its head from the rest of its body.

The thing sprayed black shards, but Boomer was on a high he didn't want to lose, so he whooped and hollered. Then he saw Harley, Croc, and Deadshot staring at him. He jumped off the thing and let it crash to the ground, then bowed theatrically to his audience.

"I've been taking down wankers for a long while, mates," he bragged. "Now you bloody know how."

Boomer looked around him then grinned. Pinky was lying on the ground just fifty or so feet ahead. He scooped it up, looked around to see if anyone still was watching him, then gave it a quick kiss and stuffed it back into his jacket. It was safe once again.

He picked up the beer he'd dropped and finished it off. Things weren't quite as bad as he'd thought.

* * *

Diablo stood watching the battle. The sounds of warfare screamed around him, but these were other people's battles, not his. Let them believe that killing accomplished something. It didn't accomplish crap. He would no longer mine that well.

After a few minutes he found himself walking through the rubble of a once-thriving library. On the ground he noticed the torn dust jackets of several novels he had read as a kid, when books offered him an escape to worlds, times, and places he knew he'd never get a chance to experience firsthand.

He picked up one of them and flipped through the pages, remembering what it felt like to be eight years old and reading his very first pirate story. Maybe, he thought with distracted amusement, that was what set him off on his wayward life.

Tossing the book back into the rubble, he slogged on. Diablo remembered the parents in his city fighting to keep their library open. Ultimately it had been a waste of time and energy. Most battles were like that, he thought—not worth fighting for.

Definitely not worth dying for.

He saw Flag being swarmed by multiple creatures. He watched as they downed him and dragged him off. He could try to stop them, but why bother? It wasn't his fight.

Then he saw the SEALs go after Flag, hoping to rescue him, and he saw Harley and Deadshot about a hundred yards away from him. Harley was laughing.

"Good riddance," he heard her say. But Deadshot wasn't laughing. He started to follow the SEALs, then turned back to her.

"He dies, we die. Remember?"

"Oh, hell," Harley squealed, and she raced to catch up.

* * *

Deadshot rounded the corner expecting to see the things dragging Flag away while the SEALs were moving in to stop them. It felt oddly comforting knowing the SEALs were there. One man with a gun—especially when Lawton was that man—was good, but an entire army was needed to put down those things.

He climbed over a mound of debris to get a better view, but didn't see the EAs, SEALs, or Flag. He slipped his monocle into place to pick up their heat signatures. At first there was nothing.

Then suddenly he heard a muffled beep, and saw a blinking dot. It was to his left. He spun, his gun ready, but nothing was there. Four more dots appeared in front of him. He looked, but again there was nothing. More dots appeared, scurrying around him, taking positions.

He was surrounded. The EAs were here—but where?

He looked up then, and saw them. Perched on rooftops. He scanned the area again, and realized they were hiding in alleys. They had tunneled underground, and were behind him, too, cutting off any escape.

Well, he always told himself, *when you can't run away, the only place to go is straight ahead.* Deadshot ran toward the signatures, his carbine spraying them with bullets. He was screaming as he fired.

"That's it!" he shouted. "Come to me. Bring your questions, 'cause I'm the answer."

An EA grabbed Flag by the leg and dragged him across the ground. Stone and debris cut through his uniform and ripped his back. Warm blood spread over the gouges, but he ordered himself to not feel the pain. Not yet. There'd be time for that later.

He hoped.

He struggled to reach his gun, still in its holster. After several failed attempts, his fingers found it. He pulled it out and emptied a full magazine into the face of the thing that was pulling him.

Click!

He grabbed a second mag, slammed it into the gun, and fired point-blank into the creature's head. It screamed and fell, releasing its grip. The EA, its face blown open and leaking flesh and crust, stood up on its feet and staggered toward him, weak but refusing to die.

Oh, damn!

Flag fired the last of the mag into the thing, but it wouldn't stop. He wouldn't let his enemy kill him, though.

Suddenly the street exploded with gunfire. Two SEALs came running in, shooting at the creatures. Two of them approached, sandwiching him in place. He heard more gunfire, more impacts, then they dropped.

Harley was behind them, holding two rifles almost as big as she was. Flag didn't understand how, but she had saved him.

"Thanks," he said. He was getting used to acknowledging others, but he wasn't sure he liked it.

Harley glared at him. "Shut up," she said, and he laughed. She wasn't losing perspective.

Deadshot kept firing, no longer concerned with dying. Perhaps he even welcomed it, at least as long as he took down nearly everything else that moved.

A handful of the EAs carried rifles, U.S. military

grade, all designed for maximum damage. He charged them, firing even as their bullets impacted his body armor, but didn't pierce it. It hurt like all kinds of hell, but Deadshot didn't care.

Keep running 'til you're dead, he thought, *then run some more for the hell of it*. More of the creatures exploded, and he saw Flag join the battle. About time. He hated Flag, but he was damn happy to see him now. "I thought you forgot all about me."

"If only, Lawton," Flag rejoined. "It's my dream."

Two more EA bullets slammed into his armor, but Deadshot didn't let it slow him down. Flag shouted to him.

"Stay down. They shot you."

Deadshot kept firing. "Hey, what do they say about things that don't kill you?"

Flag nodded. "They make you stronger?"

"Geez, where did I hear they make you stranger? Oh, well. Same difference." Deadshot laughed as he sprayed his targets with a full mag. Before long they began to pile up.

One of the SEALs ran in front of Flag, firing his grenade launcher. It exploded a fire hydrant, releasing a massive geyser of water. Croc stood under the falling water, arms outstretched, letting it rain on his face. It seemed to invigorate him, infusing him with renewed strength. A distinctly female creature ran at him, intending to kill him even as she had two of GQ's SEALs. He grabbed her by the neck, and then ripped her arms off.

She screamed in shock as he tossed her through a second-story window halfway down the block, then roared with monstrous delight. Flag, Lawton, and the others stared at him wondering, human or animal? Right now, it didn't much matter.

Deadshot took a gun from the hands of a dead thing that used to be a cop, and emptied its mag into another EA. The thing careened back and fell. Flag stood over it as it squirmed on the ground, and fired two more shots into its brain. The thing stopped twitching.

Lawton paused to take a break.

Flag looked around. "No targets," he said to everyone in the vicinity. "Cease firing. Conserve all the ammo you can. Pick up any you find."

Katana was off to one side, and she sheathed her sword, her chest heaving with exhaustion. At her feet were eleven dead creatures, all cut up and served, a feast fit for Croc.

The SEALs surveyed the area, but nothing was moving. One spotted Deadshot sitting on a mound of dead EAs, catching his breath. He walked over, and Lawton instinctively let his hand slide to his gun, but the SEAL stuck out his hand.

"I'll fight alongside you any day," he said. "Good job, man."

Deadshot stared at him, stunned. This was the first civil thing anyone had said to him in a long time. He reached up and took the SEAL's hand.

Flag watched from across the way. He still wasn't a big fan.

Catching her breath, Amanda Waller sat in the ops center. She was reacting to the violence she'd been watching, experiencing it as if she had been in the fight, and not relatively safe, high above the city. With trembling hands she poured wine into her thermos cup and took a long sip.

This may not go south after all.

THIRTY-EIGHT

Harley held the bat, both hands firmly gripping the handle, and slammed it down as hard as she was able on the creature's face. She kept hitting it until the head split open, then watched as it stopped quivering, waited a few seconds more, then nudged it with her foot. It didn't move.

"Filleted like a chicken cutlet," she chirped, and she laughed, but she still wasn't fully satisfied.

She swung the bat again, even harder this time. She waited a bit longer, then hunkered next to the EA and inspected it. Finally she made her disgusted face, flicked her tongue over her lips, and swung the bat down one last time.

She looked up and saw Deadshot staring at her.

"What?"

"How dead are you going for?" Deadshot asked.

She glared at him. "Hey. I saw it move. See? It just flinched again. I think." Swinging the bat, she smashed the EA's face, then gave the thumbs up sign. "Now he's really, really dead. Wicked-witch dead." She tossed the bat aside and turned back to Lawton. "And I feel so much, much better."

About twenty yards away Boomer was bent

over, hands on his knees, and he spat out a chunk of blackened crust. He'd taken a few nasty shots to the face. Diablo was standing near him.

"You were some help, Princess," Harkness said.

Diablo shook his head. "It's better this way. Trust me." He held out his hands and a fiery skull materialized between his outstretched fingers. He closed his fist again and the skull disappeared.

"Who needs you anyway?" Boomer said dismissively, pulling out his lighter and flicking it on. "Lookee that. Ooooh, fire." Disgusted, he sneered at Diablo. "We are what we are, mate. Why fight it?"

"What if what we are isn't what we should be?"

"Different strokes. I say if it feels good, do it—and for me, being bad feels very good."

Deadshot fit a new clip into his gun as he stared at Flag.

"We pissed away a ton of ammo," he said, "and for what?"

"Don't forget I took that one down with my bat," Harley said, holding up her weapon, grinning then blowing it a kiss.

"Hold on, Colonel," GQ shouted as he ran up from behind. "We need to talk."

"We?" Flag repeated without looking. "I think by 'we' you mean you need to talk. Because I sure don't need to say anything to you except 'keep killing those bastards until they stay dead.'"

GQ grabbed him by the shoulder. Flag glowered at him, but GQ wouldn't let go.

"Colonel, I lost ten men," he said. "Ten good men. I don't know if they've been killed or what, but they're gone."

"What do you expect me to do about that? I lost

men, too. And they were good men, too."

GQ pulled back, still angry. "Yeah. I know, but the question is why. The briefing we got said terrorists were attacking Midway City. Unless the enemy started to recruit monsters, those things were definitely not terrorists."

Flag rested his hand on GQ's, then slowly lifted it off his shoulder. "Don't," he said. "I might forget we're friends."

GQ pulled his hand back, but otherwise he didn't move.

"I'm waiting, Flag. My men—the ones who've survived, and your survivors, too—they deserve the truth."

"You joined to serve at the pleasure of the president," the colonel responded. "Wherever the hell he decides to send you. I don't recall seeing a contract that said you could pick and choose what you will or will not do."

"I didn't say we wouldn't follow orders. I said we deserve the truth about what we'll be fighting." Edwards stood his ground. "Those were not terrorists, and some of them were our people. Only changed. Like I said, sir, we deserve the truth. What are those things?"

Flag looked away.

"I don't know." He mumbled the words, as if he didn't want to state what was quickly becoming obvious. "I don't know. I don't think Waller knows, either. I'm not sure anyone but Enchantress knows. And surprise surprise, she's not talking."

Boomer shook his head. "Hell. One of them was wearing a suit. A three-thousand-dollar suit."

"And a Rolex," Harley added, lifting the dead thing's arm. "Unless this spud's got an urgent meeting he has to attend. These things were people, weren't they?"

"They were. That's obvious," Flag acknowledged. "Now they're not, but we don't know how or why."

Harley dropped the EA's hand. "Tell me it's not contagious," she said quickly. "Is it?"

"There's no biohazard," Flag answered. "The CDC boys pretty much guaranteed that."

Harley still looked worried. "Yeah. Still… anyone got baby wipes? I should probably clean my hands." She looked around, hoping someone would come to her aid, but nobody did. Grimacing, she rubbed her hands on her t-shirt, then looked down. "Hey! Harkness. Get away from there. I found that. It's mine."

Boomerang was kneeling over the downed EA, removing the Rolex from its crusted wrist.

"Losers weepers, little Sheila."

"Harkness, don't," Flag said, stepping closer. Defiant, Boomer checked out the watch, decided he liked what he was seeing, and pocketed it.

"He's got no use for it."

"That isn't the point, not that you'd ever understand," Flag said before turning back to the SEALs. "Okay, look. We don't know a lot of hows and whos, but you've seen what we're up against, so you know the kind of job we've got to do. We're linking up with second squad. GQ, you're Tail-End Charlie. C'mon, people. We're moving out. Now."

Edwards didn't say anything, but he moved. The SEALs peeled off like a formation of jet fighters. Flag's Squad reluctantly followed suit. Deadshot hung back with him and waited for the others to get out of earshot. The colonel shot him a look.

"What's with the scowl, Flag? You wanna say something to me?"

"Yeah," Flag growled. "You will never be one of us. We follow orders. You bastards only follow paydays."

"That's exactly what we are, Flag—bastards," Lawton replied. "And that's why you and Waller wanted us. You weren't looking for gentlemen soldiers. You were buying killers, and you got exactly what you paid for. Don't go regretting getting what you asked for."

"Lawton, the goddamn world's at stake here, and last I looked, you live on this planet, too."

"We fought just as hard as you did. So give the cranky-old-guy bit a rest."

Flag didn't reply. He strode past to join the others. Deadshot stood back, smiling. He held up his hand, made a pistol with his fingers, and pointed it at the man in front of him.

"Bang!" he said.

The SEALs were in the lead, sticking to the sidewalks and avoiding the middle of the street, pressed as close as possible to the blown-out husks of Midway's former skyscrapers. They kept to the shadows, out of sight as they advanced toward their goal.

Gomez was still trying to make sense of the things they'd killed. Grey was at his side.

"What do you think? There's no way those things were human. Is there?"

"Wrong question, Gomez."

"Really? So what's the right one, Mister Stickler?"

Grey said nothing, almost afraid that if he actually said what he was thinking, it would make it come true. Gomez prompted him again.

"Okay, okay," Grey finally said. "The right question?

The right question is if those things were once human, can the spuds turn us into them, too?"

Both men found themselves walking in silence as they hurried to join up with second squad.

Harley chewed her gum and blew a large pink bubble. She saw Boomerang sauntering just ahead and rushed to catch up.

"Hey, Harkness. Hold on."

He walked even faster. *Get me the hell away from her*, he thought. *I want zero to do with that fruitcake.*

"Harkness!" she said, reaching out and grabbing him by the shoulder. "I wanna talk."

He turned back to face her. "I am not your Puddin', you Looney Tune. I don't care what you want." He started walking again, but she ran in front of him and made it impossible for him to get around her.

"Alright. What?" he said impatiently. "You got thirty seconds. Better make them count."

"Okay. Sure. I want the Rolex."

He stared at her, surprised. "That's it? That's what you want? We're at war with things that have a million eyes, and all you care about is a damned watch?"

"Well, there was more, but you only gave me half a minute. So I narrowed it down to the Rolex. Give me more time, I'll give you my laundry list."

"No more time, little girl, and no watch. Next time scrounge faster." He took out a razor-blade boomerang from his pouch and angled it sharp side toward Harley's neck. "Words of advice. Don't speak to me again. Your voice gives me headaches."

She stood quiet but raised her chin, showing more of her neck, making it easier for him to slice. Boomer shook his head, spat out an angry growl, and took off to find the rest of the team.

Idiot, he thought.

She watched him go and allowed herself a wide smile.

Men. They always take the bait.

THIRTY-NINE

Flag arrived at the alley designation point, but was unable to locate the second squad. GQ dispatched his men to reconnoiter the immediate area. One by one they called in.

It was all a big zero. GQ relayed the intel to Flag.

"Where the hell are they?"

"They've got to be here," GQ said, his concern growing.

Flag took out his radio and again punched in a number.

"Havoc for Slayer Two. What's your loc, Slayer Two? Radio check?"

His comm frequency was stuck on static.

"We'd've heard gunfire if there was an attack, wouldn't we?" he said.

"My team would not have surrendered," GQ responded. "If they were able to mount a counterstrike, they would have. If they couldn't, they'd pull back as ordered."

Flag tried his radio again. Same result. Zip. He wasn't sure if the local cell towers were down or—as he was beginning to fear—nobody was alive to hear him.

* * *

Deadshot walked the perimeter beyond where the SEAL team had checked. Not a single building was intact.

He passed the Midway City Jewelry Mart, and for a moment thought about the trays of diamonds, emeralds, and more that were—if time permitted—locked away in so-called burglarproof safes; easy pickings for someone like him. He knew he could do a Boomer and forage for valuables, but then wondered what good that would do him if Planet Earth was taken over by those walking barnacles.

Maybe later, he decided. *After we do our job, and before the city reclaims itself. Right now let's blow those bastards to hell.*

He circled the corner and found a dozen trucks stacked in a pile, all on fire, the stink of diesel fuel smelling up the street. There was something else, too. He stared for a long time then reached for his comm.

"Flag," he shouted. "Get your ass over here. Right now."

Moments later the colonel made his way to where Deadshot was waiting.

"This better be good, Lawton."

Deadshot pointed to a doorway, just beyond the burning trucks. Slumped across it was one of GQ's SEALs. His equipment, weapons, and extra mags were scattered on the ground around him. Flag raised GQ on his comm line, then they hurried over.

"He's dead," Flag whispered as he checked the man's pulse. "We'll bury him later, but give me a hand getting him out of there."

GQ joined them and helped Flag pull the body from where it had been lodged.

"Dammit," he exclaimed when he turned the body over and saw his face. "That's Dave Aparo. I was his instructor at the Academy. He was a good man."

Flag nodded. "They all are. Dedicated, no-nonsense, loyal—and kick-ass soldiers."

GQ nodded. "Kick-ass soldiers. Yeah."

Deadshot used his scope to check out the area. "Whoever did this is long gone. I'm not seeing anyone else. I'm thinking those spuds came and snatched up your boys. This one probably fought back and got himself killed."

GQ agreed. "Fighting back was his style. Never gave up." He turned to Flag, eyes red with anger. "We don't leave teammates behind. Let's get our people back."

Flag shook his head. "Negative," he said flatly. "We're continuing the mission. They've been taken by those things, they're already dead."

"Rick, you don't know that."

Flag shot him a look that said, *Yeah. I do.*

GQ's anger swelled suddenly. He saw images of funerals and broken families. Aparo was a personal friend, but then most of his boys were. It was the way buddies got after spending days huddled together in trenches on the field of combat. There was nobody closer to you than the people you knew who were watching your back, and expected that you'd be watching theirs.

The other SEALs surrounded Flag, GQ, and Deadshot, and they were joined moments later by the rest of Flag's Squad. The colonel looked them over. Nobody had ankled.

"Okay, I want the Two-Forty on point, Diamond

formation. Start picking 'em and putting 'em down. The objective ain't walking to meet us."

GQ wanted to find his lost men and rescue them, but he was a special warfare officer to the bone. The mission, and his orders, always came first.

"Yessir," he said, saluting his superior officer. "Understood, sir." His men started out, with GQ in the lead.

FORTY

The battle was a short one.

The SEALs made their way to Devin Drive in an attempt to engage the enemy from behind, effectively cutting off their escape routes. The SEALs had expected to find well-armed soldiers, the enemy's version of their own team, equipped as they were, with similar high-tech weapons.

They thought the monsters, whatever their origins, were the grunts—point men sent out to test the enemy. The real enemies, they thought, would be men, just like them. Men who, when the war was over and done with, might someday become allies, like World War Two's Germany and Japan. Like Cuba. Like Vietnam.

Instead, they found themselves attacked by more of those things. The monsters weren't an advance squad. They were the army. The first wave of creatures easily pushed through the SEALs as if they were little girls at a backyard tea party. Four soldiers were killed in the first seconds of combat.

Whatever the SEALs were expecting, this wasn't remotely it. The enemy downed Grant and Moore, then dragged them away. Their frightened cries chilled GQ to the bone. Brubaker and Lopez were hunkered in the remains of the Reed building, shooting at creatures as they scurried into view. The bullets slowed them down, even ripped out chunks of them, but they couldn't stop them.

The things turned to their attackers and squealed. Groups of them came together and scurried toward the SEALs. The screams could be heard from a block away.

Sweating and frightened, the soldiers took position behind a stack of demolished trucks. The things rushed past, dragging away SEALs still alive and resisting.

Enchantress looked pleased as the SEAL was tossed down in front of her. His name was Joe Anderson.

The captured SEALs stared at her, not yet believing what they were seeing. If the giant was a god, she looked like she was a goddess, breathtaking in her glowing crown and robe of light.

Their briefing called her Enchantress. Perhaps she had godlike power, but she was also a murdering witch. They had heard Waller talk about this one, to Flag. Enchantress was evil, Waller had said.

"Not the Goddess she claims she is, but definitely a devil."

A glowing septagram had been painted on the wall behind her. Its points were formed by seven gravity-defying creatures, hovering cross-legged in the air. Somehow the very sight of it emanated pure evil. Without warning Enchantress embraced one of the SEALs. He tried to pull away, but somehow she was too strong for him. She held him close and immobile.

"The change cannot be contested," she said loudly enough that everyone could hear every word. "But it will not hurt if you surrender to the light. Accept what is already done." She wrapped her robe around him and kissed him. Her lips pressed to his as a chrysalis of light surrounded them both. A similar glow came from the septagram, and writhed around them.

The witch held him a few seconds more before releasing him. Then she smiled.

The SEAL gasped, and cursed under his breath.

Her kiss somehow turned him into one of those things. This was where those creatures came from, he realized. The would-be goddess took his people, his friends, and turned them into more of her blasphemous monsters.

The SEAL couldn't look away. He bowed deeply, took a weapon from a large pile, and joined the line of Enchantress's slaves. The decent man he had been was gone. This thing was an enemy now. Something they might have to kill—if they survived long enough.

Killing their friends—killing their family—that wasn't what any of them had signed on to do.

FORTY-ONE

Fifth Avenue was a decimated wasteland, most of its buildings leveled to the ground, shattered glass and other debris strewn across the street.

A window shattered.

Harley batted aside the few remaining glass shards from the window of Northern Lights, a stylish clothing store frequented mostly by millennials aged twenty-one through thirty. She had stolen some of her favorite outfits from the Northern Lights store in Gotham City.

She reached in and pulled an expensive crystal purse off of its display pedestal. When she turned back to the street, everyone was staring at her. Except for Flag.

Flag glared at her. "Seriously? What is it with you people?"

Unfazed, she swung the little purse over her shoulder, and rolled her eyes at him.

"We're bad guys, remember. It's what we do."

Harley struck a pose and checked her reflection in the mirror. "How does this look?" Arms out, she danced a bit, reveling in her new acquisition. "Me likee."

* * *

Flag shook his head and walked off. He hoped when push came to shove, they'd do the job he needed them to do. Until then, might as well let them have their little fun.

They'll pay for it all later, he thought optimistically.

Lawton saw Croc standing about thirty yards away. Then Croc gestured for him. Deadshot looked back and saw Flag was deep in conversation with GQ and a few of the other SEALs, probably arguing over who had the biggest gun.

They call themselves heroes, but they're just as ridiculous as everyone else, he mused. Then he let Croc come to him. "You want something?"

"Yeah," Croc said. "When we're back in Gotham City I have a list for you. Names I want scratched out."

Now that was unexpected.

"You have any idea what my fee is?" he said dismissively.

Croc laughed, or gave what Deadshot took as a laugh. It was deep, guttural, and nasty.

"You killed a man once," Croc said.

"More than once. That's my job. I do it well."

"Whatever. He was an important man. You cut out his heart and sent it to the client."

Then Deadshot remembered the job. The client's requests were twisted, but he paid big for it.

"I don't discuss my business," Deadshot said.

Croc laughed again. "I was the client. I know what you cost."

Deadshot stared, studying him. There were deeper levels to this... man... than he would have expected. He'd have to take the job offer seriously.

Suddenly Flag shouted.

"Everyone take a knee," he bellowed. The SEALs immediately formed a perimeter around the Squad. They watched as Flag double-checked his map, then pointed to the Federal Building just four blocks away. "Our VIP's at the top of that building. We get up there, pull the target out of the vault, and make it to the roof. Helos will be waiting for us.

"After that, it's Miller time."

Deadshot took his monocle and used it to bring the Federal Building into clear focus. Nothing seemed out of the ordinary.

"Who's up there?" he asked curiously.

Flag started toward their destination. "Not your concern," he said, as the others joined, following behind.

Deadshot wasn't pleased. *Why do I think this is all turning to crap?* he thought, but he held his tongue.

FORTY-TWO

The Federal Building was less than a hundred fifty yards away. Flag kneeled behind an overturned garbage truck, and watched EAs move in and out of the area, doing whatever the hell EAs did. He gestured to the SEALs, about twenty yards behind him.

We're ready. Let's do this.

Moving in pairs, they scurried to their new positions, their rifles locked and loaded, and ready if any of the creatures spotted them.

None did. Waller believed they were of a hive mind, fixed on a given task to the exclusion of all others. Unless programmed to do so, a single EA couldn't directly dictate the actions of another. Flag hoped that was true. It might make it easier for them to slip past.

With the SEALs in place, Flag darted ahead. He waited for the crowd of EAs to thin out, then gave the sign for the SEALs to leapfrog him again. They would continue that way until they were inside the building.

Deadshot hunkered behind the chain-link fence that surrounded the Federal Building. He was rapidly growing impatient with Flag and the SEALs and their snail-pace dance. At their current dead-man-walking speed, it would take them another twenty minutes to get inside. What was needed, he decided, wasn't a cotillion, but a little rock 'n' roll.

He slipped through a break in the fence and made his way to the front door. The creatures, involved with their own tasks, paid no attention to him. Group mind. Waller's analysis appeared to be on target.

He waved to Flag and company, opened the door, and stepped inside.

Amanda Waller watched the drone feed from inside the ops center. She shook her head as Deadshot disobeyed his orders and calmly walked into the building. She held the remote detonator, deciding what to do.

That bastard's going to get everyone killed. At the same time she almost admired him—at least he got things done. So she put down the detonator and turned to the tech assigned to direct the camera. "Any visible threats?" she asked.

The tech maneuvered the drone over the Federal Building rooftop and had it do a 360° scan of the area.

"No, ma'am," he answered. "All clear."

Waller sat back in her chair, her hands nervously clasped together behind her head. Something was going to screw this up, she feared. Somehow, this mission was going to go south. But she said nothing. She needed the techs to do their jobs, and she didn't want to add anything into the mix that might distract them.

Deadshot used his carbine sight to scan the Federal Building lobby. It was clear. Either the EAs were lousy tacticians and forgot to place guards, or they weren't at all worried that the humans might find them. He prayed it was the former, but he knew better.

He crossed to the guard desk and checked the security monitors, which were still active—they had to have an internal power source. Each was focused on a different area of the building.

"All sectors are clear," he said as Flag and the others entered.

"You were supposed to follow orders, Lawton," the colonel growled, "and that meant following me, not going off on your little scavenger hunt."

"If I listened to you, we'd still be outside."

Flag turned to scan the monitors. "You do know you're an asshole."

"Better believe it," Deadshot replied. "It's on my business card. 'Floyd Lawton, asshole assassin.' You want, I can tell you where to get 'em printed. All you'd need to do is change the name."

"I don't see the problem, mates," Boomer said, interrupting. "Looks like we had a spot of luck. A walk in the park. Easy peasy."

"Will you please shut up," Deadshot said. "Getting inside was the easy part. Finding our target won't be."

"That was the easy part?" Boomer asked, concerned.

"We're still alive," Deadshot answered.

"What's the hard part?"

"When we're not."

Flag checked the building's blueprints on his tablet. Satisfied, he put it back into its case and walked off to the left.

"Atrium's this way. The stairs up are on the far end.

FORTY-THREE

Squad and SEALs followed Flag out of the lobby toward the building's second quad. None of them noticed the slight movement on the guard desk's main security monitor. For just an instant an EA looked at the camera, then scurried past, out of range.

"Any of you wankers got a clue why we're doing this?" Boomer asked as they made their way through one endless stark white corridor after another. "Just saying, I'd rather be safe behind bars than get myself killed. Anyone else thinking about that?"

Flag tapped his cell phone holster. "Feel free to make a break for it, Harkness. I'm all for it."

"Calm down, you two," Deadshot said.

Croc stared at Lawton. "Something going on here I don't know? When did you become Mister Peace Between All Nations?"

"When they put their damned bomb in my neck. It's powerful enough to blow even you to tiny bits."

"There is that, mate," Boomer said, nodding. "We don't have any choice. But, Flaggy, I hope you realize that also means we're not actually on your side.

We're just going along for the ride, until we don't have to anymore."

Flag kept walking. "I don't need your loyalty, Harkness. All I want from you are your boomerangs, doing whatever the hell I need them to do."

"I can just hand 'em over to you, and then go back to sleep in my cell. I'd enjoy watching you try to handle them."

Diablo sided up to Boomer and put a hand on his shoulder. For just an instant Harkness thought the big man might be getting ready to set him on fire, but Diablo just wanted to talk.

"This is not the time to fight among ourselves," he said somberly, "and it's definitely not the time to argue with him. Flag holds all the cards."

"Yeah, well, according to you, it's never the time to fight. So when, exactly, did you become a loser?"

"When I figured out that fighting destroys you, and killing doesn't strengthen you. Never. Believe me. I know."

"I like fighting and I like killing," Boomerang said, and he laughed. "And when I kill I feel good. So your theory's all shot to hell."

"But that blissful feeling is only temporary. Kills are like drugs. You need more and more to get that same feeling again. Today it's one kill. Tomorrow two. Next week it'll take a dozen. Not only is there no end in sight, but after a while you forget why you ever started. Your need for relief, rather than your intellect, takes over—and it is insatiable."

Boomerang laughed and looked to Deadshot. "Lawton, you're an assassin, mate. You wanna tell the boys what you think about killing?"

"I don't," Deadshot responded. "It's just my job.

How I pay the rent. Nothing to get emotional about."

Flag turned to him with a look of disgust. "And what does your daughter think about it? How much of that part of your life have you shown to Zoe?"

Lawton didn't like the question. He had always tried to separate his life from his work. He never told Zoe exactly what he did, and he never wanted her to learn the truth.

"She... she said she still loves me."

"Because of, or in spite of?"

Deadshot closed his eyes, and again took control of his anger.

Later, he thought fiercely. *Not now. When the time is right. When Zoe is mine again. When this bastard can't separate us again. Nothing else matters. Nothing but Zoe.*

"Screw you, Flag," he said aloud. "Don't we have VIPs to rescue and monsters to kill? So how about we shut up and do our job?"

It was only a few minutes later when they reached the atrium, a soaring, inspiring cathedral of glass in the center court of the vast government complex. Flag checked the blueprints then headed toward the closest stairwell.

"This way," he said. "Elevator's not trustworthy. We're taking the stairs. It'll be good for your cardio."

"The stairs? For crap's sake," Boomer said. "I definitely did not sign up for that." He looked at the stairs, then back to the others. "Hey. Where's the cuckoo bird? She's not here."

"Maybe a dingo ate her," Deadshot retorted.

Boomer laughed. "We can hope, mate. We can only hope."

* * *

Harley leaned against the door to the glass elevator, bat propped by her side, cell phone in hand. She typed a quick message then hit "send." Less than a minute later the phone buzzed. The reply.

I am close. Be ready.

The header said it had been sent by Mr. J.

Harley beamed with anticipation. As the elevator rose, she saw Deadshot staring up at her. She waved, but he was pointing frantically.

She looked up just as an EA punched through the roof panel and dropped inside. It lunged for her. She fell back and somersaulted over it, kicking while in mid-spin.

The thing slammed into the elevator's glass wall, but used the impact to push itself back into Harley. It forced her to the ground and grabbed her by the throat. She twisted her legs around its head and snapped it back. It flipped over and landed on its feet, readying itself for another attack.

The monster was a horrifying sight, all that darkness covered over with dozens—if not hundreds—of eyes, staring at her, anxious to kill her. She was sick to her stomach, but she knew she couldn't stop fighting long enough to throw up. Every second mattered.

Harley leapt and grabbed the EA by its head, smashing it again into the glass wall. This time it stayed down. She jumped on it, kneeing its mid-section, then remembered her gun, at home in the holster hanging from her belt. She tried to grab it, but the thing kicked up and slammed her to the other side of the elevator.

It scrambled back to its feet and lunged for her. Its hands grabbed her throat again, but this time with more force. Instantly she was having trouble breathing.

White explosions blinded her. She tried to knee it again, but she didn't have the strength to drive it back. Hands still wrapped around her throat, it pushed her to the floor and squeezed her even harder.

Her hands reached for her gun, but the thing lifted her by the neck and slammed her into the wall. It stared into her eyes and growled. Her eyes rolled up into her head even as her hand finally found her gun.

She didn't have to see the thing that was strangling her—she knew exactly where it was. She shoved the magnum under its chin and fired.

BAM! BAM! BAM!

"Go to hell, you stupid turd," she screamed.

Its head exploded from its body. Black shards smashed her in the face. As the headless form slid to the ground, she wiped its parts from her eyes and spat out the remnants that had lodged in her mouth. Then she fell to the ground, heaving, trying to catch her breath. She needed a minute to regain control, maybe longer.

But she wasn't allowed it.

A second EA swung down from the elevator roof and smashed its way through a pane of the elevator's glass wall. She saw it stand to its full height. All its eyes stared at her. It looked hungry, anxious for the kill.

She ducked as it tried to grab her—spun, wrapped her legs around its feet, and pulled them out from under it. The thing fell to the floor. In an instant Harley was on top of it.

She was still holding her gun. She pushed it under the thing's jaw, intending to blow it into pieces as she'd done with the other one, but it kicked her into the wall. She struggled to her feet, but the thing's foot rested on a sharp piece of debris. It kicked up, propelling itself into her, causing her to drop her gun in surprise. The creature was on her before she could retrieve it.

It became a hand-to-hand fight.

The EA was bigger than she was, and stronger, but Harley was more agile. She dove between the thing's legs and then cannoned her feet into its back, kicking it into the glass.

It jumped back to its feet and tried to punch her. She ducked under its fist and, with both hands locked together, slammed it hard.

She barely fazed the beast. It tried to punch her again, and this time it connected. Hard. Harley reeled, saw bursts of light flashing all around her. Stunned, she fell back to the floor. She felt her bat on the floor next to her. She grabbed its grip and as the EA reached for her she swung it, smashing it into the thing's face. Chunks of black exploded from it. Even with only half a face, though, it was still coming for her.

Harley slammed her bat into it again, separating its head from its shoulders. It wavered back and forth, but wasn't yet going down for the count. She somersaulted at it and slammed her legs into its chest. For an instant nothing happened, but then the thing fell back, crashed through the shattered glass, and fell into the elevator shaft, disappearing into the darkness.

Deadshot and Croc ran to the elevator to join the fight, but when the doors opened, they saw Harley holding her bat over her shoulders, whistling as she calmly exited the elevator as if nothing had happened.

"Hi, guys," she said merrily. "Don't we have some big-bads to slaughter?"

Flag and the others approached. He looked at Harley, saw the shattered glass and a dead EA still in the elevator, and nodded approval.

"Okay," he said, looking at the corpse. "Now we know they're here. Keep moving. Stay together." They made their way down a long corridor, offices on all sides. Flag paused in front of a dark office.

"Ready?"

Deadshot felt the hairs on his neck bristle. "We're walking into a shooting gallery, aren't we? You sure about this?"

Flag shook his head. "I don't like it, either, but it's the only way in. Let's do it."

He opened the door and they entered.

FORTY-FOUR

The office area was larger than he'd expected. Workstation cubicles filled nearly every open space. The lights were down, and Flag and the others, weapons ready, entered carefully. More than likely EAs were everywhere in the building. They had to be here, too.

The cubicles were designed in a clear grid, giving them a series of easy paths via which to conduct their search. Sticking close together, they started by moving up the left-most aisle, pausing before each self-contained space, their guns leading them.

Looking for the enemy. Praying none were there.

Nothing.

At the end of the aisle they turned right and started down the second row. They paused at each cubicle.

Then they heard breathing. Heavy and labored.

Something was in here with them. Whatever it was, it was too close.

"Who's there?" Flag shouted. He wanted to add, "We're the good guys," but considering who was with him, he didn't see how he could. "We're feds," he continued. "Navy SEALs... and others. We're on your side."

Close enough for government work.

No answer, but the heavy breathing became louder. Coming from straight ahead. Somewhere down this aisle.

Flag dispatched a small group of the SEALs to go back the way they came, then to circle around and come up from behind the source of the sound, effectively trapping the heavy breather between the two groups.

"Hello," Flag said again. If there were human beings here, he wanted to give them every possible chance to get past their fears.

No response.

They'd seen how hard it was to kill the bastards, they were severely lacking ammo, and they had no idea how many of the damned things were laying in wait.

"This is gonna be a bloodbath," Boomerang whispered nervously. Flag shot him a dirty look.

Shut up, idiot, it said. For once Boomer obeyed a direct order.

They found it crouched behind a desk in a far cubicle. Breathing ominously. It was wearing the tatters of what had once been a uniform.

A SEAL uniform.

Its eyes were red with hate and less than an hour before this monster had been one of them. Other creatures were crouched behind him. Their eyes, too, red with bloodlust and hate. All of their hundreds of eyes. Kane, Pérez, Levitz, Sprang, Winslow—GQ's friends and teammates. People with whom he had once trusted his life. Monsters who now only wanted to kill him.

They were waiting.
They were ready.

* * *

Time seemed to slow down. Flag signaled for his crew to stop. Deadshot saw the eyes burning red. He pulled on his mask and flipped its monocle into place. Then he saw Harley staring at him, shaking her head, laughing.

"Weakling," she said. "Not tough enough? Afraid of them? Did I tell you I took out two? All by myself."

"Shut up," Deadshot snapped back. "I'll knock you out cold. I don't care if you are a girl."

Harley laughed again. "Promises, promises. It's like I—"

All hell broke loose before she could even finish her sentence.

The EAs opened fire. Flag and the others jumped for cover.

"Ambush front," Flag bellowed. "Move."

Deadshot was overwhelmed. Three more creatures rushed in through the door. He saw Flag run toward the opposite side of the room, firing at anything that moved.

"Where the hell are you going, Flag?" Deadshot fired at the scurrying monsters. Though it was close quarters, they were damned hard to hit in the darkness.

"We're out in the open, waiting to be picked off," Flag replied. "We need cover. Find a corner. It'll be easier to defend."

Deadshot agreed. "Front. Right. Go."

Flag ran down the rightmost aisle. He shot at the eyes of the creatures following him, then there was the sound of shattering glass. More EAs streamed in through what had been a side window, and were on his tail. The way ahead was cut off, too, sandwiching him in, leaving him no place to run.

Deadshot quickly scanned the room. The things

ignored the SEALs and the Squad—they were all targeting Flag. For just a moment Deadshot laughed—the bastard deserved whatever he got—but then the instant joy he felt was gone.

"They're after Flag," he shouted to his Squad.

"His problem," Boomer said. "I got my own."

"No. They're leaving us alone... maybe just for now. Circle up. Circle around him. We gotta save him."

"You're crazy," Boomer said.

"Do what I say, dammit."

Flag was surrounded, but he kept his ice-cold calm as he unloaded mags into the things. Suddenly Deadshot grabbed him by the wrist and pulled him back. The Squad formed into a circle, and Lawton tossed him into the middle of it.

"Get in here," he ordered.

Flag stared at him. "You crazy? Let me fight."

"You die, I die. So you ain't dying." The circle closed around Flag. The convicts he hated were saving him. The world had turned upside down when he wasn't looking.

"They're trying to kill me," Flag shouted.

Deadshot grinned. "They're gonna have to get in line behind me."

More of the things. GQ recognized too damn many of them. They swarmed through the office and rushed the circle, ready to breach it and tear apart Flag.

"Shoot!" Deadshot shouted. "Don't stop 'til I tell you to."

GQ raised his gun and aimed it at an approaching creature. Then he stared at it, surprised and horrified.

"Doug?" He stared at Doug Wagner's face,

instantly wondering if he had balls enough to shoot a man who for better than a decade had been his closest friend. But then Wagner charged him, and GQ fired instinctively.

It took ten rounds to explode Wagner's head. His legs buckled under him and he collapsed. GQ stared at the body and took out a handkerchief to dry his eyes before anyone else saw him.

General William Sherman was so damn right it hurt. *War is hell.*

An EA took out Dave Bolland and Brian Conway, two of the SEALs assigned to protect Flag. Three other creatures grabbed their legs and dragged them away, while still more spotted Flag and rushed toward him. There was a quiet whoosh, followed by the thud of their two heads crashing to the floor. Their bodies collapsed only a second later.

Katana stood behind them and ran her hand down her blade.

"You have already absorbed so many souls," she whispered to it. "Sadly the day is still young."

Another EA leapt at her, pushed her to the ground then dragged itself up to her face. Its thousand eyes stared at her.

"A thousand eyes but you see nothing," Katana said as her blade ripped up through the creature's chest and into its throat. She twisted and the head fell free, reluctantly joining the others she'd severed.

More streamed into the room. They ignored the SEALs and Squad and ran toward Flag. Deadshot shot him a look.

"They really only want you," he said questioningly.

"They're ignoring the rest of us. Maybe we should let 'em have you."

"They know who the big kahuna is," Flag responded. "Lop off the boss, and the rest will follow."

"You wish," Lawton replied.

"Then I'll see you in hell, won't I?"

"Behind you. Shut up and duck." Lawton opened fire. It took three full mags before their crusted, barnacled faces had been reduced to little more than mush. He stared at his gun and felt his heart jump.

He was out of ammo.

More EAs rushed him. He saw Grey, the huge Dutchman he had saved less than an hour earlier. He was no longer a soldier. No longer human.

Harley was right. Sometimes things just sucked.

His wrist magnums flipped into position. Each had a full mag in it. He emptied both into the big guy, but Grey refused to go down. He grabbed Flag in a tight bear hug and started to squeeze. Deadshot rushed across the room and retrieved the gun Dave Bolland had dropped when the EAs took him out.

In a practiced move he checked that the mag was fresh. He then spun and unloaded it. Simultaneously Flag pulled out his hunting knife and hammered the pommel into the thing's face. Again and again.

Grey refused to fall. He kneed Flag in the balls and the soldier collapsed to his knees, gasping for breath. The big Dutchman raised both fists to finish him off, but abruptly shuddered, then fell forward.

Croc was behind him, and he punched the EA again. Grey turned, roaring in anger and pain, and charged him. He had a new target to kill.

Croc backed away to give himself more room. He stared at his attacker and goaded him.

"Whatcha gonna do, bitch? You think you can hurt me?" He slammed his fist into the EA's gut, dropping him to his knees. Croc rushed him, but the thing climbed back to his feet and somehow blocked the punch.

Grey was weak and trembling. He tried to throw another punch, but Croc easily ducked it, then smashed his fist through Grey's face, burying it deep into his eyes, mashing them into pulp. The EA again fell to his knees, then shuddered and collapsed to the ground. Croc slammed his foot into Grey's face and finished him off.

"If I were you, I wouldn't move," he growled with reptilian menace. "Ever again." The EA was dead but its body was still quivering. Croc stared at it angrily. "I warned you," he said as he raised his foot again.

Flag stopped him.

"He used to be one of us."

"Used to be one of yours, not mine." Croc slammed his foot down hard, watched the EA's body spasm one last time, then stepped off him. "Now he's nobody's."

Deadshot secured another rifle and several mags of ammo. In perfect form he delivered one headshot after another, dropping assailants with each clip, reducing their numbers.

An arm suddenly grabbed him from behind. Lawton saw that the flesh under its torn uniform had crusted over. He could make out a half-dozen eyes just on this one small section of the thing's arm. He jammed the wrist magnum into the EA's face and fired.

The thing jerked back and fell, releasing its grip. Lawton aimed his magnum to finish it off, but Harley stepped in his way. She brought her heavy wooden bat down onto the hideous face and smashed it into pieces. Then she held up the bat like it was a trophy and did a small victory dance.

"And that is how it's done," she chirped. "You put 'em down, I flatten 'em."

"Not bad, Quinn," Boomerang called to her. "You know, for a Looney Tune."

She giggled. "Well, personally, I prefer Merrie Melodies. They were so much funnier. But hey, nice slice 'n' dice, Down Under."

He looked at the creature he'd just beaten, and saw it twitch.

"Not quite dead enough. Hold on a sec." Boomer rested his foot on the thing's chest, then raised a razor-edged boomerang over his head. As the blade plunged down, the EA jerked to the side. The blade cut a deep gash into its neck but just missed severing it from its head.

The creature pulled back and freed its hand. It was holding a knife. It thrust up and sunk it into Boomer's chest.

With a gasp, Boomer fell back.

Harley stared at him, falling to his knees. "Oh my God. Boomer." She shrieked, "That thing killed Boomer!"

Boomer was confused and frightened. He stared at the knife, then angrily turned back to the EA and slammed his boomerang into its neck, this time slicing through flesh and bone. Its head lobbed to the side.

Harley ran to him, staring at the knife still embedded in his chest.

"Omigod, why aren't you dead? You should be dead." She turned to Flag, who was also staring. "He should be dead, shouldn't he?" Harley asked again.

Boomer pulled the knife from his chest and tossed it aside. He opened his vest and revealed underneath thick packs of money, recently appropriated from the Midway Bank. Miraculously, they had protected him from the blade. Boomer pulled out a pack of bills and kissed them. "Who said money can't buy happiness?"

Flag stared at him, and just shook his head.

"For once I'm speechless."

Harley looked at the bills, then glared at Harkness. "Tell me you brought enough for everyone?"

Boomer shrugged his answer.

"Get back," GQ ordered. A grenade launcher rested on his shoulder as he got into position.

"What the hell is G.I. Joe doing?" Deadshot asked. "Nothing's standing for you to knock down."

"There're still nests of EAs. Might as well thin the herd."

Deadshot agreed. "Sounds good." He turned to Diablo and chuckled. "They used to be people, you know. Moms, dads, kids. How does wiping out entire families sound to you, big guy?"

Diablo stared back at him, and it was clear that the words had struck home. His eyes flashed with anger, and he clenched and unclenched his fists.

"How dare you?" he shouted. His hands erupted with fire, his fingers flaming candles. "You've crossed the line, Lawton."

The skin on his face reddened, and Deadshot was suddenly very afraid. In his mind he saw that old video of Diablo, taken so many years earlier. How many did he burn to death in that prison? How many had he incinerated over the years?

Lawton edged back, away from Diablo.

"Hey. I'm sorry," he said, the uncommon fear washing over him. "I didn't mean anything. I swear it. I went way overboard and I know it. I'm sorry."

Diablo turned away and reclaimed his calm.

"Never again, Lawton. Never talk to me again."

Deadshot nodded. "You got it, man. What you say. Good with me." He turned to the others. "What the hell was I thinking?"

Flag was grim. "Just don't repeat it."

"No way, man. Never."

As they backed away, GQ launched a 40mm grenade deep into the office building. They watched and waited.

"Five seconds. Four…

"Three…

"Two…"

The grenade detonated. The front windows blew out. Stone, steel, and plaster exploded in all directions. The building shook, blasting creatures off the ceiling, shredding others into pieces. Half an EA crashed close to Flag and Deadshot. It was still holding its rifle and somehow it was still alive. A SEAL picked up his gun, about to shoot it through the head, but the thing shot first, killing the SEAL.

Croc stared at the dead SEAL, then he slammed his foot down on the EA's face, smashing it into pulp.

No additional combatants appeared, and the inmates whooped, high-fiving one another and celebrating their kills.

Flag stepped back and away, and let them have their moment. They were killers, and he still hated the idea of working with them, but when push came to shove they actually worked together. They were becoming a team. He hadn't thought that would ever happen.

When they finally calmed down, Flag called out to them.

"It's time," he said. "We're on the clock. Move it. Get off the X." He headed for the exit, not looking back but confident they were following close behind.

Maybe there was some hope for this motley crew after all.

FORTY-FIVE

The atrium balcony circled the government complex, imposing a deep vertigo effect on anyone who saw it, from new visitors to long-term employees. Amanda Waller had worked there for years but she still had to grab the handrail when she made her way from office to office.

Waller was rooted to the ops center, monitoring the enemy as well as Flag and his soldiers. Time was running out, she thought. Her Suicide Squad still had too many EAs to fight before they could complete their mission.

She looked to her tech. "Center on Flag," she barked, "but give me a wide shot. I need to see exactly where he's taking them."

"Yes, ma'am," he said as he reoriented the drone camera. She watched Flag and the others circle the dizzying balcony.

"They're heading for the stairs," she said. "That's good. That's exactly where I need them to go. How much further?"

The tech punched up a distance ruler and laid it over the scene.

"Approximately eight hundred fifty yards, ma'am."

"Okay… good. He has his bases covered. Thank God." Flag was doing his job. Waller had expected nothing less.

She'd harbored serious doubts about his temper, once upon a time, and worried if its quick burn would hamper the assignment. Flag was known to humiliate soldiers if they didn't snap to attention and follow his orders. The man didn't have a clue how to play with others, but he was the best tactician Waller had ever known. She'd decided long ago to put up with his quirks, as long as he achieved the desired results.

Still, she had a reason to be nervous. If he pushed the wrong way with soldiers, they were required to follow his orders. But if he tried pulling his crap with the villains, they could just as easily burn him before she could activate their detonators.

With Flag she'd traded charm for proficiency. Her rule of thumb had always been, you put the best you got on the field then let them do what they do. As far as this mission was concerned, Waller would hire Hitler himself if he'd get the job done.

Flag was a pro. He'd fought this assignment, but ultimately she'd pulled rank and made it impossible for him to turn it down.

She sat back as the tech scanned the balcony ahead of the soldiers.

Nothing on the horizon. Good.

"Ma'am," the tech suddenly said. "See that?" He pointed at a shadow moving across the wall behind Flag.

"What is it?"

The tech scrunched his eyes and stared at the monitors. "Not sure, but I think it's coming from the catwalk. Hold on a sec, ma'am. Let me pull focus and adjust the drone's video range."

Waller watched as the picture on the monitor tilted up, revealing the glass catwalk about twenty feet above the balcony and mirroring its position.

A dozen armed EAs skittered across it.

"Ma'am, that's what caused the shadows."

"You think?" She glanced at the tech, sitting at his station, waiting for orders. "Idiot. Why are you just sitting there? Sound the alert," she ordered.

The frightened tech hit the alarm, but it was too late. The newly arrived EAs were firing at the Squad, and Flag and his men were already running for cover.

Waller quietly cursed. Time was running out.

Flag and the remaining SEALs dove into offices, then leaned back out, returning fire.

"You know what to do," he shouted, his voice tinny over the speakers. "Aim for their eyes."

"You think?" Boomer retorted.

Waller saw two EAs explode. She glanced at another monitor, focused a few yards away, and saw Harkness throwing his explosive boomerangs at the EAs.

Not bad, she mused. *He's actually holding up his end of the deal. I wasn't a hundred percent certain he would.*

Deadshot crouched behind an overturned desk and fired at the enemy. He fired into two different creatures, then watched, grinning, as the EAs blew apart into thick black chunks.

Diablo stood a few yards away, and stared at him, doing nothing else. "Hey, Matchstick," Lawton shouted over the carnage. "We could use your help."

Diablo shook his head. "This is not my fight. I'm not your savior." Then he frowned. "And I told you never to talk to me."

What the hell—might as well go for broke. Angry as piss, Deadshot dove over to Diablo and stabbed a finger in the big man's chest.

"Okay, Mr. 'Walk the Earth in Peace.' Do whatever the hell you want to do to me, but man, you are the worst. I thought I no longer had much to live for, but dammit, you just straight gave up."

Diablo wasn't fazed. "I did not ask to be sent here. I warned everyone before this began. I do not engage in violence. Not any more. If you want to live, it's all on you. Leave me out of it."

"Yeah, hell no. You're not turning into a loser on my watch." Deadshot stared at him then turned to Flag. "Hey. Yo! Use your remote thingie. Blow this cat's head right the hell off. Do him the favor, huh?"

"I'm kinda busy here, Lawton, in case you couldn't tell." Flag was firing at the creatures closest to him. It took at least two full mags to bring them to their knees, and another to put them out of their misery.

Deadshot turned again to Diablo.

"You're a punk," he shouted, lashing out. "You know that? We're all getting smoked and you wanna go out like a bitch?" Diablo tried to ignore him, but his face went flushed. He mumbled something he used to keep himself calm, but Deadshot kept yelling at him. Kept hitting him.

Lawton saw Diablo's hands redden and knew he was finally getting to him. He had to be careful now. Very careful.

He slammed his fist into Diablo's face.

"C'mon, baby. Do something," he shouted. The big man's skin turned a deep red, and began steaming. "You can do it, little girl. You can fight back. You can be a man."

"Do something," he screamed. *"Do something."*

A SEAL crouched nearby, firing at a creature that calmly made its way toward him. The EA aimed his rifle and fired. The SEAL stared plaintively at Diablo, and died.

"What are you waiting for, you baby?" Deadshot kept hitting the big man, trying to get him to react. Trying to wake him from his stupor and help save them, because no one else could. "You know if you helped, these soldiers wouldn't have to die. Why won't you help them? Why won't you do something? *Anything*?"

Diablo looked at the dead SEAL. Then, suddenly, he felt a sting in his arm. He stared, and saw that the creature who killed the SEAL had fired again—this time at him. He looked back at the dead SEAL, then at the EA.

He screamed with rage and frustration.

Deadshot started to say something, but Diablo shoved him aside. He raised his hands and flames appeared.

He screamed again and launched a column of fire at the creature. It burst into flame and writhed in pain as the fires burned through it, melting it, incinerating it.

"Hey, c'mon, man," Deadshot said, and there was panic in his voice. "Be cool. You don't wanna roast me. I was just trying to get you there. We need you, man—to save the whole of Planet Earth, and look. You showed them you're a hero. You know what that means. You're the big time, man. The Fire Man. Hero of the people, and all you gotta do is focus."

Diablo peered venomously at Deadshot. He reached out to grab him, and his hands were still on fire, hungry to burn.

Harley pushed past Deadshot and gazed intensely at Diablo.

"It's true, you know," she shouted, "what he said. You were wonderful, D. You saved us, and even better, my big, fiery hero, you saved me." She was standing on her toes, and she gave him a kiss on the cheek.

"Oooh, D, you make me so hot 'n' bothered. Touching you is like canoodling a furnace. Maybe a little hotter, but I think I like it."

He stared at her, knew she was trying to control him, but it had been so long since anyone had touched him like that. He lowered his internal heat, and returned to normal.

"I am sorry if I frightened you, Harley," he said. "I would never have hurt you."

"Hey, D. I know that," she responded. "I mean, you and me. Would we make a real hot couple or what?"

"Good job, Diablo," Flag said. "Thanks for finally joining the rest of us."

Deadshot leaned in. "Ignore him, but you did good. Real good."

Flag rested against the balcony wall. The Squad was coming together, but still they were just a handful of nutjobs and psychopaths, acting like heroes. They were about to go into a battle against a pair of big bads who could create as many deadly creatures as they needed.

They were overwhelmed and underprepared. Despite this victory, it wouldn't be long before they fell before the greater power.

Deadshot joined Flag and stared out across the balcony. A few EAs appeared here and there, but GQ and his SEALs dealt with them as quickly as they could. They watched another SEAL die, but not before taking down five bad guys. They didn't need to calculate numbers to know that they would run out of fighters long before the spuds did.

"You know, in the beginning, it was impossible to stop them," Deadshot commented. "Less impossible now. Maybe they're cranking out these things too fast. Not giving their babies time to grow up."

Flag thought about it. "Could be," he replied. "Doesn't matter, though. Easy or hard, they still gotta die, and we gotta be the ones to make sure they do."

"So, Flag," Deadshot said, "why are they after you like that? I mean, it's obvious you are the man they're after, and since it sure ain't your swap meet cologne, what's your secret?"

"I have no idea," Flag lied.

The EA shook himself awake. Everyone thought he was dead.

Everyone was wrong.

He rose to his feet, pulled himself together and staggered away.

FORTY-SIX

The SEALs and the Squad proceeded up the stairs. Harley kept climbing even as she took a deep breath.

"I am definitely out of shape," she said as soldiers rushed past her as if she were standing still. "God, do I need to work on my cardio."

Moments later she was alone on the stairs, the others already two landings higher. She looked down the center column and saw the stairs winding toward the basement, disappearing from view.

Memories, dark and joyful, flooded through her.

It had been raining for more than a week. He was dragging her up a menacing-looking steel stairwell. She giggled as she looked around, getting the lay of the land.

They were inside a large, sprawling factory, at least the size of a football field. Harleen stared at the massive network of tubes and pipes anchored just below its ceiling, all with bottom vents that emptied some glowing liquid into immense room-sized vats.

A hammered steel sign was welded into the side of the vat.

ACE CHEMICALS

FOUNDED 1921

"There," he said, interrupting her thoughts, but she didn't care. He was talking to her. "I was born down there."

In the vats.

She stared into one, mesmerized by the swirling chemical bath below. His birthplace. His mother. Harleen desperately wanted the same.

He grabbed her by the shoulders and stared into her soul with his madly hypnotic eyes, the same color as his chemical birthplace. "Would you die for me?" he asked.

Quinzel nodded with certainty.

"Yes."

"No. That's too easy." He leaned in closer, his eyes drawing her in. "Would you live for me?" He then smiled The Smile, and it scared the hell out of her.

Quinzel trembled. There was a power about him she could not deny, and she wanted that power to ravage her. He was a lion about to swallow a mouse, and she could hardly wait another instant to be devoured.

But he wouldn't let her go. Not now. Not yet.

"Will you embrace me and only me?" he demanded. She nodded vigorously.

Of course. There'll never be anyone else.

"Will you bind your spirit to mine, in hate?"

If not you, who else? Bind me. Bind me any way you want.

"Do you consign your soul to me?"

Duh. What do you think I've been trying to do? C'mon. Let's do this already.

"Do you laugh at the world in disgust?"

Always have. Always will. 'Specially if we can laugh at it together.

All she said to him was, "Yes."

Joker backed away. He stared at her, studied her. He was the doctor now, and she the patient, but he still needed to make sure.

"Do not say this oath thoughtlessly," he said, his expression serious. "Desire becomes surrender. Surrender becomes power. Do you want it? Do you really want it?"

She looked at him with undying love in her eyes.

"I do," she joyously said. "I do."

"Then goodbye, Dr. Quinzel." He took a step back and gestured toward the edge of the vat. Without hesitating, she stepped off the platform and plunged into the churning liquid below.

Impressed, he watched her disappear into the hellish brew. She was gone.

Forever, he thought. *Problem solved.* He turned from the edge of the platform and dusted off his hands, but then he paused and touched his heart.

"What is this? I feel something. Pain? Maybe. Food poisoning? That's a possibility. Love? Impossible. No way. Could never happen."

The pain was in his heart, and it wasn't going away. "Nonono… This can't be. I do not fall in love. Certainly not with a crackpot. I don't need someone to complete me. I'm loony enough for two families."

He turned back and stared into the vat, but still wasn't seeing her bobbing to the surface, choking on the chemicals, then floating face down in the gunk and dying. Which was the plan he'd had for her.

Without another thought, he jumped off the edge of the platform and dove into the churning mass below.

He disappeared into the vat. Time ticked by.

Tick…

Tick…

Tick.

Suddenly, he broke the surface. The girl was limp in his arms. As they floated, he looked at her and began giggling. Her flesh had been bleached white, just like his. Only she was a babe, and her skin had an alluring alabaster glow to it.

He stared at her for many more ticks before he realized she wasn't moving. Or breathing. Was she already dead?

"Nononono," he said. "I'm not done with you. I've got many years of humiliation I want to heap upon you, Doctor." He put his lips over hers and breathed life back into her tiny, little, sexy, sexy body.

Finally, her eyes opened.

"Wait, wait," he said. "You're not Dr. Quinzel." He didn't know if he should be overjoyed that she was still alive, or angry that she was no longer the woman who wanted to die for his sins. "Your eyes. Your skin. Your hair. It's all different. If you're not Dr. Harleen Quinzel, eminent psychiatrist to the outrageous and crazy, then who are you?"

She looked up at the Joker and grinned.

"I'm Harley Quinn," she said. "You're my Puddin'."

Joker moved in and kissed her hard on the lips while she began gnawing on his.

When they came up for air, she added, "You're my Mister J."

* * *

Good times. Harley sat on the stairs, eyes closed, a distant smile on her face, tears streaming down.

She wanted to be with him now, and wished Mister J would put on his armor and ride in on his big white horse and stomp all these crazy men into so much street pizza. Then the two of them would ride off together and show the world how to really have fun.

There was a muffled sound behind her.

Her eyes snapped open suddenly. Someone was there.

"Mister J!" she exclaimed, hoping against hope. Nevertheless, she pulled out her handgun, and was ready to kill.

"You," she said, disappointed, staring at Deadshot.

"Yo. Hey, it's me."

"Yeah. I know. What do you want?"

Deadshot pointed to her gun. "For starters, you can holster that bad boy. I'm on your side."

"That would make one, but okay. I won't blast a hole the size of Wyoming into you. Least not this time."

"Just making sure you're all right," he said. "You fell behind. I didn't see you."

Harley fluttered her eyes at him. "You like me. You really like me," she said, laughing. "Who cares why you're here. I got a question."

"Shoot."

"You might wanna rephrase that. I mean, knowing me."

Deadshot laughed. "I got to say, Quinn, I used to think you were just insane, but you actually got a sense of humor. Will wonders never cease. Okay, ask away."

Harley thought about what she wanted, but couldn't find a subtle way to start the conversation.

"So. You ever been in love?"

"No." Deadshot shook his head. "Never."

This time she laughed at him. "Bullshit."

He walked to the edge of the landing and looked down, away from her.

"You don't kill as many people as I do and sleep like a kitten at night if you feel love or empathy."

Harley stared at him. "Figures. Another textbook sociopath—and that's my certified professional opinion. Or maybe it's 'certifiable.' Anyway, what do you call this?" she said, touching her heart.

Deadshot thought about it for a second before responding.

"Need," he said. "Nothing more."

"Sure," she said after a moment. "Why not?"

They heard explosions in the distance. Something had triggered one of the claymore mines.

"EA," he said, professional again. "On the stairs above us."

"Eewww," she said back. They had their weapons back in hand even before they separated. "I hear somethin' up there. You ready?" she asked.

"You really think I'm into delayed gratification?"

She glanced at him and grinned like a tigress before dinner. "Consider yourself lucky. I was about to destroy you."

Deadshot shot her a dirty look. "I'm the assassin."

Harley chuckled. "Nah. You're just the first syllable, and I'm the last. Ass meet sin."

He stepped back. "Can't wait to go running back to him, huh? When's the last time someone was nice to you?"

Harley stared at him, unable to respond as he hit the

FORTY-SEVEN

They made their way to the top floor, then stopped in front of the huge steel vault door marked EMERGENCY OPERATIONS. It blocked them from continuing on. Croc tried to push it open but it stood firm.

"Came all this way and now we can't get inside," he growled. "Flag, this your idea of a joke?"

"Want me to blow up that baby?" Boomer said, holding a boomerang embedded with C-4. "I got just the right 'rang."

"Don't be an idiot," Flag retorted. "This entire floor is mined. One wrong move and that's all she wrote."

"So what do we do?" Croc asked. "Get on our knees and pray someone gives us the right combination?"

"I've got this covered," Flag said. "First, we need to secure the roof and sweep for shooters, so we can bring in our aviation assets. GQ, think you can handle that?"

"Next time come up with something that's a challenge," GQ said, saluting.

Flag laughed. "I'll try better. Be careful."

GQ and his SEALs headed back to the roof access. Flag crossed to the steel door and punched a code into the keypad. He turned to Croc.

"No need for someone else to give us the combo when I already have it."

Croc nodded. "Definitely makes it easier. For once, I approve." Then he added, "Why didn't you say something before?"

"I like hearing you complain about nothing. The revelations keep you humble."

"That's never gonna happen," Deadshot said. "We're supposed to be in this together. Next time just give us the frickin' intel."

Ignoring him, Flag entered the last number then stepped back. They heard the rollers retract as the vault door eased open. Flag stepped through then turned back to the others.

"I'm going in," he said. "You stay here. Don't wanna give our VIP a heart attack."

Harley grinned and tapped a little dance. "Aww, so sweet. He's embarrassed of us. You're such a cutie."

Deadshot glared at the colonel. "This whole mission just sucks. I'd be better off back in Belle Reve, serving twenty. Least they'd tell me what I was supposed to do."

"That can be arranged," Flag replied. "And by the way, who says we'd let you go back? Detonator, remember?"

"Bite me," Deadshot said. "This guy better cure cancer after all this." Flag gave him a twisted smile then headed through the vault door.

FORTY-EIGHT

The room was filled with computers and monitors. A block-by-block satellite view of downtown Midway was displayed across a dozen screens. One showed GQ's SEALs scurrying across the roof.

Big Brother was watching, and for once Flag was glad of it.

Amanda Waller was sitting at the comm, impatient as always, staring at him. He could tell she was going to complain. She always did, but he'd learned years ago to tune out most of what she babbled.

"About time, Flag," she said. "I've been monitoring your progress. There were at least a dozen ways you could have gotten to me faster."

"Yeah, feel free to write me up after I get you back home, maybe even in one piece. You ready?"

"I've been ready ever since this began."

"So why are we waiting?"

She stood up and took a last look at the room into which she had sealed herself to protect her from the inhuman hordes. A.R.G.U.S. techs still manned the computers, keeping track of EA interference. Flag saw his Suicide Squad on one of the larger screens, waiting at the vault as instructed. Maybe they were capable of following some orders after all. Especially those that instructed them to do nothing.

"You wouldn't have made it without them," Waller said. She nodded toward the screen. Flag gave her a *Yeah, so what?* look.

"We got lucky," he responded, "and I don't do luck. I do planning and precision."

She scooped up important papers and stuffed them in her shoulder bag. "Admit it, Rick. I was right."

"We can agree to disagree on that. I told you to get on the damn truck with me, but you said no. Then, with the infestation, you got yourself trapped here, and we had to squander a whole slew of precious lives to save you. From yourself. Why'd you stay, Amanda?"

Waller stared at the monitors, watching the different elements move across the screens.

"You know I've been studying your girlfriend."

Flag didn't want to talk about June. His personal life had nothing to do with Task Force X. He stared at one of the monitors—this one displaying a high-angle shot of the rail station. It was ringed by a palisade of stacked cars.

"What the hell did that?" he asked. "And why? There's gotta be easier ways to construct a fence."

Waller pushed the monitor so it faced away. "I'm talking now," she said. "You listen. So, your girlfriend, she takes an average person—a yoga mom, an elderly retiree—and she turns them into soldiers who can take a headshot and still fight. Better, they don't argue with their superiors. Sounds like heaven."

Flag was listening. He wanted to hear where she was going.

"You know, it takes the military years to stamp out someone like you, Flag. She does it in a minute.

Poof. An instant army." She turned to one of the techs and barked an order. "Clip four hundred and seven." He quickly typed in the info and the monitor displayed an exterior view of the station. A platoon of EAs exited the front doors and marched in perfect lockstep.

"Great," Flag said. "They're the damned Rockettes. So what's the plan to stop her?"

To his surprise, Waller actually looked defeated. Flag had never quite seen her that way.

"There is no plan," she said. "The suggestion box is wide open."

He thought for a second. "They're hard as hell to kill. I don't think the government has enough bullets to put them all down, not if she can keep growing more. We have to nuke the place."

Waller pointed to a different monitor, which showed a large ring of debris somehow floating above the station. "We thought of that, and acted," she said flatly. "There's a dozen W88 warheads trapped in that ring up there."

Caught off guard, Flag stared at the ring and tried to make sense of it.

"How the hell is that floating? Are there wires hidden someplace I'm not seeing?" Waller enjoyed watching his confusion. As they watched, the ring began to pulse with a dark, strobing light. Somehow it felt evil to him. "What's it doing now?"

Waller didn't answer. She resumed stuffing papers into her bag.

"Waller," he said again, a little louder, but she went to her desk and removed the case that contained Enchantress's heart. She opened it to make sure the object was still inside. Flag noted it looked like a pincushion with who knew how many needles stuck in it.

"That's the heart, isn't it?" he said. "Her heart?"

Waller finally turned to him; her face betrayed both fear and anger.

"How'd she do it, Flag? How'd she game the system? With you watching her every move?"

Flag clenched his jaw. He looked at her and shook his head.

"I'll accept the consequences." But Waller was not going to let him off the hook.

"I'm your damned consequences, Rick." Waller shoved the heart back in its case, shut the lid, then put the case into her bag. She looked up, and involuntarily let out a gasp. Deadshot was standing in the doorway. With his mask on, she couldn't tell what he was thinking. How much did he overhear?

He walked over to Flag, then nodded toward Waller.

"I'd be careful out there," he said calmly. "Everyone thinks we're rescuing Nelson Mandela or something. Certainly not you."

Waller didn't care what he thought. "I can take care of myself." She turned to the techs. "Shut it down. Wipe the drives."

The techs rushed into action. They pushed buttons. Screens went blank, replaced by the programming code for self-deletion. Within seconds all information linked to the EAs and Task Force X was gone. As far as the databases were concerned, none of them ever existed.

He watched as monitor after monitor turned itself off. He turned to Flag, repulsed yet still in awe.

"You won't believe me, because you're locked in your temple of soldierly self-righteousness." His jaw tightened. "A dude as two-faced as you wouldn't last but a minute in the streets."

"Says the guy who shoots people for money." Flag laughed.

"Yeah, but you've seen all my cards." Deadshot shrugged. "I don't hide what I am."

Flag turned away. "You really pride yourself on being bad. Don't. That's starting off on the wrong foot. My way got it done, and that's good enough for me. End of argument."

"Yeah, well. We're both pretty much the same—but you know, when it comes down to people lying face down in the streets, our little differences don't make a helluva difference."

Gunshots suddenly exploded behind Deadshot and Flag. Waller was emptying her Glock into the technicians. Three bullets. Three headshots.

"What the hell?" Deadshot exclaimed. The fourth tech had time to react. Cowering, he tried to hide, but Waller coldly finished him off. Deadshot softly applauded.

"Lady, that was gangster. You get the golf clap for that."

Flag just stared at her, surprised and confused.

"Why? They're your people?"

"They're not cleared for any of this." She put away her gun then turned to him. "Any of it. You can live with it?"

Flag shrugged. "I've buried a lot of mistakes, too."

Waller almost smiled at him. "We're bonded by this. Never forget it." Then they headed for the exit.

Waller might have been smiling at him—in her own weird way—but Flag knew she'd put that gun to his head and kill him in half a heartbeat, if she needed to.

For now she still needed him.

When she no longer did, he'd make sure he was more than prepared to take her out first.

FORTY-NINE

The Squad saw Deadshot heading back toward them. Flag followed. Then Amanda Waller appeared behind them.

"No. Way," Harley said, and she stared. She had to be hallucinating. Waller walked past her and the others, not even acknowledging their presence.

"What the hell's going on, Flag?" Boomer asked.

Flag pushed in until they were nose to nose.

"Need to know, Harkness," he growled, and he didn't look happy. "Count your blessings rescuing her was this simple. Travel should be waiting for us on the roof. Follow me."

"Getting here was simple?" Boomer echoed. "What parallel universe spawned you, Flag?" They headed for the stairs to the roof. Harley shook her head back and forth, refusing to believe this.

"We're done," Flag bellowed. "Everyone shut up and let's go home."

"Yeah, right," Boomer said. "Mission accomplished. What could go wrong now?" He turned to Harley— she was walking beside him. "There's gonna be a nine-point-seven any minute now," he whispered.

Harley agreed. The part of her that had been Dr.

Harleen Quinzel knew exactly what Boomerang was thinking, even while couching his words.

"I bet you walk under ladders and chase black cats, too," she said, giggling. He grinned back at her.

"I make my own luck, darling," he said. "I say we kill both of 'em. Right now. Before they kill us."

She was about to respond when Katana, silent as always, came up behind them.

"Later," Harley whispered. "We're gonna need a bigger boat." She looked at Croc and Boomer. They were in. Diablo was hit and miss, and she wasn't sure she could trust Lawton any longer. Still, they'd make do with what they had.

Katana moved in closer to Waller, but the woman held up her detonator. She didn't need protecting.

"Y'all made it this far," she said, grim as ever. "Don't get high spirited on me now, and ruin a good thing."

Croc watched as she pushed open the door and walked onto the roof.

"She's a rock. Nasty, too. I like her."

Boomer shook his head. "Whatta bunch a' wankers. You guys got no self-respect."

Harley laughed. "A village in Australia is missing its idiot. You should call home."

"That I will, sweet thing," he said "And tell 'em exactly where they can find you."

The SEALs were waiting on the roof. They watched the Chinook as it circled over them, then arced down to come in for a landing.

"Ride's here," GQ called.

Moving to the edge, the Squad stared down from the roof at the remains of what had been a thriving city. So many buildings were lying in rubble now. Others burned out of control. Everywhere they looked they saw terrible devastation. They doubted there had been time to save anything. Good for looting, they all thought, but given a choice, all of them knew they would rather get the hell out of there.

Deadshot saw Flag staring at him. He knew they were both thinking the same thing.

It's over and we didn't kill each other.

Flag looked up and watched the Chinook hover just above them. Something was wrong but he was unable to put a finger on it.

He traded looks with Waller.

She had the same hunch.

The floor of the chopper was littered with the bodies of Special Forces soldiers. Each had had his or her throat slit, and was lying in their own blood. The Joker found it all so funny, but he didn't have time for the already dead when there were so many others still breathing.

The pilots knew about the Joker. They knew he could kill them both while the chopper was still flying, and risk crashing to Earth, too. Or he might suddenly decide to let them go free, and give them a million dollars each for their inconvenience. They had no clue how he would react, or what they might do that could set him off. So they both tried to stay professional, do what was ordered and not talk back.

Joker glanced into the cockpit and saw his Panda Man standing behind the pilot and co-pilot, holding his gun close.

"Nice job, boys," Panda Man said. "Keep it up and I won't turn your heads into Swiss cheese." Joker laughed. Somehow the words "Swiss cheese" always got to him. Like "spaghetti" and "weapons of mass destruction."

Frost sat behind, watching the nanite expert, Dr. Van Criss, use a spectrum analyzer to find the signal of the bomb Waller's people had implanted in Harley's neck.

The Joker was impatient. He tapped his glowing purple shoes against the chopper's metal floor, then began to pace back and forth.

"We're waiting, Doctor."

Van Criss's heart almost jumped out of his skin. He was in a helicopter with a madman. No. *The* madman. Every second the doctor still lived was a second that brought him closer to death. He knew that to extend those seconds as long as he could he had to do everything the Joker demanded, then somehow indicate he had further value down the road. If the Joker thought he might need him, perhaps he would let him live.

"Everything's working, sir, just as I said it would," he insisted. "But I need to be closer to isolate her specific signal. Can you get the pilots to do that, sir?"

The Joker leaned close to the pilot and gave him his broadest smile.

"Closer," he said. Both pilots nodded. *Absolutely. Whatever you want. Anything you say.*

"So," the Joker started, "you were saying, Doctor, that it's all working? You're not lying to me, are you?"

His heart beating like a trip-hammer, Van Criss looked up.

"No. No. I'd never do that, sir. It works. It really does. Just as you wanted."

The madman leaned into him and gave him a big,

toothy smile. "You definitely are my new best friend."

Van Criss grinned. Happy. But then, he didn't know what the Joker had done to his previous best friends.

FIFTY

Flag and Waller stared at the Chinook hovering directly over the Federal building, but not descending to its landing dock. Why wasn't it landing? Something was wrong.

GQ shouted into his comm. "Savior One Zero. Why are you holding? Savior One Zero, respond, please. What the hell is going on up there, Savior One Zero?"

There was no answer. GQ traded looks with Flag.

"They're not talking to me."

Flag turned to the Squad. These were exactly the kind of scum who would throw a curveball like this. He turned back to GQ.

"Our bird's been hijacked," he said with certainty. "Light it up." He thought it could be interesting to see how his killers reacted.

GQ and the SEALs opened fire on the Chinook. It suddenly slipped sideways, circling to reveal the tail ramp. Flag could see a big man inside it, spinning a six-barrelled chain gun. It pumped lead like water in a fire hose.

Flag shouted at his Squad. "Get down. Now."

They scattered in different directions.

One of the SEALs let out a gasp then fell to the

ground. A bullet tunneled through his forehead and exploded out the back. The other SEALs hit the deck, taking cover behind the roof's parapet.

Harley hunkered down just a few yards from Deadshot. She saw him staring weirdly at her neck.

"What? I got a hickey or something?"

He looked at the indicator light just under her skin. It was blinking green.

"Your nanite's disarmed."

She felt her palm buzz. She unclenched her fingers and looked at the tiny cell phone the Joker had given her. She'd gotten a text.

Now. It's time.

Finally she saw the Joker step out onto the Chinook's tail ramp. Her eyes widened with joy and her heart almost burst from her chest.

This is the most romantic thing anyone has ever done for anyone else in the whole history of the world, she thought with fierce love. *That's why he's my one and only Puddin'.*

Frost hosed down the roof with his chain gun, scattering SEALs and the Squad team. Next to him the Joker tossed out a rope. It unrolled down to the roof, then dragged toward the edge.

"Harley, it's up to you now," he said over the sound of the rotors.

Without hesitation, she ran for the edge of the roof and leapt to catch the rope. As she held on, the chopper nosed down and veered away. Frost kept firing at the rooftop to keep Flag and company pinned down. He only stopped shooting after they cleared the immediate area.

* * *

Deadshot stared at Harley climbing the rope to the copter. Joker impatiently waited for her inside.

"C'mon, babe," the maniac shouted. "Quit taking your time. We got killing to do."

"Mr. Lawton," Waller said. "You kill that woman. Right now."

Deadshot glared at her. "What's she done to me?"

"You're a hitman, right? I got a contract. Kill Harley Quinn. For your freedom and your kid."

Deadshot nodded. He lifted his carbine and aimed it at Harley, her copter rapidly receding into the distance. He stared at her; she was square in his crosshairs. What Boomer had said. Easy peasy.

"This won't be easy, lady," he said to Waller. "They're already so damn far. And I don't have time to calibrate wind velocity. Good as I am, I make no promises."

"I'll hold you to one anyway. Kill her."

He didn't know what to do, and that bothered him. Was he growing a damned conscience? After all this time? He was pretty sure that would be a "no." He would never allow that to happen. That would be the death of Deadshot.

He tightened his finger on the trigger.

"Now, Lawton. For your daughter."

He squeezed it.

Harley had nearly reached the open tail ramp. Her Puddin' was waiting there for her. He'd risked everything to save her, and she was definitely going to show him how grateful she was.

She heard the bullet explode from Deadshot's

M4A1. A second later it impacted, less than an inch from Harley's ear. She glanced back at the Federal Building. Deadshot was standing in front of Waller. She was dressing him down.

"Sorry," he said. "I missed."

"Yeah. Like hell."

"No. It was the wind. There was no way to compensate for it. Not without my equipment, and certainly not while the target was moving in an unsteady chopper. Trust me. I've got no love for that nutjob, but you were asking for the impossible. Despite everything, I came damn close."

Waller stalked off angry as hell. Deadshot stood, watching as Boomer gave him a reassuring pat on the back.

"Good one, mate."

They looked up and saw Harley pull herself into the Chinook. Its tailgate closed behind her. Deadshot was surrounded by the Squad—they were cheering him for his "accidental miss."

Waller was livid, but Flag looked at Lawton and smiled.

The head of A.R.G.U.S. reached for her phone and punched in a preset.

"Savior One Zero's been hijacked," she shouted. "Shoot it down." She was determined to get her kill, Deadshot knew.

He decided he didn't care, and turned back to Boomer, Croc, and Diablo.

"Well, this's become a brown-eyed mullet," Boomer complained. "We started with six. Now we're four."

"Not sure we needed Quinn," Lawton said. "Maybe

if she was taking her meds, but she's a loose cannon. And we certainly didn't need what's his name?"

Boomer laughed. "Slipshod. Sliprope. Slip something. Who cares? But the real stinker here is we're bein' run by a knocker who'd shoot us all herself, if we gave her half a reason."

"We're better off alone," Deadshot agreed. "Just the four of us."

Harley was staring at the ocean, looking at it from the Chinook's tail ramp. The water was beautiful, seductive, overwhelming, and it seemed to be endless.

Two of a kind, she thought. *The ocean and Harley.*

"C'mon. Get inside," the Joker ordered. He grabbed her by the wrist and pulled her toward him. "What the hell are you waiting for? We got murdering to do."

She turned back to her rescuer and gave him the biggest, most sincere smile she had. But he wasn't smiling back.

"I tell you, the crap I do for you," he said.

"Puddin'?" Harley stammered, confused. After all, he had just put his life on the line to rescue her. What could she have done wrong? Harley decided maybe they got off to a bad start. She rushed closer to hug him.

He answered by pushing her back.

"We'll talk about this," he said sternly. "Later."

"Okay. Sure." She nodded her head, still confused, but he was her Puddin', her Mister J. Whatever her man said worked for her.

Frost broke the tension.

"Boss. We got problems."

FIFTY-ONE

The Blackhawk helicopter had been circling Midway City, spotting enemy combatants as well as the few idiot looters who thought they had the place to themselves. They quickly learned otherwise.

Captain Hawk was the pilot. New orders came over the comm, relayed to the chopper by Amanda Waller. The Joker had stolen a Chinook, and likely murdered its crew. The captain's orders were to find it, and then blow it the hell out of the sky.

Waller didn't want prisoners. She wanted body parts.

The captain's people linked into the Chinook's GPS signal, then sent Hawk a new course that would enable the Blackhawk to intercept the chopper over the city's downtown. The Joker wasn't going to get away.

"First monsters, and now I'm hunting super-villains." Captain Hawk chuckled. "Never a boring day."

"We have our target, sir." Steve Gardner, Hawk's second in command, pointed to the radar. "Five hundred ninety yards due west. Just behind the Kane Tower complex." Hawk entered the data into the nav computer, then felt the Blackhawk bank as it adapted to its new orders.

Within minutes they were shooting toward the Chinook at an interception angle. Before the target could respond, they cut it off and shifted into firing position.

The Chinook pulled up and hovered.

Hawk hit the button that launched a hellfire missile.

The Joker shouted for the pilot to evade, but it was too late. The missile slammed into the front of the Chinook, blowing the pilots out of the cockpit. The impact disabled Dr. Van Criss's equipment.

Joker grabbed onto a handhold and angrily turned to Harley.

"We gotta get out of here fast," he shouted.

They rushed toward the tail ramp when the chopper swerved and spun. Harley fell forward, out the open ramp, even as the Joker fell back, into the plunging copter.

Before she knew what was happening, Harley was hurtling out of the helicopter. The loud sound of the rotors was replaced by the whoosh of empty air. She was plummeting toward the ground, but she also had forward momentum, and it carried her over the roof of a low building.

I'm flying, she thought. *Gliding*. The city below spiraled crazily, but Harley closed her eyes, spread her arms out like the wings she knew they were, stuck out her tongue, and let the winds and momentum carry her wherever they might.

She came in at a low angle and skidded across a building's roof rather than pancaking directly into it. Scraping painfully along the rough surface, letting out a couple of unladylike grunts, she finally rolled to a stop. Sure, she might have a broken bone or two, but miraculously she was still breathing.

Best. Landing. Ever!

Lying on the rooftop, bloody and partially broken, she looked up to see the Chinook spiral down, then crash into the Groiler building. It exploded on contact.

"No. Nonono. Puddin'!" she exclaimed. Tears streaked her face. She howled in pain even as the Blackhawk thundered overhead, heading back for the Federal Building.

FIFTY-TWO

Flag and the others stood on the Federal Building roof as the Blackhawk arrived and hovered alongside the edge. Captain George Hawk opened the door as Katana and Flag helped Waller board.

"Stand by," she ordered. "I'll send another helo for the rest of you." The Blackhawk lifted, moved off, then screamed to the street in a near freefall, leveling just yards before it would have hit the ground. It slowly regained altitude and fired off amber flares behind it to distract any incoming missiles.

She leaves us behind and takes off all by her lonesome, Lawton thought. *That's one paranoid bitch.*

"Okay, let's go," Waller said to Hawk. "The fun's just beginning."

He laughed. He'd known Waller since the day she started at A.R.G.U.S. She was a self-professed bitch on wheels then, and she hadn't changed the slightest in all these years. There was little reason to. Despite her style, she was usually right.

Hawk flew the Blackhawk as low as he safely could, maneuvering it between the fallen skyscrapers and damaged buildings that had yet to crumble. He needed to keep them off enemy radar.

Deadshot watched as the Blackhawk disappeared into the distance.

Why the hell didn't Waller let any of them join her? They certainly had room for most of the Squad. Then again, Waller only cared about Waller, and he knew that would never change.

Well, he thought, *she has to live with herself.* In the back of his mind he knew others said the same about him, but he had resolved that problem years ago.

He turned to Flag. "Signed, sealed, and delivered, big guy. Time to pay the bill."

"You earned it." Flag sighed in relief. His job had been to use the Squad to rescue Waller, not specifically to fight the EAs. Waller and the Army were better set up to do that.

Deadshot looked to the ground and saw something metal glistening in the light. He picked it up and recognized it. Harley's cell phone. He slipped it into his pocket. Might as well keep it.

She wouldn't need it any more.

FIFTY-THREE

The Midway City Bank building was completed in 1926 and somehow managed to make it through the 1929 Great Depression, an uneasy economy during the war years, and the bank closures of the early 21st century. It survived the EA's initial bombardments and as SEALs, Army, and Marines joined and launched their assault against the beasts, it continued to stand as a tall and proud reminder of the way things had been and could be again.

Then hell plummeted from the sky in the guise of a crippled, out of control Chinook helicopter that skidded across rooftops and shredded its way down Ninth Street, only to careen into the bank's facade, destroying glass, stone, and mortar before its sturdy all-steel vault put an abrupt stop to the aircraft.

The copter was on fire. Nothing inside could have survived.

From across the way, on another rooftop, the Joker watched the flames rising into the sky. He had jumped just in time. If he had waited even another ten seconds, he would now be little more than ash.

He watched as the bank erupted into a blazing inferno. The fire consumed the building, destroying ninety years of solvency. What the Great Depression couldn't shutter, the Joker did without even trying.

He picked himself up and laughed as the bank burned. It was a glorious sight, knowing that millions of dollars of cold, hard samolians were being reduced to worthless ash.

What's next, he wondered, but he already knew the answer.

He had to find Harley.

He'd accepted that one day she'd be the death of him, and perhaps that was why she was so enticing. Every day with her was like running through a shifting mine field. Having to survive kept him stimulated. Knowing one day he'd strangle the very life out of her kept him focused. Life with Harley was always an adventure. A dangerous, corrosive one, but hey, he was the Joker.

How could he complain?

He checked his weapons, then turned back to the bank and breathed in deeply.

"God," he said, "I love the smell of burning cash in the morning."

Hawk angled the Blackhawk low to the ground and sped through the city canyons.

"Are we at all close to being in the clear yet?" Waller asked.

Hawk checked the GPS. "Less than a mile, ma'am. Just a few more minutes, then it'll be all she wrote."

Waller sighed. "Thank you, George," she said. "This turned out to be a real hell-storm. How could we have known?"

Hawk didn't answer. Whatever she was talking

about was above his pay grade, and she knew it. He was a convenient listening post, and with him there would be zero recriminations.

"Ma'am," Hawk shouted suddenly. She looked up.

He was pointing to a figure standing in the distance. A man, far taller than a normal human being. Waller saw him raise his hands. She saw them glow, and then he released a bolt of burning energy. Toward them.

"Evade," she shouted. "Get us the hell out of here. Hurry."

Hawk adjusted the throttle as he pushed up the collective. The Blackhawk jerked upward, but the bolt struck home, shearing off the Blackhawk's rotor, dissolving its metal frame.

Hawk turned to Waller.

"Ma'am, I hope your seatbelt's fastened. This isn't going to be gentle."

She held on as the Blackhawk belly flopped onto the street, then ground up the asphalt while spitting sparks and smoke, until finally it plowed into an abandoned bus.

As they came to a rest, Waller checked herself out, looking for blood, feeling for broken bones.

"I think I'm okay, George," she shouted. "You did great. We survived. I don't know how you did it or where we are, but we're breathing. Thank God for that.

"George?" she said. "*George*?"

He didn't answer.

She leaned to look into the cockpit. It was a jumble of twisted steel. The cabin had been crushed when the Blackhawk slammed into the bus. Hawk wasn't moving. Parts of the helicopter's steel frame had skewered him.

She told herself not to panic, recited her mantra, coined when she was still in the field, before she became one of the top brass she used to hate.

If you get yourself into a bad situation, you can get yourself out of it. The pounding of her heart, so loud she could hear it in her ears, started to abate.

Waller saw several EAs skittering over the debris. They were headed for the Blackhawk. One of them was wearing a SEAL uniform.

She tried to get out of her seat, but she was still belted in. Smoke was filling the cabin and she could smell the stink of hydraulic fuel. It was dripping into the broken remains.

Propelled by sheer instinct, she clawed at the seatbelt until the buckle finally released. She tried to push herself out of the seat, but her left leg was trapped in the twisted steel tangle. Controlling her growing panic, she tried to pull her leg free.

George's neck had broken in the crash. She reached for his carbine, lying on the floor beside him. She hooked a finger on the sling and dragged it to her.

There was a reflection in Hawk's window.

She whirled and fired through the cabin's aluminum wall. Kept firing until the carbine ran dry. She reached for Hawk again—his chest rig was filled with full magazines. She strained to reach one of the mags and managed to pull it free with two fingers, but it slipped and fell to the ground, just out of reach.

She keyed her radio.

Flag was on the roof of the Federal Building, along with GQ and the others, when his comm feed buzzed. He saw Waller's ID flash across his screen.

"Queen Bee," he said. "You copy? Havoc for Queen Bee."

GQ lowered his own phone. "Operations just confirmed she's down on K West."

Flag turned to Deadshot, but Lawton already guessed what was coming next.

"Let's go," the colonel said. "The mission's not over."

"It is for me." Deadshot stepped back. He wasn't having any of this. "We had a deal."

Flag shook his head. "The deal was to get her to safety. She's not there." He turned and raced down the stairwell, followed by Katana, GQ, and the half-dozen or so surviving SEALs. Deadshot and the Suicide Squad watched, angry about the sudden shift in events.

"So, what now?" Diablo asked.

Deadshot was seething. "Got no choice," he said. "The rescue blew up in our faces. Let's get this the hell over with."

"Hooray. I'm back!"

As they exited the Federal Building, Harley sat on the hood of a Beemer, looking beat-up beautiful.

"I missed you guys sooo much."

She was smiling at them, but Deadshot could tell the grin was forced. Grime clung to her face where there had been tears.

"Aren't you dead?" Croc said.

"I got better," she replied. "These things happen, you know."

Deadshot gave her a thumbs up. "Well, I don't believe I'm saying this, but I'm glad you made it," he said, offering his hand to help her off the car.

She took it and slid to the pavement.

"So who are we supposed to kill now?" She leaned close to Deadshot and talked to him in a stage whisper for everyone to hear. "Tell me it's him," she said, theatrically pointing at Flag, who was staring back at her.

"You're hilarious, Quinn," the colonel said.

She curtsied then danced off, joining the others.

"That's exactly what Mister J always tells me."

"Hey, Craziness!" the deep voice called to her. She turned, catching the baseball cap Boomer tossed to her. She laughed as she dropped it on her head and thumbed it to a sexy tilt.

Like it or not, she was one of the guys.

PART THREE
THE GODS

FIFTY-FOUR

Before the Eyes of the Adversary, hundreds of thousands of suburban commuters yawned their way into the crowded subway cars each day, to begin the hour-long journey into the Midway City Rail Station, only to reverse the trip nine hours later.

Amanda Waller didn't care about the efficiency of Midway's transit system. She was being dragged against her will into its bowels by two hideous creatures, one still wearing his SEAL uniform, the other her police blues.

Waller resisted and tried to squirm free, but their grip was firm. She saw one of the EAs hunkered by the case that contained Enchantress's desiccated heart. Incubus stood behind him, towering over the creatures that were scurrying about. Enchantress joined them at the man's side.

"Bring her here," Enchantress ordered. "Her thumb goes on the machine."

Waller tried to pull back, but they held her firmly.

"I'll fight you all the way to hell."

Incubus looked down at her and smiled. "Resist and we will cut off your thumb and put it into the machine."

Enchantress laughed as she watched Waller squirm. "We would prefer to preserve your living flesh for as long as we might need it, but we will do whatever we need to. One way or another, my heart will be freed and returned to me."

The two EAs forced Waller's thumb to the scanner. She heard the machine tick as if gears were grinding into place. The case lid slid open and Incubus looked inside. He was pleased.

"It is here, sister. Ready to rejoin with you." He held up the shriveled organ and showed it to her. She lightly brushed her hand over it, caressing it.

"Now, brother," she said. "I do not want to wait a moment longer."

He carefully picked up the heart with both hands and pressed it into her chest, pushing it inside her ribcage. It started to beat again, and grow. They could both see it glowing green through luminous skin that was crisscrossed with thick black veins. She seemed to be wearing a cape made of smoke that pumped out of her body, and looked like a demonic god.

She thought she was one, too.

Waller stared at her in horror. *What have we set loose?* The witch had been waiting for this moment for a very long time.

She waved her hands and created an image between them. Flag was walking on a street, just outside the rail station. He was holding a weapon, looking worried, maybe even frightened, but he wasn't about to stop.

"You see him," Enchantress said. "The soldier. He's outside now, coming for you." Waller stared at the ghostly image, and she prayed somehow that Flag would find a way to save her.

"You look to him with hope in your eyes, but long

before he finds you, we will eliminate him. After all, as important to him as you think you are, I have what he truly wants.

"Thank you," she said to Waller. "For everything. You were so useful."

"I never liked you," Waller said, still thrown by that ghastly, shrunken image. "I should have had you killed when I had the chance."

"Too little, too late—it is your problem, and not mine," Enchantress said as she removed her robe and tossed it to the floor. "Anyway, he will die, but you... well, as the saying goes, it is better to reign in Hell than serve in Heaven. Isn't that right?"

Waller squirmed as she tried to free herself from the creatures' grip.

"And you are going to serve me very well in Hell. Oh. In case you wanted to know. I am an extremely unpleasant boss."

"Do your worst, bitch," Waller shouted.

Enchantress laughed. "How original, but it does cut right to the meat. Speaking of, I think I'll start by slicing into all the precious secrets you keep hidden in your mind. You know the secrets I'm talking about. The ones about your leaders and their wonderful machines."

Waller reacted with a sudden shiver as Enchantress stood and spread her arms out wide. Thick, clear tendrils poured from her spine and snaked forward.

"Don't hold anything back, Amanda," she said. "It will hurt a lot less if you work with me."

FIFTY-FIVE

Harley Quinn jumped up and down, waving her hands, whooping and whistling.

"Guys, over here! Guys. Hey, c'mon! Lookee what I found," she squealed, pointing to the crashed Blackhawk. "I found it. Can I keep it?"

Flag ignored her and peered inside the shattered cockpit. "Waller's not here," he announced. "Where the hell is she?"

"She could have been thrown from it," Deadshot suggested. "If that happened while they were still in the air, she's street pizza now."

Flag didn't want to hear that. "Or she crawled out, which means she could be alive."

"I vote with Lawton," Boomer added, "and don't tell me you don't secretly agree. She is not a nice person."

"Same could be said about you, Boomer."

"Yeah, but I call myself a villain. I'm not pretending to be something I'm not."

Flag crawled into the copter and rummaged for clues. "Oh come on, Harkness. You wear that villain crap like it's a badge of honor, but you might just as well say, 'I hurt people for my own benefit,' because that's what it comes down to. You do whatever the hell you feel like doing, and everyone else be damned. So just shut the hell up and do what you're told."

"We got ourselves lots of restocks," Kowalski said as he and GQ unloaded ammunition from the rear of the downed aircraft.

"Take a case but leave the rest behind," Flag said. "We can't carry any more."

"Not a problem," Kowalski responded. "We can always go back and get more if we have to."

"You see anything, Colonel?" GQ asked.

"Only enough to know she's not here," Flag said as he pulled himself out of the Blackhawk. "That means she either got out on her own, or was helped out."

"By the monsters?" Croc asked. "Then she's history."

Flag didn't agree. "Depends on why they took her."

"If they took her," Deadshot added. "We don't know that yet. She could be one of them by now."

"Until we know, we keep looking," Flag said. "Let's go." They moved away from the wreckage.

Harley followed in the rear, walking alongside Katana.

"So what do you think, Gabby?" she asked. "Alive or dead? I'm starting an office pool. Five bucks to get in. Whoever's closest to what really happened wins it all."

Katana turned to her and shook her head. "Do you ever keep any thoughts to yourself?"

Harley grinned. "Share the wealth, Mister J always says."

"Hey, Looney Tunes, ten bucks on that's where we're going," Deadshot said. He pointed to the impossible sight ahead and above them.

Hovering above the rail station was a large suspended ring of abandoned vehicles, trash, and other street debris, all floating around a beam of bright, white light that was shooting up into space.

"That's where we're going, right? I mean, cause we're certifiable idiots, so why wouldn't we?"

Flag stared at the floating ring, a wave of conflicting thoughts and emotions washing across his features. Finally he seemed to come to a conclusion.

"Load up," he said. "We're in for a fight."

"You think," Deadshot replied, still staring at the floating ring of junk. As Flag motioned for them to move out, he wormed back into the Blackhawk for another helping of extra ammo. Enough was not nearly enough.

He reached for a box and saw Waller's backpack and binder. On it was stenciled "Task Force X: TOP SECRET." He flipped through it, studying the photos of Enchantress and the EAs. There was also a selection of surveillance photos of a huge man, taken in the subway.

Deadshot's face tightened with anger.

The colonel was in the lead, talking with GQ as they prepared to head toward the rail station. The soldiers were getting ready and moving into position.

"Hey, Flag!" Deadshot called out. He looked pissed, and threw Waller's binder at him. "Dammit, Flag, you knew exactly what we were walking into, didn't you?"

Flag shot him a look. "I tell you what you need to know only when you need to know it. It's how things work. Do you know I own a pickup truck with a blown engine? Not everything is relevant."

"Lover's spat, guys?" Harley rested her chin on

her hands, and stared at them. She shook her head sadly. Croc, Diablo, and Boomer joined them. "Tell them," Deadshot said, still staring daggers. "Tell them everything, because they deserve to hear it."

GQ leaned in and whispered to Flag so the others wouldn't hear him.

"He's right. It's the least we owe them."

Flag didn't like giving in to lowlifes. They didn't deserve consideration, but the mission was too important to risk defections now.

"Okay, it won't make one helluva difference far as you're concerned, but you want the dirt? Fine." He flipped through Waller's binder and took out several photos of a ten-foot-tall man, walking the streets of Midway City, laying waste to hundreds of soldiers. He put out dozens of photos, each one horrifying.

"Three days ago a non-human entity appeared in a subway station. It called itself Incubus. First the city government sent cops to check it out. It killed them without raising a sweat. Then the military sent in the Army. Despite being outfitted with every state-of-the-art weapon, the thing, Incubus, took them out, too. In less than thirty seconds. So now they've sent me."

Flag rifled through the photographs. "If you were wondering, these are drone shots. When they tried to send in photographers, the thing killed them, too."

Boomer turned to Deadshot and gave a laugh. "All those killings yet Flag's still breathing. Why do only the good die young?"

Deadshot shot him a "shut up" look. He'd seen the photos, and understood that this was far more serious than anyone expected—Flag included.

"You have to understand the extent of Incubus's power." Flag tossed several other drone photos for them to look at. "Army Rangers were sent to confront the creature. They shot at it, but the science team said our bullets impacted against its glowing armor, flared brightly for a second or two, then dissolved.

"They tried to engage with it physically," he continued, "but he used his powers, or whatever you want to call them, and he reduced the Rangers to crystalline blotches. Nobody could get near it. And that's what we're up against."

"So they thought they'd send us to die, too?" Croc said. "Were you using the alien as a convenient alternative to lethal injection?"

Flag was about to give a snarky response, but considered how he might have interpreted what he'd told them.

"No, not at all, Croc," he said, almost apologetically. "None of us could get near it. You couldn't either—but she could," he said, picking up a picture of June. "The witch could."

"So why are we here? It doesn't sound like you need us," Diablo asked.

"Waller's plan—and I championed it—was to hand June a nanite demolition charge. She was supposed to drop it at the thing's feet, use her witch powers to warp her way out of there, then we fly economy back to DC."

"You still haven't said why we're here."

"You asked for the truth," he growled. "Shut up and I'll get to it." Flag picked out several more photos and lay them down for the Squad to see. They showed Flag with four Delta Operatives, moving through the subway tunnel. Flag was wearing a heavy backpack. June Moone was walking beside him.

Harley stared at the pictures of the two of them,

studying their body language. She turned to the colonel and gave him a broad smile.

"Look at you two, you rascal, you!" she squealed gleefully. "You guys totally did it, didn't you? Right in the middle of World War Three Thousand. You rock, Flag."

He wasn't listening to her. He was staring at the picture of June.

"Anyway, they sent in me, and a woman with incredible abilities." He paused, and added, "She's a witch."

Harley snorted a laugh. "She twitch her nose, too?"

Flag glared at her. "This isn't a joke, Quinn. This is real. She's a witch, as in brooms and black cats. She could turn you into a frog without even thinking. I may even suggest that to her."

Harley thought about it, and nodded excitedly. "That would be so cool. Ribbit ribbit. When can she start?"

Exasperated, Flag shook his head. "Someone put a gag on her, or I swear I'll personally cut out her tongue." Deadshot gave her a look and she suddenly clamped her hands over her mouth, then motioned to zipper it shut.

"Done," Lawton said. "Right?" He looked at Harley. She bobbed her head up and down in silent agreement.

"I had the nanite charge in my backpack. I took it out and set the timer for two seconds. June was watching." Flag picked up the photo of him, June, and the Delta operatives. That was where everything had changed.

"Are you sure?" Flag had asked her.

June looked frightened, but she nodded yes. "I have to. I'm the only one who can."

He held onto her and kissed her. "Okay," he said. "You're on."

She held Flag and whispered the one word.

"Enchantress."

In an instant June was gone, only to be replaced by the witch. Flag hesitated a moment to remind himself that this person—the thing he was holding—was not the woman he loved. That only through a bizarre twist of fate or magic or something inexplicable, they were sharing the same space and time.

He showed her the bomb and pointed to a button on the detonator.

"Once you put it in place, just push this button and drop it. It's set to explode in two seconds. That should give you time enough to poof your way out of there."

Enchantress smiled at Flag, not wanting to let him go.

"Darling," she said, "I'd like to show you the world."

"Seen it. Not impressed," he said, calibrating the bomb's timing mechanism. "Okay. It's ready. You can take it."

Enchantress only laughed. She leaned in, gave him a kiss, pressed the button then disappeared in an instant...

...leaving Flag holding the armed bomb.

Two seconds.

That was all he needed.

FIFTY-SIX

The top button armed the bomb, but it was designed with an emergency override, for ordinary soldiers who couldn't just drop it and disappear. He turned the bomb over and found the small, unmarked pressure plate. He tapped it and the timer disengaged.

Alone in a room just off the ops center, Amanda Waller was holding Enchantress's heart in her hand when Flag called to tell her the witch had disappeared.

She hung up, then angrily and repeatedly stabbed the heart with her pen.

Although her heart was no longer inside her, Enchantress felt excruciating pain radiating outward from her chest. With it she felt Waller's rage and hatred, growing stronger with each furious strike.

Waller was trying to kill her before she could reclaim the power to resist.

Enchantress reached out through the agony to find Incubus, and located him in a subway tunnel. She closed her eyes and concentrated. Finally, she disappeared.

When she opened her eyes again she was lying on a subway platform, not far behind her brother, who was standing at the edge of the platform, staring into the tunnel. She recognized the signs of the battle that had been waged all around him. Then more pain ripped through her and she moaned, breaking Incubus's concentration.

"Sister, what is it?" he said, horrified to see Enchantress crying out in agony.

"Quickly. Help me, brother. The woman, Waller, she is trying to destroy my heart. I need your power. I need your strength."

He leaned next to his sister and took her hands in his, funneling his energy into her.

"Where is it?" he asked.

"Do not worry, brother. I will get it back. Until then you'll sustain me."

"But I do worry, sister. I fear we are not ready."

"We will be. You can trust me. We will be." Enchantress jerked as another spasm rippled through her. She trembled from the pain, from having her heart stabbed again and again, but with Incubus giving her his power, she began to feel stronger. "Brother, I will need you to help me build the machine. It is our time."

"You'll use the machine to destroy their world?" he said.

"No, brother, but we will grind it into our dreams. Trust me. You know this is what must be done." She looked into his eyes and knew he would cooperate. He believed in her completely. She kissed him and placed his hand over her missing heart.

Incubus concentrated, focusing even more energy into her. She glowed and her flesh turned translucent. As her withered body grew, she spread her arms wide, taking in all of the energies Incubus gave her.

"You agree with me, do you not, brother?" she asked, holding him so he could not back away. However, he had no intention of leaving his sister's grasp.

"Yes, this is what must be done," he repeated. "To become the gods we were born to be."

When she was ready, Enchantress gently peeled away from him. She saw a wounded Delta operative lying on the ground, writhing yet staring at her, transfixed. She leaned closer, smiled, held his face close to hers then gently kissed him.

Easy prey, she thought. *They are all easy prey.*

"Did we blow up and die?" Harley asked. "You can tell me. Am I seeing dead people?"

Deadshot shot her another look. "I know you're intelligent. Why do you act like an idiot?" he asked.

Harley laughed. "Break the tension? It's fun? I really am an idiot?" She grinned at him innocently. "Multiple choice, choose one or choose 'em all."

Harley stared at Flag, about to say something she knew was definitely hilarious, but she decided instead to say nothing.

Deadshot gave her a quick smile.

"Better."

FIFTY-SEVEN

The batteries in the crashed Blackhawk were still functional, so GQ used them to light the area. As they prepared for the conflict ahead, Flag paused and addressed the entire Squad.

"We okay?" he said. Two words, but they carried a tremendous weight. He had to know he could count on them.

Harley squeaked. "Can I talk now?"

Flag rolled his eyes. She'd never stopped talking, but he nodded yes. Quinn took a deep breath, as if about to launch into another long, pointless diatribe.

"Yeah. I'm good."

Boomer turned to the others. "Really?" he said. "Seriously? We've been fighting thousand-eyed monsters who suck up three mags before they croak, and you're all good with this?"

"He spoke the truth," Diablo said. "That is all I wanted to hear."

Croc agreed. "Maybe he lied to us before, or withheld truths, but these monsters deserve to be destroyed. If they destroy mankind, they will certainly destroy us, too."

Exasperated, Boomer paced and shook his arms wildly.

"So, let me get this straight. Nobody here is the slightest bit crackers that we're going to war against magical monsters and a crazy witch, who by the way may even be crazier than fruit loops here," he said, glancing at Harley. "No offense."

She shrugged.

"Yeah, pretty much," Deadshot responded.

"Yes. That is acceptable," Diablo echoed.

Croc just nodded and said, "Yes."

"Hey, I don't agree," Harley said, looking around the group. "You are wrong."

Boomer pointed to her, smiling. "At last. Someone with some sense."

"Yeah, and I totally disagree with what Stickman said. Witch Nutso's crazier than me? I beg to differ. Nobody's crazier than me. Mister J told me so himself."

Deadshot shot Boomer a smile. "She's got you there. Stickman."

"Can't argue with the lady," Flag added.

"Certifiable." Harley crossed her arms over her chest and slammed her foot down. "Toldja."

Deadshot glanced at the others then looked up to a floating ring of debris, still another block away. "I don't know about you, but I need a drink." He headed across the street to The Golden Tree, a bar that probably was shuttered when the war began. He turned to Flag and waved.

"Go ahead and kill me, or trust that I'll be back when I'm good and sloshed. Your decision. I already made mine."

Flag ran after him. "Gonna kill me?" Lawton asked. "If so, can you do me a big favor and wait until after my first drink? I think I earned that much."

"Deadshot, I need your help."

Lawton paused. "No. You need a miracle." He broke the lock, headed into the bar, and checked out the bottles behind the counter. "Not bad," he said as Boomer followed him inside. "I expected all this would have been stolen or destroyed, depending on who got here first."

Diablo and Croc entered behind them and sat down at the bar. A moment later Harley entered. She paused at the door, sashayed back and forth, turned and saw Flag still outside. She flipped him off, gave a curtsy then headed in to join Deadshot behind the bar.

"Sit down, big guy," she said, reaching for a bottle of bourbon. "Used to tend bar during grad school." She poured him the drink and eased it over to him.

"Keep a tab going," he said. "I'm going to need more than one."

"You got it, pal. So let's see if I can figure out everyone's drink o' choice." She sidled up to Boomer and fluttered her eyes at him.

"You know what I like, sugar."

"That you don't get, mate. I belong to my Puddin' and nobody else," Harley laughed. "So let's see. You're an Aussie. Well, I don't see a Darwin Stubby or a VB anywhere on these shelves, but you probably like a good Black and Tan. Am I close?"

"Not even, sweet cheeks. I'm a Gurgle's Ale mate. So, were you any good pouring drinks?"

"Never had to take out a student loan."

Next Harley walked over to Croc and studied him. "You're a hard one to read, KC." She sniffed him and made a face. "Hard to tell your beverage of choice when all I smell is five-day-old sewer."

Deadshot took a sip and joined the fun.

"I'm betting he's a Bloody Mary man. Emphasis on

the blood, and a whole side of Mary."

Croc shook his head. "Nothing for me. Drink dulls the mind."

"Precisely, my giant alligator pal," Deadshot said, gesturing for Harley to fill his glass up again. "You really want a sharp mind going after those things we saw? The duller the better for me."

Croc stared at him, then shrugged. "Okay. Beer."

Boomer clapped his hands and gave a whoop. "There he is. A man after my own heart. Don't take that literally. Sweet-lips, pour the big guy a Gurgle's. No. Make that five."

Harley turned to Diablo. He interrupted her before she got a chance to guess.

"Water."

"Says the man who can set the world on fire. Good idea, honey."

She poured it from the tap and handed it over. Deadshot raised his shot glass.

"Here's to honor among thieves," he said merrily as they clinked glasses.

"No. Not thieves," Boomer said, raising his glass again. "Asset relocation specialists."

"I like that," Harley said, carefully fitting a handful of tiny cocktail umbrellas into some God-knows-what blue tropical drink.

Deadshot swirled his drink hypnotically. "We almost pulled it off. Despite what everyone thought."

"We weren't picked to succeed," Diablo interrupted. "We were chosen to fail."

"Think I don't know that?" Deadshot laughed and poured himself a third bourbon. "They'll blame us for what went down here. They don't need no one knowin' the truth. We're the cover-up. The patsies. The bad guys."

Croc raised his glass. "To the bad guys. You know, I never think of myself as a bad guy. I just got needs that others don't always agree with."

"That is so true," Harley added. "It's all perspective. Say you got people attacking the government, they'll be treated like terrorists. Unless you're the American revolution, and suddenly you're rag-tag patriots."

Croc agreed. "Or you're in *Star Wars* and you're the rebel alliance."

"You got it, Wally Gator," Harley added. "Good and bad, they change depending on who's writing the history books. So what did Flag promise you?" she asked Lawton. "What were you gonna get outta this?"

"Same thing Waller offered me to kill you, sweetie. A shot at being a father. Life outside the suburbs."

Harley raised her glass. "I owe you one," she said as she downed the cab.

"No, you don't. I trusted Flag. I was a jerk."

Diablo slammed down his glass. "Flag had you chasing a carrot on a stick. You played yourself."

They all nodded, agreeing. "There's some real truth in that," Harley said as she sidled up next to him. She put an arm around him and held up her cell phone with the other. "I love this guy," she said. "Smile for the selfie, hot stuff."

Diablo looked at her. "This *is* me smiling," he said as she snapped the picture.

"We'll work on that later."

Deadshot chugged his drink, then slammed the glass down on the bar. The bottle in front of him was empty. "Maybe I played myself, but right now I'm having a drink, and for two seconds I had hope."

Diablo shook his head. "Hope don't stop the wheel from turning, my brother. It's coming back around for you. So, how many people you killed?" Deadshot stared at him, then turned to Harley and raised his glass again.

"Hey, Craziness, you got any more back there?" She rummaged through the bottles and found a bourbon in the back, behind the ryes and Scotches.

"The last one," she announced. "Savor it, honey." He nodded and turned back to Diablo.

"You're a street guy. You know you don't ask that crap."

"You never whacked no women or kids?"

Deadshot held up his glass, but just stared at it. "Naw, man. I do not kill women and children."

Diablo leaned in close, whispering, but loud enough for them all to hear.

"I do."

FIFTY-EIGHT

They could hear a pin drop.

Diablo turned his hands palms-up, and a flaming figure of a woman appeared between them, swaying back and forth. It was his wife, only she was alive and laughing.

"I was born with the devil's gift," he said. "Kept it hidden most of my life, but the older I got, the stronger it got. So I started using it for business."

The flames were still dancing. He was creating pictures with them that demanded everyone stop what they were doing and watch. Diablo's show was magical. Hypnotic, and frightening.

They saw a house in East Los Angeles. It looked like every other house on the block, but then it seemed to explode in fire and sparks. Diablo calmly opened the burning door, and just as calmly walked through the fire out to the street. He was holding a bottle of tequila, and he was smiling, and there was evil in his eyes.

He paused on the walkway and looked back to the house that was being reduced to ash. He noticed that his shirt was on fire, stripped it off, and tossed it back into the inferno. He took another gulp of tequila, crawled inside a waiting car, and drove off.

The woman stopped dancing. Deadshot, Harley, Croc, and Boomer were staring at him.

"The more power I got on the street, the more firepower I got. Like it went together. The world was mine for the taking. After a minute, no one dared tell me no."

Boomer laughed. "Money. Power. Obedience. Yeah, I can see why you're so damned morose all the time. What a hard-knock life you've led."

"You'd think so," Diablo said, his voice soft, barely above a whisper. "But you know what they say about appearances being deceiving."

His hands ignited again and the flames continued to tell their story. He was in that house before he burned it to the ground. He was sitting at the dinner table, eating breakfast. His wife, Grace, angrily tossed the *LA Times* on the table. Its headline read, "Six Die In Arson Fire."

"Yeah, nobody dared say no to me. Except my lady. She prayed for me. Even when I didn't want it. God didn't give me this. Why should he take it away?"

Grace stared at the newspaper then back at him. She looked deep into his eyes, desperate to find his soul, wondering if there was any good left in him at all.

Then more flames appeared and took on the shape of two children, a boy and a girl, both sitting at the table, both watching their parents. They were laughing and thinking their mother was being funny as she emptied a box filled with money on the table. She tossed thousands of dollars in front of her husband, then brought out another box, this one filled with handguns, and emptied it for their children to see.

"Our kids sleep here!" she shouted at him.

The Squad watched him mouth the words, but it sounded as if she was the one speaking. "What if they found these? This is our home. Whatever you're doing on the street stays on the street."

Diablo let the flames die and he looked at the others. His eyes were empty and lost.

"When I get mad... When I got mad, I lost control. I blacked out, and I never knew what I did. Not until it was done and I woke up." The flames on his hands ignited again. In them, Diablo was standing in front of his wife.

Crying, he reached out to apologize to Grace, but as he held her his body ignited. They were both engulfed in flames. He roared in horror as he held her, unable to let her go. He was screaming to God to protect her, to save her from him, but if God had heard him, he certainly didn't interfere.

He held his wife as she crumbled to ash in his arms. He saw his kids staring at him in horror. He unleashed a howl of utter anguish as his flames filled the room and consumed everything.

Everything.

The flames dancing between his hands looked like the woman trying to run away but then her image disappeared. Diablo had placed his water glass upside down over the flames and watched them fade as the air was used up. He was back in The Golden Tree, staring at what had been his wife. Then he looked at the others. All bad people, he knew, but none of them nearly as bad as he.

"And the kids?" Boomer asked, still in shock, not quite understanding what he'd seen. Diablo's look answered his question.

"You killed them. Didn't you?" Harley said.

Diablo looked at her, his eyes wet and red with grief. "I lost them to my own hands."

Harley leaned close to Diablo and put her hand on his.

"You have to own that stuff," she said emphatically. "Own it."

Diablo looked away.

"I own it with every breath," he finally said.

Harley didn't step away. She leaned in even closer. For a moment the others could see the psychiatrist she had once been.

"What'd you think would happen? You could have a happy family and coach little league and make car payments? Normal's a setting on a dryer. People like us, we don't get normal."

Boomer stared at her. "Why's it a knife fight every time you open your mouth? Outside, you're amazing. Inside, you're… ugly."

"We all are," she said, then turned to Croc. "Except him. He's ugly on the outside, too."

They heard the door open and turned toward it. Flag was entering the bar.

He didn't say a word. He saw Deadshot standing behind the bar and sat down across from him. Deadshot poured him a whiskey. Flag chugged it then put it down for another. Deadshot complied.

There was no pretense here. No bravado. Just weary honesty.

He took another swig then held the shot glass with both hands and stared into it, swirling the amber back and forth.

"Get to the part in that binder saying I was sleeping with her?"

Deadshot nodded. "I did. That's why they come after you, isn't it? Those things. You got a connection with part of her. 'Cause'a that, the witch is scared of you."

Flag took another sip. "The only woman I've ever loved is trapped inside her. If I can wake her up, I can end this. We don't stop the witch, it's over. Everything is over."

"So what's your plan now?"

"Plan? Hell, I'm low on ammo and shooters, but I'm seeing it through. Me and the boys. Who better to die with. My tribe. My family." He stared at his drink, then finished it off.

Deadshot watched Flag put down the glass. There was a spark in his eyes. He had shambled into the Tree looking half dead and praying for the other half to take him, but now he was somehow gathering whatever the hell strength he needed to finish his job.

Lawton recognized that Flag was a very different creature than he. Flag was a soldier. When he was weak, he rallied. A man of honor. Of duty. He stared at his Squad and wondered if any of those things were in their hearts.

Somehow he knew every one of them was wondering the same thing.

Flag pulled the detonator out of his pocket. They panicked as he lightly tapped the screen. A moment later all their arming lights tuned green. Then he twisted the device and broke it into pieces.

"You're free now. Do what you want."

Realization instantly clicked with Boomerang. As fast as he could he ran out of the Tree. Deadshot watched Harkness disappear and shook his head, but he understood where Boomer was coming from.

Every man for himself.

Flag reached into his backpack and set a thick wad

of letters on the bar. They were all addressed to Floyd Lawton. The return address on all of them said they came from Zoe Lawton.

"I was going to give you these anyway, no matter what happened. Might as well do it now." Lawton flipped through the envelopes. "She wrote to you every day, Lawton. Every. Single. Day. The rest are waiting for you at the office."

Deadshot stared at them and crumbled. He clawed at the envelopes, unable to open and read them through his tears. Harley was watching and reached out to grab his arm reassuringly.

Flag finished his drink and turned to leave. Deadshot grabbed him by the vest and spun him around.

"I'm going with you."

The others stared at him.

"I'll get you there and you'll stop this," Deadshot continued, "and it's gonna be like a chapter in the Bible. Everyone's gonna know what we did, and my girl will know her dad... her dad was..."

He didn't need to finish.

Flag reached out and shook his hand, then turned to leave again, the others still watching. One by one they turned to each other. Harley was the first to stand.

"What? Got something better to do?"

FIFTY-NINE

They rejoined the SEALs and made their way a block south to Neon Street, Midway's nightclub district. Parties started every night at one minute before midnight and refused to shut down until just before noon the next day. That nightly ritual ended just three days ago, when the EAs appeared, when the electricity went out and the clubs went dark.

The railway station was one street south. They were prepared to fight for those final yards, no matter what was sent against them.

They saw Boomer heading toward them. He glared, but fell back in line.

"I hate you guys," he said.

"Same here," Deadshot laughed. "Oh. And welcome back."

Flag suppressed a smile. "This is it. Ready or not."

Gripping their weapons tightly, they marched forward.

Together.

The railway station was diagonally across the street, protected behind a barricade of stacked cars and trucks.

Flag gestured for the SEALs to guard the perimeter. They took their positions without another word.

"Something's glowing. Up there," Deadshot said, pointing to an otherworldly light emanating from the station windows.

"Lawton, it's more than just light," Croc said. "Can you feel it?"

"It?"

"The power. Like electricity in the air. Only stronger. It has an almost bitter smell."

"Yeah, whatever's causing that and the light inside, we need to see it."

GQ followed Flag. "If you're putting this up for a vote, Colonel, mine is no. Least not yet."

"Any reason?" Flag asked.

"Our heat sensors are picking up a treasure trove of EAs. We'll be spotted the second we attempt to breach their barricade. I'm suggesting we scope it out, and don't invade until we have the full lay of the land."

"Hey, if we can't go in," Boomer interrupted, "will a visual tour do instead?"

"That would certainly help. How?"

Boomer held up a drone boomerang. "Bluetooth-enabled with a camera you can follow on your smart phones."

Flag was impressed. "Looks to me like it'll work," he said to GQ. "'Sides, it's not like we have a lot of alternatives." He turned to Boomer. "Do it."

Boomerang threw the drone, then punched up the video feed on his phone. "I downloaded the app to your phones, too. You all can watch." The drone silently whooshed toward the railway station roof. Boomerang controlled its pitch and arced it toward one of the shattered glass windows.

"Can you get her inside?" GQ asked.

"This would be a big waste if I couldn't."

The drone hovered and scanned the window's measurements. The first window was too small for it to fit through. It moved over the next one, which proved the right size.

"We got us a bingo," Boomer said. "We can dot the 'I' now."

The drone slipped through the window and glided into the station.

Flag enlarged the video on his cell. "Can you move it over to the right? About forty-five degrees? I think I see something."

"Yeah, mate. I'm seeing it, too." An image of Incubus filled the screen. He was talking to his sister.

"Our big bads," Deadshot said.

Incubus went still for just a moment then he turned and looked at them. Harley watched as he lifted a hand and pointed at the camera.

"Holy pizza," she said. "He sees us. He knows we're watching." Incubus made a flicking movement with his hand and a pulsing tentacle of light shot from his fingers. A moment later the video turned to static, and died. "Something tells me that is *not* a technical error."

Boomer shook his head. "Wish it was, Looney Tunes. But no."

Flag stared at the static-covered screen as if by staring long and hard enough, he would make the video return. But nothing happened.

"Boomer, you got another drone in your coat?"

"Another big fat no, mate."

"Well, that really sucks." Harley blew a gum bubble, then burst it when it was the size of her head. "What do we do now?"

GQ stared at the blank screen, trying to come up with possible alternatives. "Flag, push comes to shove I have only one real idea. It might even work."

"Yeah? What?"

"The demo charge is still in the subway."

Flag shook his head. "No. I thought about that, too, and I ruled it out."

GQ wasn't about to let it go. "Why not? There's a tunnel right under the building. I believe it can take out the big one, if we get in its face and distract it. I can do it."

Flag was adamant. "No. The problem is you only have two seconds once you arm it. Enchantress could have magically transported herself away in time, but you can't. None of us can. It would be a one-way trip."

"I know," GQ said. "I understand, but we literally have no other choice."

"The concept is acceptable. The choice of personnel isn't. I need you with me here. If we do this, you have to choose a man."

GQ wasn't about to let Flag dictate terms to him. "I understand, but I'm not going to ask any of my men to do something like that."

"Then do it by lottery. Give them the chance to be the hero. It doesn't have to be you."

"It means exactly that. None of them have the training I have. Flag, trust me, I went through all the possibilities. Ultimately there's only one choice who can get it done. You're looking at him."

Flag didn't want to give in. Letting him go meant he'd never see GQ alive again, but he also recognized that there was no way GQ would send someone else in his place.

They embraced, and GQ went off to brief his men.

Each one tried to change his mind, each one wanted to take his place, but he overruled them all.

Croc watched from a short distance away as GQ and Kowalski inventoried their explosives. They had hand grenades, 40mm grenades, blocks of C-4, and detcord. Kowalski dumped his ruck and a large magnetic limpet mine fell out. GQ saw it and laughed.

"Seriously, Kowalski? We're not here to sink a Russian destroyer."

Kowalski stared at it. "Huh? Oh, right—that's from my last op."

"Just thought of something," GQ said as he saw Gomez walk past. "Gomez, you, Kowalski, and the others come with me. We passed a sporting goods store about a block back. We're going to need some stuff." He turned back to Kowalski. "And the limpet mine stays here."

"Yes, sir," Kowalski saluted. "It stays here."

The door to the sporting goods shop was locked and its windows were still intact. During the apocalypse, people would break into food, bars, and weapons stores, but baseball gear wouldn't necessarily enter their minds.

GQ kicked down the door, then stepped inside.

"We need scuba tanks, filled, masks, and swim fins."

Kowalski looked confused. "There probably are more expensive things we could loot, sir."

Gomez shook his head. "The subway's flooded, dumbass, but don't trip. I'll pay for it on your card."

* * *

Croc entered the store and found the SEALs. "I'm going with you," he said, not expecting an argument. He wasn't used to dealing with SEALs.

"We got this," GQ said. "I'm sure Flag needs you for something."

"I'm not asking, bruh." Croc stood next to the man, trying to intimidate him. "I live underground. You're just tourists."

"Two things, Scales," the SEAL replied. "One, you're right. You'd be an asset down there. But two, don't stick your face in mine. Try that again and we'll see if a lizard can grow another head."

"My name is Croc. As in crocodile. Not a lizard. Not an alligator. Crocodile."

"And how is that my problem?" GQ said as he pushed past Croc and led his men back to Flag and company.

Croc definitely wasn't used to dealing with Navy SEALs. But he was a fast learner.

SIXTY

The SEALs and the Suicide Squad prepped for their dual assaults.

Flag checked his gear. Harkness inspected each of his boomerangs, gauging them to determine the perfect aerodynamics. A nick here or cut there would throw off their balance and spell the difference between success and death.

Harley checked her magnum, aiming it like a movie detective going against the mob. Done, she twirled the gun and slipped it into its holster.

"Ready when you are, boys," she said, chuckling.

Diablo was on one knee, praying. Katana crouched, going through her daily ritual. She held her sword as if it was a baby, and whispered to it.

"What's up with her?" Boomer asked. "She one of yours or one of ours?"

"Some things are hard to know for sure."

"True that, Flag, but what's her story with the sword? I mean, c'mon, mate. She's yakkin' at it like it's listening."

"The man who killed her husband used that sword," he replied. "His soul is now trapped inside. That's who she's talking to."

"His soul is inside the sword? Right. You do know that makes no sense."

Deadshot was walking past but stopped. "We got a guy with us who makes fires come out of his fingers. You're sure you know the boundaries between sense and nonsense?"

Katana completed her ritual. Boomer turned away.

"Well, you know what they say about the crazy ones?"

Deadshot turned to see Harley blowing more gum bubbles.

"Yeah. I know."

Flag waved for everyone to quiet down. Boomer leaned in to Deadshot and whispered.

"This when we get the big, rousing booyah speech? You know, how we're all a team and crap?" Before Deadshot could answer, Flag started to speak.

"Everyone stay in line. We're bugging out now." He headed out and the others followed. Boomer stared at Deadshot, confused.

"That was the big 'win one for the Gipper' speech?"

"One way or another, it's going to be a short fight," Lawton observed. "Maybe he thought a short speech is all it deserved. 'Sides, we're fighting for our lives. Do we really need a speech to do our best?" Deadshot cocked his wrist magnums and followed the others out.

Boomer stood for a while longer. Then he shrugged and followed.

Everyone dies eventually.

"Pay attention, everyone," Flag said. "Bad as it's been, something tells me it's about to get that much worse. Listen to my instructions and most of us might just survive."

"You're a real cheerleader, Flag," Deadshot said. "Makes us all tingly inside wanting to follow your lead."

"Whatever turns you on," Flag said, smiling.

Wearing the scuba tanks they appropriated from the sporting goods store, GQ and his SEALs swam through the darkness, their mask lights barely piercing the murky water.

Croc didn't require gear or light. He moved on his own through the dark. He found an air pocket at the top of the tunnel, surfaced, took in a deep breath, then plunged back into the water and pressed forward. The body of a drowned man floated in front of him, blocking his way. Nonchalantly, he pushed it aside and swam on.

Flag and the others made their way inside the station. They quickly moved past the fallen soldiers, then headed for the subway platform. Deadshot walked alongside Flag.

"You must really love this girl—and no way you look like the loving kind," he said. "No offense meant."

"I'm not. I always thought love was bullshit." Flag shot Lawton a glance. "Hey, don't look at me like I'm nuts. I'm being serious."

"Yeah, I know," Deadshot said. "Just hard to believe. I mean, you know what kind of person I am, but even I found love."

"She left you."

"Yeah, there is that, but I found it. And it was mine

to lose. Which I did—and that's my point."

"Actually, Lawton, that's *my* point. Love's tenuous. It doesn't last. Hell, I don't think it can last. Look, I get lust, desire, mutual benefit… whatever. But actual love? I rated that with UFOs. Lots of believers, but no proof."

"Then you met June," Deadshot said.

Flag nodded. "Yeah. Then I met June."

They walked another few hundred feet in silence. Then Deadshot turned to Flag, as serious as Flag had ever seen him.

"Well, whatever you have to do, know I got your back."

Flag was taken by surprise. The world was most definitely changing. Faster than he could believe. Faster than he could adapt. But for once, Flag approved of the change.

Hell, he thought. Even while marching into hell Flag realized he was actually happy for once. *Yeah. The changes keep coming. Who'd have ever guessed?*

They quietly moved through a tunnel, ready for whatever the enemy brought to them. Deadshot scanned the place with his monocle. No heat patterns ahead. They were in the clear. They reached the staircase leading up—to where the drone had showed Enchantress was waiting.

June would soon be his again, but Flag wasn't sure what he'd find when he found her. If it was June, he knew he'd have to find a way to prevent Enchantress from ever taking her over again, but if it was the witch, he knew there was no alternative but to go into battle against a woman who would kill them all without a moment of regret.

SIXTY-ONE

Enchantress anxiously paced the hall at the far end of the building. The septagram was behind her, like the one Flag had seen in June's bathroom, mystically floating off the ground, covering the entirety of the back wall. It looked like a mechanical bonfire with rows of gears that brought to mind a hungry, clamorous grinder.

"Okay, so tell me," Harley said as quietly as she was capable of being. "Am I dreaming that thing, or does everyone else see all that trippy magic stuff? I mean, I'm off my meds, so you can't go by me."

"Hell yeah, it's real," Boomer said. "It's like I'm flashing back to my college days, only I was never that high."

"None of it's making any sense," Harley agreed. "And that's coming from me."

Deadshot turned to Flag. "C'mon, man," Lawton said as he pointed to Enchantress, swaying to music only she could hear. "Your girlfriend's there, right? So run up to her. Give her a big kiss and tell her to stop this garbage."

Flag disagreed. "We need to follow the plan we already have. We draw out the big one, and then my guys detonate the bomb under him."

"Yeah, fine, but where is the big guy?"

Enchantress was too busy powering the machine to pay attention as Flag and company moved deeper into the room, searching for Incubus. Then she spoke.

"Colonel Flag, is that you?" she said, her voice a mockery of June's. "Good. I've been waiting all night. You can step out of the shadows now."

Deadshot grabbed Harley's arm before she could do something stupid, and pulled her close to him.

"Stay with me and stay quiet."

"Why are you here?" Enchantress said, feeling their presence even if she couldn't see them. "Is it because the soldier led you here? For Waller? But, boys—and I include you too, Harley Quinn—why do you serve those who cage you? I am your ally, and I know what you want.

"Exactly what you want."

Wind and white light exploded suddenly in the room.

They are lost in timeless white space, and they are overwhelmed by it.

Deadshot is surrounded by the white. He feels his arm being tugged. He looks down and sees Zoe trying to pull him away. He looks up again and he is on a sidewalk in Gotham City. It is still night.

He smiles at her, confused, but the feeling of love is rushing through him.

"Zoe? But how did we get here?"

"C'mon, Daddy," Zoe says, tugging at him. "We have to go. Before he comes."

"Who?"

Suddenly, a dark-gloved hand grabs his shoulder.
Batman.

Batman tries to pull him away from Zoe, but Deadshot launches himself at his attacker, punching him in the face, sending him staggering back. The Bat, frightened, starts to turn. Deadshot activates his wrist magnums and fires them. Batman falls to the ground, shot between the eyes with a hollow-point.

"Daddy," Zoe cries out. She is staring at her father. Bewildered, he sweeps her up in his arms and they run.

Harley Quinn's vision blurs from the white blast.

She rubs the light from her eyes and realizes she is dressed in purple sweats. One baby is attached to her hip while a toddler holds onto her leg.

The kitchen is something to behold, with large, colorful appliances ready to perform any task a modern woman can possibly need. She stirs the oatmeal on the gas stove while she texts her daycare providers. Harley Quinn is a busy mom.

Actually, her name is now Harley Ker. She embroidered it on a lovely cross-stitch sampler. She sees her loving husband, Jo, enter the room amidst wild applause and great laughter. He is dressed in a natty purple business suit, just the article of clothing necessary for a busy exec.

Harley immediately has a glass of freshly squeezed orange juice in her hand. The oranges come from their backyard garden. Jo Ker checks his smart phone calendar.

"Honey, what's for dinner tonight? I'll pick up some wine on the way home."

Harley shivers in anticipation. "I'll make your favorite potato knishes. Good luck, honey."

"I don't need luck, honey. Not when I've got you."

Harley stands on the tip of her toes and kisses him. Jo starts to leave, but stops as he remembers to take his tablet. He scoops it up and exits. Grinning ear to ear, Harley holds herself and giggles.

What a great life.

Rick Flag is fast asleep in the California king as the dreams begin. Suddenly, he screams and starts to grunt and throw wild punches.

"Rick. Honey. Rick," June says, worried as she tries to shake her husband awake. "Wake up. Please wake up."

Flag draws in a deep gasp and looks around, confused. June cradles him like he is a child.

"It's okay, honey. You're here. You're with me." Flag stares at her as the world begins to make some sense. "You were having a bad dream."

"Just a dream?" he asks. "It was so real."

He reaches up and sweetly brushes the back of his hand across her face. He loves her and is forever grateful she loves him back.

Digger Harkness sits cross-legged in the outback, his hands on his knees. His eyes are closed. He is listening to the sounds of the night, feeling that same sense of serenity he had experienced when he was all of fourteen. That spiritual walkabout took him nearly four months to complete, and once he returned home he thought he could hold onto that wonderful peace and it would guide him into adulthood.

His life since then has been harsh and violent, and he decides, finally, to do something about it.

He opens his eyes and looks behind him, to the fire he built. Hundreds of his boomerangs are on fire, roasting inside the inferno, blackening the weapons he once held so dear, turning them into soft, crumbling ash.

"No more death," he says to himself. "Never again." He closes his eyes and accepts the night. This time, perhaps, life will not be so cruel.

The TV is droning on and on but Diablo has stopped watching and listening. He doesn't need to be entertained. All he cares about is nestling with his kids who are sleeping on the couch next to him.

They are both so beautiful and so innocent and he loves them more than he ever thought he could love anyone.

Grace enters the TV room and sets a beer on the coffee table next to him. She looks at her sleeping kids and smiles at him. She is so proud of them, and so happy to be with him.

"Help me put them to bed?"

He stares at her and then the kids. Something is wrong, and he's not quite certain why.

"Babe, what is it?" she asks him. "You look, dare I say it, troubled?"

He keeps staring at her. He gets up and steam begins to bubble up from his skin. The wallpaper behind him blisters from the heat. He looks down at the table and the beer is boiling.

"You're scaring me," Grace says, reaching to pull the kids away.

Diablo stares at her and screams.

"I can't change what I did, and neither can you."

The whiteness dissolved, replaced by harsh reality.

"What the hell happened?" Harley asked. The others looked like they were all coming out of the same trance.

Diablo knew better, though. He had broken free on his own. He accepted the truth of what he was, and he never tried to hide from it.

"It's not real," he shouted. "No matter how good it felt, you don't want it. We shouldn't have it."

Harley crouched, her face hidden behind her hands.

"Speak for yourself, Torchy. You shoulda seen my place. It coulda been the life."

"No," Diablo said. "Whatever you saw belonged to another. Before your path changed. Even if you were to change, and fully embrace it, that way is gone. You would have to build a different road." He stepped from the shadows.

The others joined him. They saw Enchantress stare at them, intrigued that her illusion had been so easily pierced.

"How long have you been able to see, Fire Man?"

"My whole life," Diablo said. "Look, lady, they're with me. You can't have them."

Enchantress laughed and smiled at him.

"But it is our time. The sun is setting and magic is rising. The metahumans are but the first sign of the change, my friend."

Diablo stepped closer, not at all intimidated by her power.

"I'm not your friend. I know what you are, and like

me, you're not supposed to be here."

Enchantress frowned at his insolence. "Stop talking," she ordered. "This should be simple. Are we friends or are we foes? And remember, we are not the ones who caged you."

Deadshot stared. She was the face of the enemy and there was no way they would ever stand side by side.

"I'm a bad guy, yeah, but you, lady, you want to destroy my world," he said. "You are evil."

The others stood beside him. They were together in this.

Enchantress glanced up to the window. There was a glowing light in the distance.

"Brother, you were right. The pets won't turn on their masters. So go ahead. Break their necks, but try not to disturb me. The machine requires my full attention now." She turned back to finish working on her machine as Incubus appeared.

"You do what you need to, sister. I will destroy our enemies."

"You are a dear, brother," she replied, and she smiled. "Have fun."

He marched to the colonnade, his magic armor fanning like a cobra hood. "I've been waiting for this for so very long." His eyes glowed. A tentacle shot from his hands and slammed into the stone column, shattering it.

Flag hit his comm and screamed into it.

"GQ. You in position? GQ? Copy."

They waited, but they heard nothing. Deadshot looked at Flag and shrugged.

"Your plan sucks. Just saying it."

"Guys," Harley shouted. "The big kahuna's doing it again. Just letting you know."

Incubus was powering up.

SIXTY-TWO

GQ was dressed in neoprene from head to toe, but he was still freezing as he swam through the flooded subway tunnels. His hood was firmly in place and he checked the collar of his wetsuit for leaks.

He felt cold splash against his neck. It was virtually impossible to create a perfect closure, but after nine years as a Navy SEAL, he was pretty sure he could deal with it.

The other SEALs followed behind. Gomez tapped his foot and pointed to the right. A half-dozen EAs were speeding toward them, knives held in crusted gnarled hands. The SEALs pulled out their own, and prepared for the fight.

Blades hacked and slashed, cutting through the neoprene. Through flesh. Through crusted skin and twisted bone.

GQ jerked back as an assailant's knife tried to slice through his air line. He twisted until he was able to thrust his own blade up into the thing's throat, lodging into its neck bone. GQ sawed the blade until he was able to yank it free, and watched as the EA fell back and floated off in a fountain of red.

Gomez wrestled with two EAs. GQ turned to assist,

but before he could, one of the creatures thrust its knife into the soldier's heart. His friend was dead before he could swim to help him.

Kowalski was fending off an attack. An EA clawed at his face, then ripped through his regulator. Streams of compressed air exploded from the hacked tube. The SEAL kept fighting, even as he ran out of air. Finally he went limp.

GQ dived at the thing that killed Kowalski, and stabbed it through its neck. In another time it might have been one of his men, someone he'd fight to protect, but that person was gone, and he desperately wanted to make certain his friends' memories wouldn't be sullied.

He cut at the creature, sawed through flesh and cartilage until its head fell from its neck and sank to the subway tracks below.

He was gasping for more air than his regulator would permit and he struggled to control his breathing. He closed his eyes and took long, steady, calming breaths. When he opened them again, he was alone, surrounded by broken combatants.

He wanted to swim to his men and carry their bodies back to the surface, but he knew that wasn't going to happen. Now, or ever. The demo charge was still waiting for him, and if fortune was on their side, the blast would be powerful enough to destroy Incubus.

Which meant it would kill him, too.

SIXTY-THREE

Enchantress glanced up from the machine to watch Incubus, calmly firing his deadly energy at Flag and his Squad. His smile warmed her. He enjoyed playing with these children, firing his bolts closer and closer, but not yet hitting them. He'd kill them soon enough, but first he wanted to have some fun.

He'd been asleep for so long.

"Brother, enjoy yourself, but can you please be a bit quieter?" Enchantress asked. "This is a delicate instrument. I need to test it without you rattling the rafters. Maybe you should just kill them and be done with it."

Incubus disagreed. "The humans no longer worship us as they once did. They even believe we are not gods. Sister, they have to pay for their affronts."

"Fine," she replied. "Hunt them down and torture them if it will make you happy—but for now, do it quietly."

Incubus prepared to fire another tendril, but then decided not to. He was powerful enough that he didn't need mystical incantations to destroy them. What he wanted now was a little physical exercise.

Enchantress stepped back and admired her machine.

Giant black gears snapped into place, increasing the energy that fed the machine.

"It's my turn now, brother. I am the power that empowers my machine. My life gives it its strength. Watch me and rejoice." She smiled, then dropped her arms.

The machine opened its maw and swallowed its black smoke. Its gears kept turning and grinding and convulsing. Then, magical energy erupted from the machine and blew an outsized hole through the station roof.

"Brother, it has begun," she cried. "This world will again be ours." Bolts of lightning crackled through the shattered roof, angled toward the ring of street debris orbiting the station. Hurricane winds slammed the train station. They were now in the eye of a super storm.

Enchantress's machine was a long-range weapons system, powered not by electricity, but by magic that had been forgotten millennia ago. Magic the modern world could no longer combat.

GQ swam to the surface and pulled himself up to the platform. He keyed in his comm.

"Rick? You up?"

Flag's voice was loud and clear. "Yeah. We're inside. You in position?"

"Negative," GQ answered. "They're down here. My guys are gone."

"Hell. I'm sorry, man, but you gotta get to the southeast corner. We'll drive him to you. Make it happen."

"You got it, Flag. Take care."

"Yeah. My thoughts are with you. Hell, the thoughts

of everyone here are with you."

GQ slipped his comm back into its case. *This is happening now. If it works, it'll soon be over.* He hesitated a moment longer, then he took a deep breath and moved on. If he wanted to help save the world, he didn't have any other choice. This was exactly what he had signed on for.

There was a heavy, thudding noise coming from behind him. Something was moving through the flooded tunnel.

Dammit. No. Not more of those monsters. His strength was mostly gone and he wasn't sure he could fight anything else. He reached for his pistol and turned to face them. If he had to die he'd take out as many as he could.

A big hand grabbed him at his wrist. He felt its scales cut into him.

Croc.

GQ looked at him and opened fire. Not at Croc but at the EA surfacing behind him, shredding it. So many shots that his pistol was hot.

Croc pulled himself out of the water and looked at the corpse floating into the tunnel.

"Who else is dead?" Croc asked.

"I'm all that's left. And you."

"Sorry about that, man. This is all bad. Real bad."

"You don't have to tell me, but I'm glad you're here. Can you help get me down this tunnel?"

"Follow me," Croc answered. "And I'm glad you made it, too. C'mon." He dived back into the tunnel. GQ followed. He wasn't sure when his reality changed, but Croc had somehow become his brother-in-arms, and he was damn happy about it.

SIXTY-FOUR

Diablo was in pain. His family was dead and nobody could bring them back. They'd never know if he was good or bad. They'd never know if he tried to save the world or condemned it to its own slow, painful death.

Deadshot was wrong. This wasn't on them. This was on him. His wife and kids would never know what he did, and they'd never care—but he knew they'd want him to prove to himself that he wasn't just the monster who slaughtered the only people who ever loved him.

He had to prove to himself that he was worth their love. Diablo looked at Deadshot and nodded.

"Thanks, brother. I got this." He stepped into the light and walked up behind Incubus. "Hey, fool. You lookin' for me? Well, I'm over here. So let's do this."

Incubus turned to face him. "You are right, burning man," he said. "Let's do this."

Diablo's arm shot out and whipped a blast of fire into Incubus's face.

"That the best you have?" Incubus said, shrugging it off, grinning at his opponent. His armor rippled and dispersed the heat. "You are trying to fight a god, but there is no way you can survive, let alone be victorious."

Incubus suddenly lunged and slammed Diablo into the station wall. The impact blinded him with pain. He yelped then slipped to the ground, unconscious.

Their most powerful warrior was downed even before he could throw the first punch.

"Well," Harley said, looking lost and frightened. "No way that went well."

Incubus turned to the others and gestured for them to come at him. He now had more toys with which to play, and he couldn't wait. The battle was just beginning.

GQ was almost in position. He glanced to his side and saw Croc swimming next to him. Somehow it gave him the confidence to go on, and yet when he thought about it, SEAL and monster made for a crazy pairing.

He'd gotten used to the scales and spikes, but he still laughed at the crazy villain name and the wild images it conjured in his mind. For some reason super-villains adopted bizarre code names like Croc. Deadshot. Boomerang. Then again, the heroes did, too.

What was wrong with using real names? Maybe Tom, Dick, or Harry simply weren't awe-inspiring for the heroes, or frightening enough for their foes. Either way, it was a strange custom, and stranger still to be thinking about it now.

GQ tried to remember if Croc had a real name. He was sure he saw it in the briefing book they gave him to read in the chopper on their way to Midway City. C'mon. What was it again? Then he remembered.

Jones. Croc's real name was Waylon Jones, and he had been born with a strain of atavism that toughened his skin into spikes and ridges, turning him into a human reptile. Edwards could only imagine what it must have been like, growing up a monster in a world that feared anything that was even slightly different. It didn't excuse all the horror Croc had caused, but he could understand how that could warp a man, even turn him against the rest of mankind. They were, after all, the ones who looked at him with disgust and revulsion.

GQ was suddenly ashamed that he had thought the same thing. When they first met, he wouldn't have believed they would one day fight as allies, but now he couldn't think of a soldier he'd rather fight beside. Whatever Jones might have done in the past—and Croc's rap sheet was disturbingly long and twisted— he proved himself now, when the world needed him the most.

Edwards looked up ahead, and saw a light in the distance. They were close to where Enchantress had tossed the explosive. Just a few more seconds to get into position, he thought, then it would almost be over.

He sliced through the water. Croc was pulling ahead. Then he felt something brush past his leg.

Suddenly one of the creatures grabbed him. GQ tamped his panic and kicked at the thing, but it stubbornly held onto his leg. He slammed it again, smashing his foot into the thing's face, cracking it open.

Still, the EA didn't let go. It pulled itself up over GQ and reached for his face. As it did, Croc grabbed it and tore it off the SEAL. The EA turned to fight its new enemy, but Croc bear-hugged it and ripped its chest open, releasing everything that was inside.

Croc was ready to pull its head off, but the thing was already dead. He let it go and it floated away into the murk.

SIXTY-FIVE

More than four thousand years ago, Incubus stood side by side with his sister against vast armies of trained warriors who swore they would destroy the two gods. Those warriors were now dead, while brother and sister stood strong, and more powerful than ever.

Now, as then, Incubus had to laugh at the pitiful humans who thought they would succeed where thousands before them had failed. They had no idea what they were fighting. Gods were meant to rule, and if he had to destroy all who challenged him to get those few who lived to serve his needs, he would.

His sister was wasting her time, doing whatever she was planning with those arcane machines. As he had repeatedly told her, they didn't need machines to force the humans to their knees. They didn't need anything but the natural powers they were born with.

Yet she let him have his fun. How could he not do the same for her? So Incubus held out his hands, both glowing with unbridled energy. Beams of light sizzled from his fingertips.

Amused, he watched the humans scatter as the beams smashed into the ground and ripped up the station platform. He enjoyed watching them run, like little mice in a maze, somehow believing they were the dominant species on Earth. It was so amazing, he thought. Humans hadn't changed in all the thousands of years he'd known them. The sheep were still as stubbornly ignorant as ever, and he wasn't sure they would ever accept their rightful place as faithful, mindless servants.

That was the best they could hope to achieve. *So be it*, he thought. It was time to destroy them. It was now time for the *real* fun to begin.

Diablo, having regained his senses, attacked with a geyser of flame while Harley fired her guns. As soon as she used up one mag, she slammed in another and kept up the attack. Incubus shrugged off these assaults.

They were little more than harmless diversions.

When Floyd Lawton joined this little coffee klatch, he'd fully expected he'd use his time either to plot his escape, or find a way to permanently end both Flag and Waller.

Somehow, between then and now, things had changed.

Sure, Flag acted like a jerk for far longer than he should have, but at some point in time Lawton realized that Colonel Stick-Up-His-Ass actually respected him. No way they'd ever play on the same rec league bowling team, but surprising as it was, they were able to work together. His talents were finally being used for something more important than just adding to his bank account. In the past, he'd never much cared what job he took. Long as it paid, a target was a target, and he never missed.

Katana was ready to fight. "Slice and dice," Lawton shouted to her, laughing. Crouching next to her, Boomer launched his boomerangs at Incubus. There were two detonations as they slammed into his face and exploded.

Incubus stumbled back and roared, but quickly shook off the momentary pain and attacked again. Flag called to Deadshot and Diablo. GQ and Croc were almost in place. It was their turn now.

"Get him into the corner. That's where the bomb's gonna be."

Incubus saw Boomer about to launch another explosive 'rang at him. He stepped back, breathed in deeply, and concentrated, forming a smoky tendril.

But Katana jumped at the giant and brought her sword down hard on his arm, slicing his hand off at the wrist. He fell back as his half-formed tendril shook and disappeared, smoky wisps dissipating into the air.

"You will suffer for that," he shouted as he launched yet another tendril at Katana.

Incubus held out his bloodied wrist, pain etched across his face. He closed his eyes and screamed as the shattered stump of bone and flesh seemed to glow and extend, building a new forearm. Regenerating a new wrist. A new hand.

As he flexed his fingers, pleased to see he could still control them, Incubus turned to Deadshot and smiled. "The woman did that to me, but you commanded her," he roared. "So you will die first, then I will take my time and kill her, too. It will be a wonderful, agonizing death. Then, when you are all dead, the rest of humanity, with no one left to fight for them, will follow."

The giant lunged for Lawton and slammed him in the chest. Deadshot helplessly skidded across the floor and crashed into a wall. Incubus stalked toward him, his hands beginning to glow again with renewed energy.

Suddenly Harley jumped onto his back, and rode him like a bucking bronco. Her fingers clawed into his neck as she tried to strangle him.

"Have fun trying to breathe, gruesome."

He stood up and shrugged her off. He then picked her up by the head and casually flipped her across the tracks.

"I'll come back for you soon enough, little girl," he said, "I have priorities, and you are low on the list."

Boomerang tried to pull Deadshot to safety. Incubus shook his head, then grabbed the Aussie and held him high so he could look the man in his eyes.

"Do you really want to fight me before I've slaughtered Flag? If so, I will be more than happy to oblige." He tossed him off the platform, and watched him bounce onto the tracks.

He turned again to Deadshot, still on the ground, weak and leaning against a station column. His face was smeared with blood, and it looked as if he'd been dead for at least a week. Weak as he was, however, he raised his arms and aimed his wrist magnums, already set to full auto.

Incubus grinned and leapt.

"When are you humans ever going to learn?"

"Never," Deadshot cried. Suddenly his emergency Glocks appeared in his hands and he fired all four weapons into Incubus's face. The bullets vaporized with bright flares as they tried to penetrate his armor. Incubus watched them disappear and again laughed at his target.

"And this is why your worthless race will soon be extinct."

SIXTY-SIX

Sprawled on the ground, Deadshot scanned the station, searching for a place to hide until he could recover. A maintenance door was about twenty yards south. He didn't know if he had the strength to drag himself there, but he also knew he couldn't give up.

Only twenty yards. He grabbed a fallen drainpipe and pulled himself up to his feet. *I can do this. I have to do this.*

Diablo turned to Flag, angry and determined.

"I'll do it," he said. "I'll get him there. I lost one family. I'm not losing another."

Flag understood, but he wasn't ready to lose another man.

"Don't."

Diablo grinned, his smile frightening.

"You ain't seen what I can really do," he said. "An', Flag?"

"Yeah?"

"You're one real son of a bitch... but thanks. Thank you." With that Diablo closed his eyes and concentrated. He had fought against his power for so long, but now he needed to embrace it. He began counting down to himself.

Leaning against the station wall for support, Deadshot slowly took a step. Then another... and another. He stifled a cry as he felt a sudden, harsh pain stab him in the side. He fell back against the wall, took several long breaths, then started again. He felt heat coming from somewhere, but he couldn't tell where.

Fifteen yards. I will do this. No matter what.

His first steps hurt like hell, but then the pain seemed to fade as if each step shoved his bones back into position. He let go of the wall and picked up his pace. *Ten yards. Only ten yards.* He made it to the maintenance door and reached to open it.

"You have to know you can't escape me." Incubus towered over him. "But I did enjoy watching your efforts." The god's hands glowed with rippling energy and he reached for Deadshot.

Then a voice came from behind the giant.

"Hey, you. Over there! Leave him alone."

Diablo stood tall, arms spread wide, hands open, fingers splayed. Then he floated up from the ground, levitating as if he was some kind of deity, too.

Incubus stared.

"I said, get away from him." Diablo was raging, nearly out of control. He wanted to hurt. He needed to kill. All his years of anger and pain boiled out of him and formed into a huge fiery skeleton, at least as tall as Incubus.

Without another thought, he lunged for the god and slammed him away.

"They are my friends," he shouted as he whipped a jet-engine blast of fire into Incubus's face. "I will not let you harm them."

Incubus shrugged it off. His iridescent armor rippled as it dispersed Diablo's attack. He unleashed another tendril, which struck Diablo, blasting him back across the train station.

But Diablo stood, surrounded by a huge skeleton of fire that formed around him. Harley Quinn stared at the giant and laughed.

"Way to go. We got us a Mega Diablo!"

They all stared as Diablo lunged at Incubus again, and thrust his fiery hands into Incubus's face, exploding the false god's flesh. Again and again Diablo slammed his burning fist into Incubus.

"We're running out of time. Drive him into the corner," Flag shouted. "Do it now."

Diablo leaped at Incubus, forcing him back toward the corner. But the god fought back, resisting.

Harley stared at the burning giant, then rubbed her eyes to clear away what was obviously a fever dream. When she opened them again, nothing had changed. Diablo and Incubus were fighting a war normal humans could never hope to understand.

"Now I get it," she said. "Why he doesn't let himself get angry."

Boomer rushed back to Deadshot's side and pulled him to safety. Lawton looked at him and laughed.

"See, if you're nice to people, they'll turn into fire skeletons and fight giant glowing man-gods."

Boomer grinned back at him. "Right. Point taken."

Showing fear, Incubus held his arms up to block

Diablo's repeated attacks. His attempts to counter Diablo's blows were clumsy, showing that he had never really faced anyone who he had actually had to fight. He had always ordered others to do whatever he needed done.

Diablo kept hitting him. Again and again, burning through his armor, then digging his fingers into its metal, forcing a gap just large enough to shove his fists inside and ignite the so-called god from within.

During it all, Diablo never stopped screaming.

GQ surfaced, and pulled himself onto the platform. He balanced the nanite demolition charge and reprogrammed the detonator, then yanked the safety ring. There was no going back now.

"Rick," he said into his comm link. "Standing by. I'm in position."

SIXTY-SEVEN

Incubus howled in pain. His arms flailed wildly, hammering at his assailant, desperate to keep him from forcing even more fire under his armor. Diablo had melted its outer layers and was now burning into Incubus's flesh.

"GQ's in place," Flag shouted. "Drive him into the corner." Diablo allowed himself a rare smile as he shouldered Incubus toward the corner.

"Our god burns, Colonel," he said. "And I am ready." Then success lessened his rage, and his power diminished with it.

Deadshot called out to Flag.

"D's losing steam. Now would be a good time."

"No, I need him to be directly over the bomb. We can't take the chance that he'll survive. Diablo, I know you're weakening, but I need you to keep pushing. Just a few more inches, man. You can do it."

Bellowing, Diablo again lunged for the giant. They both tumbled back, into the corner, directly over the SEAL and his explosives.

"Stand by, GQ," Flag said. "Almost..."

Diablo's fires were slowly fading, but he didn't back down. Realization appeared on Incubus's face, and the god fought furiously to escape.

"Diablo, get out of there. It's time to ankle," Flag said. "GQ, on my order!" he bellowed into the comm. Diablo's fire skeleton dissipated, yet he refused to let go.

"I said get outta there," Flag shouted. "*Get clear*."

"Flag. I can't let him go." Diablo was still caged in flame as the two combatants returned to their normal sizes. "I'm losing strength, man. Blow the bomb. Do it now."

Harley looked to Flag. "He's going to die saving us?"

"Not just us. The world."

Everyone was in place. There could be no more delays. Reluctantly, Flag spoke into his comm. "GQ. Diablo. The world owes you both."

Time had run out.

"GQ," Flag said. "Now."

Directly below Diablo and Incubus, in the dark, flooded tunnels, GQ held his breath, then pulled the pin.

He closed his eyes and smiled.

The world would be safe.

The platform floor erupted in a succession of massive underground explosions, geysering brick and water, obliterating the main tunnel and the other passageways connected to it. Flames crawled up the walls then hung from the tiled ceiling. The fire was everywhere.

There was a ball of fire, as Incubus's mortal form shattered into an uncountable number of pieces, like soft chunks of amber.

Then inexplicable consciousness, as he peered

through his own eyes again. Although there was no sound, he knew he was screaming.

For a moment there was motion.

In that instant, Incubus knew his screaming would continue throughout eternity.

Flag and the others were lost in the horror.

GQ was gone. The SEAL had sacrificed himself, which was what they had been trained to do. GQ was a hero, and the whole world would know that. But Croc and Diablo—men Flag once thought were little more than barbaric murderers—had also died. Died saving the lives of all his friends. Perhaps saving the planet itself.

Deadshot reached out and put a hand on his shoulder.

"You had no choice."

"I know. Doesn't make it any easier. Lost three men. Three damn good men."

Deadshot nodded. "The best."

Katana saw Incubus's head lying alone and looking lost on the station floor, a faint glimmer of life somehow still sparking in his eyes. He was looking up at her, his fight not yet gone.

She stared at the head, fractured and bloody, then plunged her sword into the former god. He howled, writhing, as it painfully wrenched free his soul.

The Soultaker was satisfied.

It was over.

Enchantress shuddered in pain. She felt her brother's death, and it hurt as nothing else ever had before.

"What have you done?" she shrieked as she

appeared on the platform. She pushed past the Squad and saw her brother's body, dead and dismembered. "This can't be." She looked up at the others, eyes red with hate. "This is a lie. You're making me see a lie."

But she knew it was her brother, and that he was dead.

Murdered by her enemies.

Her head pounded and her eyes felt like drills had been taken to them. She whirled, raging, toward Flag and his Squad, but she could barely see them through the unrelenting, hammering pain. Her legs gave out and she sank to her knees.

"Brother!" she screamed.

Her shrieks became hurricane winds which battered the Squad. They watched helplessly as the powerful gale blew the weapons from their hands. Boomerangs, Magnums, Glocks, even the Soultaker disappeared into the storm.

Enchantress began to exact her revenge.

A pulse of coruscating, multi-colored energy washed over them, and they saw the witch as a prismatic, other-dimensional vision—not at all real, but still deadly and frightening.

Deadshot shouted at her.

"You're next," he screamed, but she only laughed.

"My spell is complete," she replied. "Once your armies are gone, my darkness will spread across your world, and it will be mine to rule."

Her machine pulsated, blasting wind and rain into the rail station. Dark, magic clouds surged with increasing power as the weapons fired, pulling scraps of metal from the ring into the main column, its lightning infusing with molten metal.

A vortex of magic clouds spread, crackling bolts of

lightning launched toward their targets, destroying everything they touched.

The Very Important People filed into the White House situation room and took their assigned seats. Tolliver looked to the others. They were in full crisis mode, and he knew it was only going to get worse.

He sat and stared at the video displays.

In space, a classified satellite exploded, shredded by bolts of magic energy. Planetside, secret military installations vaporized in the terrifying barrage of magic.

Either Incubus or Enchantress was behind its destruction. Admiral Olsen, seated next to Tolliver, scrolled through a report on his phone, and leaned over.

"That was our main satellite facility," he whispered. "Worldwide military comms are down. We're fighting blind." He shook his head. "It was a secret facility. How the hell did the witch know to hit it? Hell. Most of you didn't even know where it was."

"Damned if I know, but this is bad." Tolliver rubbed the exhaustion from his eyes and sat back in his chair. "This is real bad."

Waller screamed.

She hung upside down as black tendrils burrowed into her ears, nose, and mouth, siphoning her thoughts and knowledge, stealing all the secrets from her mind. She was unable to resist.

Enchantress shrugged off the tendrils attached to her, connecting her to her machine, and she began to change, reverting to her feral self—the creature June Moone had found hidden away in that cave.

A thing of evil.

Deadshot tried to wipe the shock from his eyes.

"Yo, Flag," he shouted over the din. "Your girlfriend needs a shower."

Boomer laughed. "More like an exorcist."

Flag stared at this thing that had taken over June. He wanted to destroy the witch then and there but knew it wasn't time. Not yet.

"If we can get her heart back, we got a chance."

"Her heart?" Harley echoed, confused. Then she brightened. "Oh, right. Bitch Hazel's got her heart stuck in a revolving door. Cool. Sick, but cool."

"So you're saying we attack?" Boomer said. "We keep fighting? Without our two strongest fighters? The matchstick and the alligator?"

"Crocodile," Harley whispered under her breath. "Not alligator. Crocodile. Like his stupid name."

"Yeah," Flag said.

Boomer shook his head. "You know that's suicide?"

"Like Lawton said," Flag replied. "That's in our name."

"Well, when you put it that way."

Weapons ready, the Squad spread out. Boomer held two explosive 'rangs. Katana recovered her Soultaker. Deadshot clicked off the safeties on his wrist magnums. Flag loaded a new magazine into his pistols.

Harley snapped her gum, grinned a big smile, and charged.

Then Enchantress disappeared.

"Guess she's scared of us, huh?" Harley laughed, blowing another large gum bubble.

Enchantress reappeared next to Deadshot. She

grabbed him by the throat then tossed him aside, into Flag. Katana lunged, but once again Enchantress disappeared.

They turned, waiting.

Seconds passed.

Still nothing…

Then Flag saw her appear behind him. He whirled, firing, but the bullets went through her as if she wasn't there. She grabbed him, again by the throat, and slammed him back into the station wall. He fell to the ground moaning in pain.

Deadshot fired, but she disappeared yet again. Five seconds passed.

Ten seconds.

Then she was back again, just inches away from Lawton, manifesting two large swords in her hands. She sliced down with them, but Lawton was already moving, sidestepping out of their path.

She fell back and pivoted, kicking Deadshot in the chest. He spun as she slid closer for another attack, and slammed Boomer to the ground.

Suddenly Katana was behind her, the Soultaker held high over her head, ready to slam down. Enchantress held up a hand, magically blocking the sword without even looking, then sent a bolt of fractal energy into the warrior, blasting her back.

She reached for Flag, sprawled on the ground, but Harley stood in her way, grinning happily and wielding the bat with anticipation. With barely a thought, Enchantress flicked her hands, magically throwing her aside. Harley pulled herself back to her feet, laughed, and attacked again.

Enchantress swung her sword but Harley dropped to the ground, the blade slicing the air just above her.

Deadshot and Flag shot continuously at Enchantress. She turned to meet each threat, but when she reached out to grab Boomer, Harley's bat connected with the back of her head, knocking her to her knees.

"Sorry?" Harley said.

Enchantress kicked her, sending her flying, then spun to face Flag. She brought her swords down on him, but Deadshot blocked the blades with his wrist magnums. She looked at Flag, grinning, blew a fake kiss, and disappeared again.

In the White House situation room, Tolliver and the others were rooted to their seats, watching as fractal energy beams slashed toward the ocean, blasting apart an aircraft carrier, killing all on board.

"We gotta put a nuke down on that witch right now."

They all agreed, but there was only one question. How?

The Squad was off balance. Where would she appear? Behind them? To the side? Alone? With an army of those thousand-eyed EAs?

Then she was there.

Behind Deadshot. Ready to slice off his head.

Boomer threw his 'rangs, knocking her sword from her hands. She turned toward him and manifested two more blades.

"Not nearly good enough to take me out, Aussie," she said. "So c'mon. Let's end this here and now."

SIXTY-EIGHT

The tunnel below the station had caved in when the explosion took out GQ and Diablo. Mountains of stone, tiled walls, and twisted track filled the narrow spaces. It would take months to clear it all out, and perhaps years to rebuild it, bringing Midway City transit back to its original level of disrepair.

For a very long time nothing moved.

Until a scaled hand pushed up through the stone, smashing aside rock and bent steel. Croc had survived the explosion but had been buried beneath the mountain of debris.

He could hear his friends fighting on the platform above. He was sure the explosion killed the false man-god, Incubus. So they were fighting the real threat. Enchantress.

As he pulled himself free from the pile and made his way back to the surface, Croc wondered how Flag was dealing with having to give orders to kill the woman he obviously loved. He smiled. If any bastard could be that heartless and cold, it was Flag. Good thing they were on the same side.

* * *

Enchantress watched the bugs as they scrambled about, forever failing to jury-rig yet another way to stop her. There was no doubt in her mind—they were going to fail. They were savages, too ignorant to understand their destiny.

They had only been able to kill Incubus because her brother was weak. He had been ready to let the humans have their world, while the two of them went off to live elsewhere.

She looked at the septagram, its machine fueled with a mystical energy. Giving her more power. The machine itself was spinning faster, as well, thundering with ferocious energies. The bugs could not survive.

A storm materialized. Rain blew sideways with unnatural intensity. The machine's gears ground with staggering torque. Whatever the humans came up with now, they were too late. The sky overhead turned black, punctuated by flashes of lightning that allowed the world to witness her glory.

As Enchantress reveled in her own wonderment, she sensed Katana behind her, ready to slice down on her. Barely recognizing the human's existence, she simply waved the sword away, flinging it out of Katana's hand. Then she turned back to Boomerang and threw a bolt at him.

He ducked and spun, throwing two explosive 'rangs at her. They detonated and she fell back. He threw another 'rang, but Enchantress waved her hand and it harmlessly exploded in mid-air. She grabbed him and pushed him to the ground, then raised her sword high.

"Your sword girl intended to cut me in half," she hissed. "Let's first try that on you." She started to bring down her sword, when her arm was suddenly grabbed by a powerful, scaly hand.

Croc. He looked down at her, his eyes glistening. His mouth twisted into a grim sneer.

"You're dead," she cried.

"I got better."

He snapped his arm and sent her hurtling toward the station wall. She disappeared just before hitting it.

"Hey," Harley called out. "You a ghost 'gator or the real thing?"

"Not a ghost, Quinn—and still not an alligator."

"That's your problem. Not mine," she replied. "But welcome back an' all that crap."

"You missed me?"

"If you mean I missed having a monster to wise off to, yeah."

"Yeah. Missed you, too, punky." He looked around him. "The witch's gone. Now what, Flag?"

"She has a nasty way of showing up when you least expect it. Keep on the alert."

"I smashed her once. Next time I'll rip her in half."

Harley laughed. "That I gotta see. Hell, I'll pay good money for a front-row seat."

"You're gonna have your chance, mates," Boomer shouted. "Behind you."

Suddenly she was on the platform, crouching in the light. Her machine was behind her, spewing water and wind. The Squad readied their weapons.

"On my command," Flag said. "We're not taking prisoners."

But then Harley stepped in front of them.

"Hey. C'mon, guys. Knock it off. I mean, what are we doing? Aren't we supposed to be heroes or something? You're talking cold-blooded murder."

"Out of our way, Quinn," Flag shouted. "She intends to destroy the world."

Harley glared at Flag as if he was speaking in Martian.

"Oh, jeez. Who cares about the world? What's the world ever done for us? C'mon. You know it better'n anyone. The world hates us. Hell. You hate us, too." She turned toward Enchantress and walked over to her. "I lost my Puddin'. You got magic powers, right? Can you bring him back to me?"

Enchantress smiled. "I can, my dear. Anything you want."

Harley paused. Katana's sword was lying on the platform by her feet. She leaned over and picked it up.

"Promise?"

"Yes, child," Enchantress said. "But now, prove your loyalty to me. The sword. Bring it to me."

Harley looked back and saw the Squad staring at her.

"Quinn. C'mon. You can't do this," Deadshot said.

"Quinn!" Flag shouted.

Enchantress held out her hand. "Give it to me. Then you only need to bow to me and swear subservience. If you do I will give you everything you have ever wanted."

"That sounds nice," Harley said.

"Don't do it, girl," Croc growled. "You *know* this is wrong."

"Yeah." She turned back for a moment and gave a defeated smile. "But she'll bring my Puddin' back to me." Harley leaned over, bowing. "I like what you've been selling, lady," Harley said as she looked up. "But there's one, tiny problem."

She held Katana's sword firmly in hand.

And grinned.

"You messed with my friends." In a single, swift movement, Harley swung the sword across

Enchantress's chest, slicing her open, exposing her heart. Then she made a face as she thrust her hand into the cavity, grabbed the pulsating organ, ripped it out, then looked at the bloody mass in her hand.

"God, that is like the weirdest garbage I've ever done," she said. "And I've done some really weird stuff." Harley turned to Flag and gave him a wink as Enchantress howled in pain.

The arcane machine began to shudder, its source of power suddenly taken from it. Flag turned to the others.

"Her heart's out," he said. "We can end this." He reached into his backpack and removed a limpet mine. "Croc," he called. "Take it."

He tossed the mine to Croc, who threw it toward the machine's grinding maw. At the same time, Harley tossed her magnum to Deadshot.

"Hey, man. I got only one shot left. So you better do that voodoo that you do so well." Lawton grabbed the gun and cocked the hammer.

One bullet. One target.

As the bomb arced toward its target, he fired the gun, and the bullet slammed directly into the explosive.

It detonated.

Abruptly the wind reversed itself, and sucked up everything and anything that hadn't been battened down. Piles of rubble, of debris, disappeared into the dark maw, ripping through the ring, shredding the machine until it could no longer contain all that it greedily absorbed.

The machine imploded, leaving behind a great, glowing cloud to mark that it had ever been there at all.

Seconds later that, too, was gone.

Fire and smoke rippled through the train station, slamming into Enchantress. She cried out as she was caught in the blast. She tried to conjure an enchantment to protect herself, but it was already too late. She was surrounded by an eruption of light and magic.

All her power, her strength, her magical energy, was gone.

It was over.

SIXTY-NINE

Deadshot stared as the machine he'd helped destroy rippled into non-existence. It was gone, he knew. Because of him.

Because of all of them.

Flag ran up and, before he could object, wrapped him in a bear hug. It hurt like hell. "You did it," he said. Deadshot pushed himself free and stepped back.

"Hey, man. I am not a hugger."

"I don't care. You did it."

"What about her?" Harley said. She stood next to Enchantress, who was lying bent on the ground, weak and fragile. "You mind giving me five minutes alone with her and my bat?"

"Watch it, Quinn," Deadshot warned. "She may do more of that witch crap."

"No." Enchantress lifted her chin to give Katana a clear shot to her throat. "Help me join my brother."

Harley gestured to her, grinning. "There you go, K. Ready to add another soul to your collection? You should number them all. You know. Collectable kills. They'll be worth a lot more that way."

Katana cocked her sword over her shoulder, ready to bring it down on Flag's command.

"Don't." The colonel stepped in her way.

"What the hell are you doing, man?" Harley said. "We're never gonna get a better chance."

"You still have her heart," he said, holding out his open hand. She looked at it, smiled, and gave it to him.

Suddenly Enchantress was frightened.

"Listen to me," she said to Harley. "The soldier and his master will only put you back in cages—but I will free you."

"June, please." Flag was no longer looking at the witch, but the woman inside. "Hear me. Hear my voice. Send the witch away."

"I am one of you," she pleaded. "Return my heart to me and I will give you anything you ask for. What can he give you beside a long incarceration?"

"June, I don't want to do this. Please."

They stared at Flag. "It's okay, man," Deadshot said. "Do what you have to."

Colonel Rick Flag looked at the heart for a long time. He had no choice. He only prayed June, wherever she was, would understand. He stared at the heart, gray and desiccated, then tightened his grip and crushed it.

Enchantress twisted in pain, jerked from side to side. Her body warped and her flesh reformed. Arms became legs, and legs arms.

She looked at Flag and spoke only one word.

"Enchantress."

Then she died. Flag stared at the corpse, dirty and primordial. He fell to the ground and grabbed at her.

"She's gone," he moaned. June was gone with her.

He turned away. Harley's hand shook as she rested it on his shoulder. He looked up at her, said nothing, but he nodded.

"Flag," Deadshot said. "Behind you."

He turned to see June Moone peeling off from Enchantress's husk. She stood, naked, dazed, and muddled, and he rushed to her. He held her and swore to himself that he would never let her go.

"She's gone," June said, sounding relieved but still afraid.

They stood in silence, staring at the now-empty train station. The ceiling had collapsed and they could see daylight outside.

"Well. That was real," Deadshot said. "Guess it's time to split. I got business in Gotham City."

Croc looked at the others and shrugged. "And if y'all don't mind, I got a sewer to crawl back into."

As the others started to walk off, Harley grimaced.

"Well, I can hotwire a car."

"Maybe, but you ain't driving," Deadshot laughed.

Boomer gave the others a salute and started to leave when they saw Waller step onto the platform.

"It's over?" she asked.

"Yeah," Flag said. He looked at the Suicide Squad. Harley, Deadshot, Boomer, and Croc. Katana, too. They were scorched, battered and bloody—emotional and physical wrecks. They were a team. They'd escaped the jaws of hell, and they were bound together.

"What now?" he asked Waller. She looked at the group as if trying to decide.

"Yes, you're right," she said to Flag, and she smiled as she held up the detonator. "Now what?"

"Aw, c'mon," Deadshot said.

Harley folded her arms over her chest. "Yeah, a thank you would be nice."

"Thank you," Waller said.

"Wait. No. That's it?" Deadshot stepped in front of her and stuck his face in hers. "We get nothing out of it? After all this?"

"Tell you what," she responded. "Any requests? What can I do for you? You can't run, but I can give you each one thing. Think hard. What do you want? What do you *really* want? Besides ten years off your sentence."

"That's not enough," Deadshot said. "I wanna see my daughter."

"Okay. Any other requests?"

"An espresso machine?" Harley said.

Croc shrugged. "BET," he said. Waller wasn't sure if he meant he wanted the entire television network, or a subscription to cable TV—then she decided they'd sort that out later. She turned to Harkness and waited for his smart-ass request.

Boomerang shook his head. "Ten years off a triple life sentence? Not even close. I wanna walk outta here a free man. Or you're gonna see what I can really do."

Waller looked at him for a long time.

SEVENTY

Floyd Lawton was in his living room. It was a simple space, plain but big enough for him to be able to help Zoe with her math homework.

"You gotta figure this length," he said, pointing to the hypotenuse. "You gotta know this angle."

Zoe tried to understand. "So, if you're up here like in a building, and you shoot a man down here on the street, the hypotenuse is how far the bullet actually travels?"

He took a sip of his coffee and hugged her. She was definitely his daughter. Then the door opened. Deadshot checked his watch. It was too soon. It was always too soon.

Flag entered with four U.S. Marshalls carrying chains and cuffs.

"It's time," he said.

Lawton hugged his daughter and she held onto him tight.

"I'll come back," he promised. "I will."

Flag nodded for the Marshalls to do their job. Lawton was ready for them to handcuff him.

"You be good," he said to Zoe. "I never want this for you."

She watched as they took him away. Flag gave her a warm pat and walked her father to his cell.

Croc was walking, not to a Belle Reve cellblock, but through the muddy waters deep below the supermax prison. They had offered him a large cell, but he preferred it here. He was no longer avoiding the rest of the inmates, but to Croc, this was home.

Of course, the food was better now, as he no longer had to forage for rats or be served rancid goat heads. They were also giving him books to read, and even promised him a videogame console.

He still had time to serve, but he was doing it in style.

Boomerang paced his cell, pissed off at the world. The others seemed to be happy here, he thought, but they were all idiots. The very idea of confinement riled him. Why the hell were they so content being cooped up here with no place to go?

Boomer wanted to be back in Australia. Lost and forgotten in the outback. Anywhere but here, in this glorified closet. He trashed his cell, shredded his mattress and set fire to this little home away from home.

"You bastards," he shouted. "Let me out."

The guards never answered his pleas. Every few days he would go on a tear and destroy everything within reach, and then when he was calm again, they would bring in new supplies and set it up all over again.

"Necessary rage," Waller had called it. That was her thank you for a job well done.

Tomorrow, he thought. *Maybe they'll finally let me go tomorrow. Who knows? It could happen.*

Harley Quinn sat in her bunk at Belle Reve, sipping a cup of coffee brewed by her new espresso machine. Her little reward for helping to save the world. She flipped through the pages of a thick magazine. "Sixteen Ways To Find A Lover."

Stupid article, she thought. She tossed the magazine away. Where the hell was she going to find sixteen lovers here? At least lovers who weren't creeps, meta-powered maniacs, or alligators?

Grumbling, she jumped out of the bunk, retrieved the magazine and decided to finish reading the article, no matter how impractical it was. Just as she picked up where she had left off, the lights went out and the alarms blared.

She perked up as she heard gunfire. She knew what that meant and she couldn't wait for him to make his appearance.

The wall behind her exploded. Paramilitary thugs in bulletproof armor and gas masks power-sawed their way into her cage.

Then he walked in. Barefoot and dancing, dressed like the finest Belle Reve guard.

And he was smiling The Smile.

ACKNOWLEDGMENTS

I want to thank everyone who made this possible.

From DC Comics, all the writers, artists, letterers and colorists who have created so many great characters, great stories and great memories.

From Warner Bros. David Ayer, who both wrote and directed the *Suicide Squad* movie, co-producer Andy Horwitz for his endless patience every time I asked yet another dumb question, and Josh Anderson, who did so much to make this process not quite easy, but definitely easy adjacent. Thanks also to Richard Suckle, Gary Barbosa, Spencer Douglas, and Shane Thompson for their invaluable input from outline through to completed manuscript.

From Titan Books: Nick Landau, Vivian Cheung, Laura Price, Natalie Laverick, Miranda Jewess, Cat Camacho, Paul Gill, Julia Lloyd, and Hayley Shepherd.

And of course my editor, Steve Saffel, for nearly everything else.

Thank you.

—Marv Wolfman
May 25, 2016

ABOUT THE AUTHOR

MARV WOLFMAN has written the adventures of many of the most famous characters in comic books, including Batman, Superman, Green Lantern, Fantastic Four, Spider-Man, and many others. He was the co-creator of the New Teen Titans, Blade the Vampire Hunter, Deathstroke the Terminator, and Nova, and wrote the universe-changing limited series *Crisis on Infinite Earths*. In the video-game world he contributed to Green Lantern, the DCU-Online massive multiplayer online game; *Superman Returns*; *Dark Knight Returns*; *Flash*, and more.

His novels include *Batman: Arkham Knight*, *Crisis on Infinite Earths*, *Superman Returns*, and *The Oz Encounter*. His awards include the Will Eisner Hall of Fame Award, the National Jewish Council Book Award, and the Scribe Award for Speculative Fiction (for *Superman Returns*).

For more fantastic fiction, author events,
competitions, limited editions and more

VISIT OUR WEBSITE
titanbooks.com

LIKE US ON FACEBOOK
facebook.com/titanbooks

FOLLOW US ON TWITTER
@TitanBooks

EMAIL US
readerfeedback@titanemail.com